ANGEL OF DARKNESS

ANGEL OF DARKNESS

Katy Munger

This first world edition published 2012
in Great Britain and in the USA by
SEVERN HOUSE PUBLISHERS LTD of
9–15 High Street, Sutton, Surrey, England, SM1 1DF.

British Library Cataloguing in Publication Data

Munger, Katy.
  Angel of darkness. – (Dead detective)
  1. Fahey, Kevin (Fictitious character) – Fiction.
  2. Delaware – Fiction. 3. Detective and mystery stories.
  I. Title II. Series
  813.6-dc23

ISBN-13: 978-0-7278-8131-1 (cased)

All Severn House titles are printed on acid-free paper.

Severn House Publishers support The Forest Stewardship Council [FSC],
the leading international forest certification organisation. All our titles that
are printed on Greenpeace-approved FSC-certified paper carry the FSC logo.

MIX
Paper from
responsible sources
FSC
www.fsc.org   FSC® C018575

Typeset by Palimpsest Book Production Ltd.,
Falkirk, Stirlingshire, Scotland.
Printed and bound in Great Britain by
MPG Books Ltd., Bodmin, Cornwall.

PROLOGUE

A young girl looks out the window at a world ruled by monsters. They swoop at her, whisper to her late at night and tell her secrets she must not reveal. She has come to know these dark creatures well. But the monster she sees creeping along the edge of the lawn this night is different. She has seen him before, in the daylight, pretending to be one of *them.*

Without warning, the earth swallows him.

She blinks and peers out into the darkness. Where has the monster gone?

She looks around to see if anyone else has noticed. The others stare at the television, minds dulled to the world. Only she has seen the monster.

'Here,' a voice says. A paper cup is thrust at her. The girl knows better than to protest. She spills the pills on to her tongue and washes them down with the grainy juice that has been proffered.

'I saw a monster,' she tells the nurse.

'You're safe in here,' the nurse assures the girl – not understanding that, this time, the monster was real.

ONE

f there is one thing I have learned from my death, it is this: secrets can destroy you. The words you cannot say, the lies you keep, the actions you pray will go undetected? They isolate you from the people who love you. They drive you into the shadows. They can divide you from yourself.

I kept many secrets during my life. Sometimes, I take them out and count them: the dreams I coveted, yet never tried to attain; the women I hid from my wife; the many times I gave up on a case, tossing the file into a drawer. But my indifference to the people I had sworn to serve was my biggest secret. Those who knew me when I was alive thought that I had stopped trying. The truth was that I had stopped caring.

These secrets shame me now as I wander through this world of mine, caught between the living and the dead, feeding on the secrets of others, like a vampire seeking life in its victim's blood. I walk the streets of my small Delaware town, unseen, peering in windows, following the furtive, savoring the mortality revealed by the secrets of others. I have seen a priest whip himself with razor-tipped wire until his back ran with blood. I have witnessed a woman following her lost love for days at a time, weeping all the while. I once glimpsed a bride tearfully bidding her young lover goodbye at the back door of a church even as a far older man waited for her at the altar. These months of watching have confirmed what I already knew: secrets can destroy you.

As proof, I point to the Holloway Institute for Mental Health, a house of secrets built high on a hill overlooking my town. At its heart, Holloway is an imposing granite mansion that towers over its lesser, more modern neighbors. Long-term patients reside in this majestic central building. If the hospital's administrators thought that living in the original wing might somehow heal the fissures in these poor souls, they were very much mistaken. The people who live in prison are lost. Their minds are alive with private worlds infinitely more compelling than the real world that awaits them. They will never return to living among others because they do not want to.

To the right of this majestic edifice, a newer three-story stone structure stands as a testament to the optimism of Holloway's founders. This is the short-term unit where the drug-addicted and depressed dwell. The people of my town send loved ones here whose lives have careened off track, spilling them in embarrassing terrain where their behavior frightens those whose more reliable lives chug onward as usual. Yet I know that little separates the despairing residents of this unit from those who live in the suburbs below and cling to the illusion that such a thing as 'normal' is even possible. It is entirely debatable as to which side suffers from the biggest delusions.

Of all the dark secrets at Holloway, none are darker than those savored by the residents who live in Holloway's third building, a stark brick box surrounded by a double chain-link fence and built on the lip of a cliff that falls abruptly to a valley below. I have sent two people to live behind the bolted doors of this unit. Both men deserved a darker fate. Both deserved to be locked up in dark barred cages far from the people whose lives they fed upon. But both men convinced a jury that their enthusiastic violence was caused by a broken mind rather than their insatiable need to inflict pain on others. I was not fooled by their acts. And I know now, that each man was a fraud, for I have visited the darkest corners of their minds, where the screams and pleas of others are stored like treasures in a museum. I have tasted their satisfaction at these memories and felt their abiding hunger for more. These men did not kill out of madness, they killed because they chose to.

One of these men died shortly after I first visited Holloway, his last thoughts dark recollections of those moments when he had taken the lives of others and gloried in his power to do so. This man died in a comfortable hospital bed, fussed over by a nurse who would have driven her syringe straight into his heart had she known the evil he savored in his final hours. I sometimes wonder where he went after his death. I did not see him go and I have not seen him since. And though

I tempt my own fate by saying so, given the punishment he deserved, I can only hope there is a Hell.

The other man still lives in the brick building on the edge of the cliff, sharing his ward with men whose madness makes them a danger to others. The inmates in this wing for the criminally insane – all men – often stand at the inner fence of the maximum security unit, fingers curled over the heavy steel strands, licking their lips and making smacking sounds at the ready-made victims cowering on the other side. They delight in the way that the patients outside their unit shrink from their shouts. They exult in their power to inspire fear.

The man I put there among them, Otis Redman Parker, spends his days blatantly bullying other inmates while bullying the orderlies in far more subtle ways. He is the worst of the worst. His most fundamental need is to have power over others. He has trained his mind to remember every detail of the pain that he caused when he was free and he spends his nights reliving his crimes, ever excited by his memories.

I can see the darkness that surrounds him like a sick, bleak fog. At rest, his mind is a terrifying landscape of gleaming skulls, scattered bones, deep pits and a perpetual night filled with terrible cries. To loose him upon the lambs of the world would lead to terrible slaughter.

Which brings me back to the most shameful secret I carry with me in death. I keep watch over this monster known by the world as Otis Redman Parker because, had I done my job better when I was alive, he would be caged deep in an impenetrable prison instead of ruling a hospital wing so quaintly labeled as for the criminally insane. These men are not insane. Indeed, they see life with more clarity than most. They see that laws are nothing more than words on a page and that there is no force in the universe that can stop them from inviting in the chaos.

Had I done my job better, Otis Parker would have died with a needle in his arm. But, like so many others before him, my incompetence proved to be his blessing. All I did was teach him to hide his hunger behind a mask of madness.

I fear what will happen the day he convinces others that he has been cured and is a man who should be set free.

TWO

I do not return to Holloway day after day to remind myself of my mistakes. The truth is that I have felt at home at Holloway since I visited it after my death.

Some patients I recognized from my prior life, but others I did not know at all. They had been at Holloway for decades, I realized, and their very existence was a profound surprise. How could they have orbited my world since I was a child, without me ever even knowing they existed?

One of these patients was a woman of faded beauty whose once-blonde hair was nearly gray and flew about her face, wild and untamed. She spent most of her days in a chair by a window where the sunshine spilled through obscenely, highlighting her indifference to its splendor. One day, soon after my first visit to Holloway, a man I had known forever came striding down the hall toward her, a bouquet of yellow roses cradled in his hands. The sight of him paralysed me with surprise.

It was Morty, a beat cop I had known when I was alive – a man we'd all ridiculed for leading a solitary life; a man we'd labeled as a eunuch.

He knelt at the woman's feet and placed the roses in her lap. Her eyes focused on his and he smiled. She did not return his smile, but she did not look away, either. She searched his face, trying to remember a life she had left long ago. Morty waited patiently, willing to give her the time she needed to place him in her world. After a moment, she reached up and caressed his jaw with her palm, her face unreadable.

They made an oddly ancient tableau: a knight kneeling before his lady.

I saw Morty often at Holloway after that day. He visited the woman several times a week, always with yellow roses, always content to say not a word. I tried to search out the cause of this devotion, but I could learn nothing from his memories. He kept his mind blank, having decided it was too painful to look back, or maybe believing that he owed his lady the honor of being in the moment with her, no matter how bleak that moment might be.

Secrets. We all have them. Even an aging beat cop who has remained unmarried for his sixty-some years, his heart imprisoned behind the walls of Holloway.

Other patients, unfamiliar to me at first, came to be a part of an imaginary family I created in my mind. Their lonely wanderings across the sculpted lawns of Holloway reminded me of my own peripatetic afterlife. Like a child with a fairy-tale family patched together in his head, I had chosen a mother, a father and a daughter for my pretend family – though in life they were not related at all and, indeed, rarely noticed one another.

A funny little man named Harold Babbitt was my patriarch. He had peaked eyebrows that matched his owl-like physique, sharp eyes that glittered and a shiny point of bald head peeping above sparse hair. Harold spent his days murmuring a strange word salad, his brain exploding with electric impulses that churned out verbal waterfalls. He spoke of himself in the third person, his mind leaping from topic to topic like quicksilver: 'Harold Babbitt is a prince among men and a man among dogs. He is a dog named Prince who knows when doves cry. He is here to fight the people who live as lions in the caves of your heart because they want to eat your soul. He is the man. He is the Harold. He is the Godfather of Soul.'

Harold was like that: ninety-nine percent nonsense, one percent brilliance. And me, with nothing better to do but follow him around each day, fell on that one percent like a bird might fall upon a breadcrumb tumbling to barren ground.

Being Harold had its dangers. At times, his benign chattering gave way to a terrifying self-violence, as if his words were lava building toward an eruption. When the explosion came, he would slam the shiny point of his head into walls, claw at the seeping blood with his hands, and then wipe it along his body as he howled for demons to take the Sun God away. The staff was ready when this happened. They would wrestle Harold to the ground and bind him in a jacket that pinned his arms to his sides. He would whimper apologies from his cocoon as they bundled him on to a stretcher and wheeled him into a room as hushed as a tomb in a lost pyramid. Its walls were padded to protect him from his madness. There, they would unstrap him from the stretcher and lead him to a corner. He'd sit, as docile as a lamb, his mutterings stuttering to a halt in the calm that settled on him in the aftermath.

I came to crave those quiet sessions with Harold in our special room. It seemed the one place in the world where my mind and my soul were still. Harold and I would take our seats, him in one corner and me in another. We would lay our heads back against the canvassed walls, listening to nothing, feeling nothing, our minds calmed by the room's artificial twilight and gently cooled air. Harold would find peace and I would find peace, too. But the respite never lasted more than a day. Soon enough, Harold was let out to roam, a soft leather helmet affixed to his head until he found a way to take it off and hide it again. After a while, the staff usually gave up trying to find it and surrendered Harold to his walking commentary. For Holloway, Harold passed as normal.

In the fairy-tale family I had constructed in my mind, Harold's wife was a patient named Olivia, whose face was wet with tears that never quite seemed to dry. I couldn't tell what the source of her sorrow was, for she would not raise the curtain on that memory in her mind. She clung resolutely to her pain, refused to acknowledge the future and did not look at the past. Whatever that memory is, she remained its prisoner, her life stalled until she can find the strength to confront it.

Sorrow had made her incandescent. She was tall and slender, with translucent skin and pale-blue eyes shaped like almonds. Her long red hair was the color of blood; it was impossible to take your eyes off it. She moved like an angel, with a slow grace made almost ritualistic by the medications she was on.

I was not the only one who noticed Olivia's beauty. Otis Redman Parker had noticed her, too. Sometimes, when I was sitting with her in Holloway's central courtyard, pretending we were friends and enjoying the fountain that she seemed to love so much, I would look up and see Parker staring at her through the fences that enclose his unit, his eyes bright and his mouth wet with desire. I hated him in those moments. He had no right to look upon her.

The final person in my imagined family was a little girl named Lily, who could not have been more than ten or eleven years old, though she, too, had been at Holloway for as long as I had visited. She was kept there by a horrifying world that cavorted in her head, a living landscape created by an unfortunate stew of chemicals and genetics at her birth. I had visited that world, seeking a way out for Lily, but she remained captive to its power. Creatures with fangs and claws and glowing eyes lurked in its darkness. Shadow figures leapt out from behind forests of twisting trees whose branches grabbed at you like hands. Strange hybrid animals with distorted limbs wandered through a post-apocalyptic countryside, sometimes stopping to turn their cartoonish faces to Lily. It was one of those creatures, a winged cat with saucer eyes and a toothy smile, who had ordered her to light a cigarette and burn her little brother up and down his arms, an act that landed her in Holloway. I know this because the cat repeated this command to her so often that the memory haunted her daily.

Lily knows what she is.

Lily was visited every week by bewildered parents unable to comprehend how it was that life handed them a child mired in such an early madness. They, like the staff, knew that Lily did not belong among adults, but the other young patients at Holloway were not safe when Lily was around, not with that wide-eyed cat in her head whispering its dark commands. So it was that the patients closest to her age stayed in a special juvenile ward in the short-term unit, but Lily was doomed to live among the lost.

I did not judge Lily or the others. I loved each of these lost beings in their own way and saw a terrible beauty in their incoherence. The world had forgotten them, but I would not do the same. I walked beside them, wishing them a peace unlikely to come.

And so it was that, on a bleak day in March whipped by high winds and cold drizzle, my two lives collided, my living and my dead, and my son Michael, age fourteen, appeared among the outcasts of Holloway, his mind as troubled as theirs.

THREE

A t first, I thought time had inverted. That I had been transported back to my own miserable teenage years and was staring at my own miserable self. That's how much Michael had come to look like me. Gone was the chubby boy with rounded features who sat silently at my funeral, his arm draped around his mother's shoulders as a sign of his determination to be a man. He now stood nearly as tall as I had been, though he was far stockier.

He had my dark hair and eyes, and certainly he had my nose, but his mouth was one hundred percent Connie. And, like his mother's, it did not look as if it had smiled in a long time. I discovered him in the short-term unit, pacing Holloway's juvenile ward, measuring the distance between the common room and his sleeping quarters.

He had his hands thrust deep in the pockets of his jeans and his hair hung in greasy strands. His skin had become mired in a no-man's land between uneven stubble and acne. Misery surrounded him in a cloud. It was a gloom that felt all too familiar to me: Michael was deep in the trough, he had descended as I had often descended, and was now chin high in crippling depression. *Had my death done this to him?*

I'd have given anything to take on my son's sorrow. But all I could do was walk by his side, unseen and unfelt. What had happened to change Michael so? Nine months ago, faced with the truth that I was no longer part of his life, I had stopped torturing myself by standing outside our old home, staring in at a world where I had been forgotten. I had forced myself to find other families to watch. I had made myself move on.

Which meant I had not been there for him during whatever crisis had landed Michael here, among the lost souls of Holloway.

Was he becoming another version of me?

Michael ignored the nurses who watched him, assessing his

behavior, trying to put a label on his troubles. He paused in the common-room doorway but gave no notice of the other young patients inside. They were gathered around a television set to watch a movie about teenage vampires. He did not notice, as I did, that the pale complexions and vacant eyes of his fellow patients were far more frightening than the stylish vampires of the movie. Michael was preoccupied and waiting for someone. His eyes kept focusing on the door at the far end of the hall before he looked quickly away, as if he were ashamed of his need for company.

He was not waiting for his mother. When Connie came through the door a few moments later, Michael slumped in disappointment. He had been hoping for someone else.

Connie exuded motherly optimism as she hugged him, but I could feel the cracks of fear spreading through her body like fissures. She was determined that Michael not sense the terror that vibrated in her like piano wire. I understood her fear. She had seen this all before. She had seen it in me. And she had learned that love alone was not enough. She knew that the darkness sometimes won.

'I brought you tee shirts,' she said. 'And some books, in case you feel like reading?'

'Why do I have to be here?' Michael asked sullenly, taking the bag she offered but refusing to meet her eyes.

'It's just for a few days. Just to give you a break.'

'I didn't wreck the car on purpose,' he protested too loudly. His voice attracted the attention of the other patients. They watched Michael and his mother warily. When it came to the war between parent and child, they knew where their loyalties lay.

'Sometimes we do things without realizing why,' Connie explained in a whisper. 'It's just getting worse, Michael, it's just getting worse.' Her voice cracked and it shocked me. This was not the steel-nerved Connie I had known. Had I taken all of her strength? Left her mired in fear of the worst?

'This place is a hellhole,' he said. 'It's not safe. Crazy people attack you all the time. The other kids told me. They have serial killers and shit locked up right next door.'

Connie's patience was being tested. 'Michael, that's just

stupid teenage rumors and don't you swear. You're perfectly safe here. Cal told me and he ought to know.'

'But end-of-grade tests are coming up,' Michael protested, trying another tack. 'You're guaranteeing that I'm going to fail.'

'It'll be OK,' she assured him, but he did not believe her. She was his mother. She had to love him. How could she possibly understand that she was the only one who did – or ever would?

This was my fault. How many times could I have stepped in when I was alive to be a real father, providing the guidance that might have kept it from coming to this?

'He's not coming back,' Connie told him gently. 'He's dead, Michael. I can't bring him back. He's never coming back to us and you have to accept it. Your life is just beginning. Don't sacrifice it to this.'

'You don't understand,' Michael insisted. He fled to his room, leaving Connie standing in the hall. I wanted to follow him, but Connie's boyfriend, the man who had taken my place in my family, entered the ward, bringing an air of efficiency with him. He was tall and graying, dressed in a nice suit, full of confidence and comfortable in this setting. The staff knew him, I saw, and they liked him, judging by their smiles.

Did he work here at Holloway? Had he been the one to convince Connie to send Michael here? Why had I not seen him here at Holloway before?

Cal. That was his name. I remembered it now. Cal: sturdy and competent and kind. He was everything I had never been.

Connie buried her head in his comforting arms. 'I can't do anything right.'

'You don't have to do anything at all,' he told her quietly. 'You've done everything that you can do. Let the people here do their jobs. They'll give you Michael back.'

'He hates me,' Connie whispered.

'He hates himself,' the man explained and I had to admit it – his voice was thick with genuine concern. He cared for them both. Who was I to begrudge him his ability to be the man I had never been?

'Where's Sean?' Connie asked him. Sean was my youngest. He was sunny and full of himself, as different from his brother as, well, as life from death.

'I dropped him off at Matt's house. His mother said he could stay as long as he needs to.'

This small kindness seemed to break her. Connie began to cry. 'I don't know what I'd do without you,' she said. 'Without you and everyone else who wants to help. I don't know what to do. I can't do this alone.'

'Just take a deep breath. You don't have to do this alone. It's going to be OK.'

'Cal?' A small woman emerged from a room near the nurse's station. She was in her mid-forties, with light-brown hair and a straightforward manner. I knew her. She was a therapist who sometimes advised the department on the psychological make-up of suspects.

'Miranda.' Cal shook her hand and then gestured toward my wife. 'This is my fiancée, Connie Fahey.'

I heard the words like a kick in the gut. Game, set, match. *Replaced.*

'How do you do?' Miranda asked. 'Wait, don't answer that. We'll get into that later.'

Connie tried to smile at the joke, but her mouth trembled with the effort.

'I know you're anxious to hear an opinion soon,' Miranda said. 'I'd like to talk to Michael alone first and then we can chat. Would that be OK?'

'Sure,' Connie agreed. 'How long will it take?'

'An hour should do it. Then I can give you my recommendation on how long I think Michael needs to stay with us and what it is we're looking at.'

'Do you think it's drugs?' Connie asked. Fear radiated from her. Addiction. Obliteration. Promises. More addiction. She'd been there before.

Miranda shook her head. 'There was nothing in his system. This is emotional in nature.'

'His father—' Connie began.

'I know,' Miranda interrupted. 'I have the family history. But let's take it one hour at a time. Michael is his own person and we've come a long way in the treatment of adolescents. Let's see what we're up against first.'

Connie nodded, glad to stave off her worst fears for the

next hour, at least. She followed Cal out of the ward while I tagged along behind Miranda, desperate to know if my death was the cause of Michael's grief. As pitiful as it sounds, I needed to know that I had mattered to him. I needed to know he remembered me.

Michael was sprawled across his narrow bed, staring at a book that I was pretty sure he wasn't really reading.

'I'm Dr Fowler,' Miranda explained, offering her hand as if he were a grown man. Michael held the grip awkwardly before letting go. He inched away from her. She made him nervous. She was too calm, too self-possessed. He was used to fighting Connie's passionate concern with sullen indifference. How do you fight calm?

'I'm going to be your therapist while you're here,' Miranda explained. 'I'm not a medical doctor. I have my PhD in clinical psychology, with a specialty in treating early adolescent depression.'

'I'm not depressed,' Michael insisted stubbornly. 'I'm just pissed off.'

'I bet you are.' Miranda dragged a chair closer to Michael. She was not going to ask that he join her in an office. She was willing to join him. 'It's appropriate for you to be pissed off right now. Your father dies, no one ever talks about it, then your mother replaces him pretty quickly, I'd have to say. On top of all that, I'm willing to bet there's not a person in this world who seems to be paying you a damn bit of attention. Did I leave anything out?'

Michael closed the book on his lap. He may even have been trying to smile. 'Yes. I'm in love with a girl who barely knows I exist,' he added. 'Even though I talk to her every day at school.'

'No!' Miranda seemed genuinely shocked. 'Now you're depressing *me*.'

Michael smiled in spite of himself. That single spark of humor gave me hope. 'My mom thinks I'm just like my dad,' he told Miranda. 'She thinks that I'm going to grow up to drink and mope and screw up all the time, and not care about anyone but myself.'

There it was: the most matter-of-fact indictment of my life I had ever heard.

'And yet you loved your father,' Miranda said. 'And I have no doubt that he loved you deeply.' *Thank you, bless you, thank you, Miranda.* 'Now his love is gone. It has to hurt, Michael. To know that his love is gone.'

Just like that, my son was fighting tears. 'I wasn't trying to kill myself when I crashed my mom's car,' he said through clenched teeth.

'Maybe not,' Miranda answered gently. 'But you did steal it. And we need to talk about that. And you could have killed the family in the other car. We need to talk about that, too. And, Michael – I don't think your mother would survive if something happened to you. Nor would your brother's world ever be the same.'

'I'm only fourteen,' he whispered.

'I know,' she said. 'It hardly seems fair, does it? That so much should be on you?'

The tears came.

I left them.

His secrets were not mine to hear.

FOUR

I wondered if Connie blamed me for what was happening to Michael. Always a glutton for punishment, I went in search of her and found her in the courtyard that marked the center of Holloway's vast grounds, holding Cal's hand as they waited for Michael's therapy session to end. If Cal was impatient to get back to work, he did not show it.

I saw Olivia, the patient I had cast in my imaginary Holloway family, sitting in her customary spot on a bench close to the fountain of marble cherubs. I joined her on the bench, where I had a good view of Connie and her fiancé, though it was hard to look at anyone other than Olivia. The hints of magenta in her hair seemed to dance in the sunlight, mesmerizing me. Her face was so pale and solemn that she looked like a Madonna sitting in repose at the feet of the angels.

It wasn't that I was trying to eavesdrop. I was just trying to find my way. Connie and Cal were waiting in a companionable silence. They fit, and it hurt.

'I come out here to be alone, you know,' Olivia said to me. I turned to her, stunned. 'You can see me?'

'I'm crazy, not blind. What unit are you in?'

'Me? I'm . . . I'm a visitor here,' I stammered. How was it that she could see me when she never had before? Only people close to death or spiraling into madness could see me. My heart sank. I knew what it had to be.

'Don't do it,' I told her.

'Do what?' She chewed at her lower lip with perfect white teeth as she stared at the cascading waters of the fountain.

'Don't hurt yourself.'

She looked up at me, startled.

'Don't ask me how I know,' I said. 'Just don't hurt yourself. You can't be more than thirty. You have your whole life ahead of you.'

'My daughter is dead,' she said matter-of-factly. 'My life died with her.'

What do you say to that?

'That's my wife,' I offered. Hey, it was the best I could come up with. I nodded at Connie, as if offering up my own sorrow might somehow make Olivia feel better about hers.

'The woman holding that guy's hand?' Olivia squinted at them. 'He works here at Holloway, you know.'

'A doctor?'

'No. I think he hires the nurses and orderlies. They all know him. Why is he sitting with your wife and holding her hand while you're sitting here with me?'

'It's a very long story,' I told her.

'OK. Maybe a better question is this: why are you just sitting there staring at them and not doing anything about it?'

'That's an even longer story,' I explained.

Olivia's gaze was like warm honey. I felt its heat and tasted its sweetness. To be seen, to be recognized, was . . . divine.

'What's your name?' she asked, letting curiosity overcome her despair.

'Kevin. I know yours. It's Olivia.'

'Well, that's not creepy at all.' She stared back at the fountain. For the first time, I noticed that all of the marble cherubs were boys and that they appeared to be peeing on one another. Good lord. What kind of message did that send to Holloway's already confused patients?

'Are you sure you're a visitor?' Olivia asked me.

'I'm sure. I just like it here. It's peaceful.'

'Like a tomb,' she agreed. 'A tomb, a tomb, a tomb.'

'What happened to your daughter?' I asked, needing to know.

'I killed her.'

I was going to say something, anything, to break the silence that followed, but the air was split with the sudden sounds of sirens approaching from far below, growing in volume as official vehicles raced toward Holloway.

'This isn't good,' Olivia predicted. 'Probably one more crazy for the hardcore unit.' She looked up at the brick building where the criminally insane were kept and I realized, with a start, that Otis Parker, the killer I'd failed to put on Death Row, was standing at the fence staring at Olivia as he idly caressed his groin.

But Parker, too, was distracted by the sound of sirens. Oddly, he hurried across the exercise yard to the back of the hospital, where a chain-link fence marked the edge of the cliff that overlooked a valley. It was almost as if he already knew what I soon realized: the approaching police cars were not headed to Holloway at all. They zoomed past the front gates and continued in a loop around the hill, down toward the river that snaked through the valley below.

'I must be going,' I told Olivia. 'We shall meet again soon.'

She stared at me, for the first time, I think, wondering if I was real.

'Don't do it,' I repeated. 'Promise me. Just wait. We can talk again.'

She looked back at the fountain, unwilling to promise, but I could not stay any longer. I had to know what was going on.

I am not bound by cliffs or walls. It was nothing for me to take the most direct route to the scene. All I had to do was pass through the unit for the criminally insane first. The men inside were pumped up from their game of basketball. The possibility of violence nearby excited them further. I could smell the tang of their sweat and feel their energy buzzing around me like angry bees as I moved through their ranks. I reached the far edge of the exercise yard and joined the inmates gathered at the inner fence overlooking the cliff. They stamped and jostled like beasts in a pen smelling a blood sacrifice.

The inmates had a bird's-eye view of the scene unfolding along the banks of the Delaware tributary below. Official cars were pulling up near a small bridge that spanned the river just before a wooded area. A group of men stood at the top of the embankment, peering down at a dark shape sprawled on the riverbank below. It had to be a body. Nothing else brought out so many badges.

Otis Parker had claimed his spot at the front of the pack and stood at the fence, inches from me. He wore a huge smile as he watched the scene unfolding below. His attention was absolute. It was as if he were watching a play that had been staged just for him. He groaned, unaware he had made the sound, and pressed his body against the fence, unconsciously grinding his hips against the metal.

That's when it hit me with an absolute certainty: Otis Parker had known this was going to happen. *He had been waiting for it.*

FIVE

E very crime scene I have ever visited is different, yet somehow the same. Invariably, the body seems smaller than you ever expect. Death itself seems smaller, almost like a let-down. Is the absence of life really this quiet, this ordinary? How is it that the world can go on around it, as if nothing has happened at all? Would death even matter if the living were not there to mark it – and fear its cold finger one day?

It was no different with the scene by the river. The area had been quickly taped off from onlookers. State troopers and county deputies were holding back the curious that had started to gather. The body had once been a young girl. Her denim miniskirt and gauzy white peasant blouse were bunched up, as if she had been dragged back toward the river by her ankles, exposing long arms and legs. Her skin seemed impossibly pale in the afternoon light. She lay face down on the grassy bank, her head and hands extending upward as if she were trying to crawl away from the river. The undisturbed grass around her made it clear that she had been killed elsewhere and left by the river to be found.

Usually when a body has been moved, I feel nothing at the dump site. The essence of the person whose life has been taken has long since wandered beyond to the place I cannot find. But that was not the case with this girl. I could feel a trace of her essence lingering nearby. I wondered if she, like me, was looking on from a twilight world, unable to move beyond, and if she, like me, wondered why she had been given so little time to live, so very little time to become who she had wanted to be. Yes, there was regret surrounding her body, a sadness and recognition of loss, but there was something else there, too: relief, perhaps, or maybe resignation. A sense of weariness and a burden put down. It seemed a heavy load for one so young. Whoever she was, she had not had an easy life.

I moved closer. Her body sprawled half in mud and half in tall grass that ruffled in the breeze. Butterflies flittered from wild flower to wild flower, only inches from her body. Her death had not disturbed the spring.

Her hair had been bleached weeks ago and her dark roots were obvious. That and her clothing told me she was probably from the neighborhood in our town that was, quite literally, 'on the other side of the tracks.' A hundred years ago, train-loads of coal from Pennsylvania had sped through that side of town, dusting the area with a black rain so sooty and persistent that the residents had named the neighborhood Helltown. These days, trains still roared through a half-dozen times a week at most, ferrying manufacturing supplies from Wilmington to New Jersey and back, still splitting the town into two sides: one for those who had everything and one for those who had almost nothing. Only people without the money to live elsewhere called Helltown home. It was filled with young girls like the one lying before me, girls whose only tickets out were their youth. This one had not even had a chance to trade hers for a better life. And now her life was over.

I heard the slam of a car door on the roadway above, followed by the sounds of someone moving fast through the bushes. I knew it must be Maggie, my replacement on the squad. Maggie always arrived at a crime scene moving as fast as she had driven there, exceeding the speed limit in both cases. She would leap from her car and be halfway across the crime scene before her car door even shut behind her. Her natural speed was surprising, given her stocky build. She was muscled with plain features and ordinary brown hair that looked as if it had been cut by someone more used to trimming men's hair. But the way she moved, parting the world around her as she claimed her way in life, made her beautiful to me. She was emphatically alive and always absolutely focused. I think she loved being alive; I think she loved being here. And I loved her for it.

Sure enough, Maggie arrived on the scene full speed ahead, taking in the girl's body and its arranged posture immediately. She wasted little time talking to the uniformed cops who had arrived at the scene before her. She liked to pick up her own first impressions. She vetted a small grassy area for evidence and then knelt by the body, running her hands over the girl meticulously, as if she were blind, consulting with the forensic technician about body and air temperature, humidity and the effect of the sun on the girl's exposed skin. From what they could tell, the body had been dumped there the night before, and discovered when a pair of retired postmen broke through the brush in search of a good fishing spot.

Though only a few yards from the edge of the road, bushes obscured the body from the view of passers-by. Yet it lay close to a path well traveled on weekends. Had that been the killer's intention, I wondered, that the body be discovered, but only after a few days of wind and sun and the forest animals had done their job? Had the fishermen spoiled his plans?

If there was anything on the body the killer had hoped might be destroyed by the elements, I knew that Maggie would find it.

Within fifteen minutes, Maggie had directed that dozens of photographs be taken and nearly as many bags of trace evidence be cataloged for transport to the lab. Finally, she was satisfied that the body could be moved. A technician helped her gently roll the dead girl over on to her back. It was impossible to tell what the kid had looked like while alive. Her eyes were closed and her features weighed against her face as if melting in the afternoon sun. A gold ring in her nose and her heavy make-up reinforced my suspicion that she was from Helltown. A bulge of white stomach peaked out from between her ruffled blouse and miniskirt, revealing a gold ring in her belly button. She had wanted to be different, to be special and stand out. There was something inexpressibly sad about the way she had been reduced to a lifeless mound of flesh and chemicals sprawled beneath the afternoon sky instead. She was too young for such a fate. However poor she was, how little educated, she should have been given a chance to make a better life for herself.

The breeze shifted and the smell of new grass wafted past. All trace of the dead girl's essence was gone. She had moved on, leaving her body to the care of others.

A huge crashing through the bushes distracted Maggie. She winced when she saw that it was her partner, Adrian Calvano. He tried hard, but his emotions often got the best of him, especially when the victim was a woman. He'd arrived at the crime scene with all the finesse of a water buffalo.

Calvano pulled up short when he saw the girl's body. He stared, gauging her age. Anger rose in him like heat. Maggie could feel it, too.

'She looks to be about fifteen years old,' Maggie said, pulling him back to the job.

Calvano pulled out his notebook and dutifully wrote the detail down. He'd have made a hell of a stenographer.

'Do you recognize her?' Maggie asked.

Calvano shook his head. 'Maybe we can take her photo around to the high schools and see who knows her?'

Maggie nodded and examined the girl's body from this new angle, receiving an assessment of the wounds that had been inflicted from the hovering medical examiner – it was likely she had been strangled and she most certainly had been assaulted. Maggie did not ask for more details yet. She had caught a glimpse of a red scar peeking out from beneath the girl's muddy blouse. Carefully, she pulled the hem up and revealed an angry red swirl the diameter of a coffee cup burned into the girl's torso. There was a puncture wound at the center, where the concentric circles ended, as if a pattern had been fashioned from a coat hanger, heated and burned into her skin – the kind of crude, home-made brand I'd seen on prison inmates marked by others.

With a start I realized I had seen the exact same symbol before. On every single one of the victims Otis Redman Parker had been accused of killing.

'That was likely done post-mortem,' the medical examiner noted softly.

Maggie nodded. She had already figured as much. 'You see this?' she asked Calvano. He nodded, looking slightly green around the gills. 'See how it's one continuous circle winding in on itself. Check out the puncture wound at the center.'

'You've seen it before?' Calvano guessed.

Maggie nodded. She had realized the importance of it, I knew, by the way her whole body stiffened. I could feel her fighting off the disbelief. Though the Otis Parker case had occurred before she joined the detective squad, Maggie would know the details of it by heart. One of the first things she had done, when named to take my place, had been to pore through my old files. Her reason, she said, was simply to get a better feel for the types of cases my small town's police force faced. But I had known with a certain shame that she felt the need to read through my case files for one reason only – because she knew that neither I nor my partner had done much to solve any of our cases in at least the last eight years of our careers. We'd been sloppy, we'd made mistakes, we'd filed cases away as 'unsolved' without ever really trying to solve them. Maggie had been cleaning up after me. She knew about Otis Parker because of it and as soon as she checked the symbol against our database, she would be certain. And probably afraid that I had to put the wrong man away. It had happened before.

'Where?' Calvano finally asked when it became obvious Maggie was lost in thought. 'Where have you seen it before?'

'It was mentioned in an old case of Fahey's from about ten years ago. They got the guy who did it. It was a series of murders, all teenage girls, two from around here and the rest up by Wilmington and over the line in New Jersey. The guy beat the rap in court. The jury bought his insanity plea and he's up on The Hill now.' Maggie nodded toward Holloway where the central building loomed like a faraway castle set on a hill, an illusion destroyed by the squat buildings on either side of the mansion and the security fences marking the limits of its perimeter. Below Holloway, the hill fell off sharply, exposing patches of red clay and crumbling cliff. A huge drainage pipe protruded out through this cliff, like a terrible dark eye that could see all.

From where we stood, Holloway looked more like a mirage then a mental hospital. But I knew that Otis Redman Parker was up there, staring down at us, pressed against the fence that held him in, watching Maggie examine a reprise of his life's work.

Calvano stared at Maggie, not quite understanding. 'What should we do?' he asked.

'Well, if I were you, I'd take a drive up to Holloway and make damn sure that Otis Parker is still inside.'

SIX

I hated Calvano's expensive suits. I hated his expensive loafers. I really hated the way he combed his hair straight back. Most of all, I hated the way women loved how he looked. But I didn't hate the actual guy. Calvano does a decent job of looking after Maggie and is as good a partner as a dumb-ass can be. So I decided to hitch a ride with him back up the hill and see how Otis Parker reacted when he realized they had connected him to the crime below.

Thanks to his badge, it didn't take long for Calvano to be processed through the gates that segregated the maximum security unit from the rest of the hospital grounds. The guard manning the entrance seemed more interested in trying to pump Calvano for details on why so many cops had gathered along the riverbank than he was in checking his credentials. Calvano was learning and knew enough to keep his mouth shut. Instead, he asked the guard if Otis Parker had been transported outside of Holloway recently.

'Why are you asking?' the guard wanted to know. 'Don't tell me Parker's got something to do with what's happening down by the river?'

Calvano shrugged. 'You tell me. When's the last time he left the grounds?'

'About six months ago,' the guard replied. 'And it's going to be another decade before we take that asshole out again. He's one of those guys you can barely contain when he's on the inside who goes straight to Looney Tunes territory when he's on the outside. Last time we brought him out of here, he broke my buddy's jaw on the way back from court, and this was after he tried to jump a bailiff. Time before that, he busted out a window in a dentist's office. The guards caught them right before he made it to the highway with his thumb out. Parker's not going anywhere but to the bathroom now, not if we can help it. His lawyer's a pain in the ass about it, but we deal.'

'What about visitors and phone calls?' Calvano asked.

The guard shook his head. 'He gets requests all the time from the crazies who send him money and want to see him, but he turns them all down flat. His scam is to place lonely hearts ads online and get women to put money in his defense fund, whatever the hell that means. You can bet his lawyer worked hard to get that scam cleared so he could get paid. But Parker doesn't even bother to thank the suckers who contribute or reply to their letters that we can see. He's a stone-cold user and he makes no bones about it. He doesn't give a crap about anyone except himself.'

'No family visitors?'

The guard shook his head again. 'Would you want to admit you were related to the guy?'

I thought he made a good point.

Calvano quickly found his way to the right hallway. Otis Parker was waiting for him. I was certain of it, and not just because Maggie had called ahead. Flanked by two orderlies, Parker wore a shit-eating grin when he entered the visitors' room and he gave off the air of a man who has a secret he just can't wait to share with others. His bravado was all the more remarkable considering that he was restrained. Although Parker was allowed to move freely within the confines of his unit, thanks to his lawyer, the orderlies took the precaution of handcuffing him to a chair bolted to the floor of the visitors' room for the interview. They didn't quite pull out the hockey mask and wheel him in on a dolly, but it was clear that they were wary of Parker.

If crazy could be evaluated by appearance, Parker was certainly insane. He had shaved and oiled his head and, although he was built like a linebacker, he had plucked his eyebrows until they were as thin as a woman's. His nose had been broken more than once and jutted to the right. He was missing teeth on both sides of his mouth, giving him the look of a jack-o'-lantern when he smiled. It was that grin that made him look so nutty and was probably what had convinced a jury that he belonged at Holloway instead of on death row.

The orderlies chose to sit as far away from Parker as protocol and security allowed. There were two of them, one a stocky black man with muscles as large as Parker's. The other orderly looked small next to Parker, though he was of ordinary build. He had red hair that badly needed cutting, his skin had a yellowish cast and his eyes were red from lack of sleep. He was rubbing his knuckles in a nervous gesture that betrayed his fear of Parker. But he was also glaring at Parker with undisguised hatred. There was bad blood between them, for sure, and I suspected the orderly probably took every opportunity to rub his authority in Parker's face. If so, it was a dangerous game to play. The first thing I had learned about Otis Parker, back when he was a suspect, was that he loathed authority of any kind.

Today, Parker was in charge and full of swagger. There are

things I can see that others miss, or perhaps it is more accurate to say that there are things that I can feel that others miss. Parker radiated a sense of triumphant self-satisfaction. He was in fine spirits. His crazy ass smile grew even wider when he spotted Calvano and he tracked his every move as Calvano took a seat and opened his notebook.

Calvano was annoying and had bungled his fair share of cases, but under Maggie's guidance he had ceased to be a complete idiot. He was not about to give away the reason why he was there. But the thing was – *he didn't have to*. I could tell by Parker's smirk that he knew full well why Calvano was there.

Calvano played it smart. Ignoring the issue of the murder being investigated in the valley below, Calvano began to ask Parker questions about the murders that had landed him inside Holloway. As Calvano continued to stubbornly avoid the subject of the new killing, Parker's cool facade began to crumble. He was not good at waiting for what he wanted. If Calvano did not bring up the new murder soon, I knew Parker would tip his hand one way or the other.

Sure enough, as the minutes passed, that insane smile of his faded and Parker began to throw specific details of the prior crimes into his answers to Calvano, choosing details that matched what had happened to the girl below, as if daring the detective to tell him why he was really there.

'I didn't choke those girls like people say, but I heard whoever did kill them choked them out,' Parker finally said. His breathing was as steady and controlled as ever, but his eyes had narrowed and his right hand kept jerking in an unconscious spasm, as if it longed to relive the experience being described. 'If I had been the one, I'd have done it slowly. Killing them quickly is a waste. I hear tell that the real fun is watching them fight their way back to a breath. That's when you start choking them again. The things I've learned in here.'

Calvano decided to provoke him. 'I don't give a shit if you did those murders or not. Maybe we have evidence you committed another murder and we're going to bring you up on that. Maybe you've been cured just in time to be sent away for life or to get that special cocktail right up your tattooed arm.'

Parker struggled against his restraints and the orderlies tensed, ready for anything.

'What's your name?' he spat at Calvano.

'Listen, dude,' Calvano said, rising as if he'd heard enough. 'My name doesn't matter. What does matter is that I'm not the sorry sack of shit who investigated you the first time. I'm not about to let you off easy this time.'

Well, excuse me.

'I've got a partner who will haunt your dreams until she brings you down,' Calvano added. 'I don't know what you think you're pulling, but you won't get away with it. Not this time.' Calvano locked eyes with Parker. 'You're gonna need ten high-priced lawyers by the time I get through with you. I'm gonna wipe that stupid grin right off your face.'

Parker's mood changed abruptly. He leaned toward Calvano and whispered, 'Face down, crawling from the mud, marked with the symbol of a harlot's lust. Another whore bites the dust.' Then he threw his head back and roared with a laughter that just as suddenly subsided into giggles that filled the room with a high-pitched, jangled frenzy. That was when I saw it: a dark and terrible shadow bloomed on the wall behind Parker, one with an elongated snout, thick body and ragged wings that beat in slow motion, as if in time to Parker's laughter.

I closed my eyes, thinking I had imagined that terrible seraphim. When I opened them again, Parker had settled back down and his mind was calm. The shadow was gone.

'We must do this again,' Calvano said pleasantly and, though I hated to admit it, I admired his style. 'Maybe we can get our eyebrows waxed together some time?'

Parker hissed and tried to lunge at him, but Calvano was already out the door. The black orderly had not changed expression since the interview began, but the red-haired orderly was laughing – and Parker knew he was laughing at him.

'You're a dead man,' Parker spat at the orderly.

'Aren't we all?' the red-haired orderly said, taunting him.

Yes, but some of us more than others.

SEVEN

I followed Calvano out, still trying to understand what I had seen in the interview room. I was grateful for the late afternoon sun and for every step that took me further away from Otis Parker. I saw my son across the lawn, talking to another kid his age. The boy was wearing a visitor's pass. I had never known Michael to have friends, although it was just as likely I had simply never noticed. Curious, I made my way over to them. The other boy was thin and pale with black hair that hung to his shoulders. He wore jeans and a work shirt and had a backpack slung over one shoulder.

'Hey, man,' he was telling Michael, 'It's just a couple of weeks and it's not like you're missing anything. There's this essay assignment due and everyone is freaking out, and you'll miss the science fair, but the same losers are going to win it again this year, so who cares? Plus they canceled the trip to Great Adventure because it would cost too much, so you're not even going to miss that. You may as well be in here where at least you'll get a break from school. I'll visit every day and tell you about all the stupid shit you're missing, I promise.'

It wasn't the most optimistic pep talk I'd ever heard, but it probably would have a bigger effect on Michael then anything his mother could ever say.

'I guess,' Michael mumbled back. 'Does everybody know I'm here? They'll think I'm a freak. Does Darcy know?'

'I don't think so, man,' his friend said. 'Darcy wasn't in school today, so I don't know about her, but I started a rumor that you had followed a band to Europe.' Michael laughed and his friend continued. 'By lunchtime, some people were saying you had moved to California, but most people were just walking around with their heads up their asses as usual. They don't even know where they are, much less where you are.'

'You sure?' Michael asked his friend. 'You know what people are like.'

'Yeah, I know what people are like.' The boy hesitated, started to say something and then stopped.

'What is it?' Michael asked. 'People are talking about me, aren't they?'

'No, man. It's not that at all.' The kid looked stricken. What was he hiding? He stared at his feet for a moment and then seemed to reach a decision. He looked up at Michael. 'You're not the only one who's been here,' he said. 'I was here. A long time ago. It really helped me. I don't think I would've made it without being here.'

'No shit,' Michael said. 'When was that? I don't remember that.'

'It was during the year I dropped out. After my mom died.'

'Oh, yeah.' Michael looked embarrassed at forgetting this monumental event in his friend's life. 'You were gone from school a long time.'

'I wasn't here the whole time,' his friend explained. 'I was only here for a month. But it really helped me. And I think it could help you, too. I'm not telling anyone you're here. You don't have to worry about that.'

His friend's admission made all the difference in the world to Michael. He was not a freak after all. 'I won't tell anyone either,' Michael promised his friend.

'I've got to go,' the other boy said. 'I've got a crapload of work to do.'

Michael nodded. Unexpectedly, he put his arms around his friend and awkwardly held on to him for a few seconds. I had never seen my son affectionate with anyone other than his mother and the gesture surprised me. But it also made me glad. My son had felt so alone while walking the halls inside Holloway. That he had someone, anyone, he could trust made me more grateful than I can say to the boy before me.

I followed the other kid out for a while but got distracted by my imaginary family. I saw Harold near the entrance to the long-term unit, enjoying the late afternoon. He had removed his protective helmet and covered the purple and yellow oint-ments that typically topped his skull with a newsboy's hat. He was busily plucking the dead petals off the flowers that had withered on the vine over the winter months. These he stored in his pockets as he filled the air with a constant monologue of nonsense. 'Harold Babbitt endorses the Flower Power Movement with the full force of his mighty power. Harold Babbitt is a rabbit, the king of the rabbits. Hop to it, King Rabbit, and try not to stab it. Dagnabit, you rabbit, dagnabit.' Harold's words flowed like the water tumbling over the fountains behind him. It was a never ceasing cascade proving that Harold was alive. Perhaps that was why he did it. Perhaps he just wanted to be sure.

I checked on Lily, the little girl who suffered from terrible hallucinations and could not be trusted with other children. She was standing with an aide, watching the sun slowly set, clutching the mutilated teddy bear she always toted around. Lily had gouged its plastic eyes out and painted the holes left behind with thick globs of red paint that dried in place like blood. The nose had also been plucked off, leaving a hole that gaped between those ghoulish eyes. I wondered what terrible sights had inspired her to blind her stuffed bear.

Then I thought back to the malevolent shadow I had seen flickering on the wall behind Otis Parker and I wondered, just for an instance, if maybe Lily's real curse was that she saw more than most. Was it possible that the ghastly creatures she obeyed were somehow real?

EIGHT

I like to wander my town at dusk in the evenings. There is something about that time of day that promises to reveal secrets. That night, I wandered past *Shenanigans,* the bar where I had spent so many nights drinking away the hours, never realizing how very few of them I had left. Inside, the television set blared sports and lonely men drank their way to oblivion surrounded by the smells of sweat and stale beer. Even the light looked unhappy with its yellowish, anemic cast. Yet I had spent most of my life in there. What had I been thinking?

I passed by the elementary school where my boys had put on many a play and suffered many defeats and important victories, all without me there to support them. Then I wandered through a park and found myself near the police station. Like a beacon, she had called me to her. I knew Maggie was inside, hard at work on the young girl's murder. I'd seen her work for forty-eight hours straight when a case was young, and double time after that until solved. Maggie was like a pit bull with a bone when she had an open case. She did not let go or give an inch. Sure enough, she was at her desk, the slender case file open before her as she examined photos of the dead girl. Calvano was leaning back in a chair next to her trash can, his feet propped up on another chair. He was explaining to Maggie what he had felt while questioning Otis Parker.

'Don't get me wrong,' he was saying, 'I think the guy is crazy as a loon. But I just have this feeling that he'd been waiting for me, that he knew we would come, and that he was enjoying every minute we spent together.'

'You think he's innocent of the five murders that put him there?' Maggie asked.

'Oh, hell no,' Calvano answered. 'What I think is that he's definitely got something to do with this latest one. I just can't figure out what his angle is and how he's involved. It drove him nuts when I didn't mention why I was really there. He wanted to hear about the murder. He was dying to roll in it. He's playing us for a reason. Could he have had a partner all along, someone who's still out there?'

Maggie shook her head. 'Parker worked alone. I've been over the earlier case files twice now and I think Fahey and Bonaventura got it right for a change.'

Um . . . thank you?

'I don't know,' Calvano said. 'I just have this gut feeling Parker's involved.'

'We can go with your hunch,' Maggie told him. 'I trust it. I'll back you up.'

'For real?' Calvano said. He wasn't used to people taking him seriously. 'It could be a copycat.'

'Maybe. Or maybe Parker has a follower doing exactly what

he's told to do. If that's the case, you can bet there's going to be another killing soon.'

'But who could it be?' Calvano asked. 'He gets no visitors, because he's a scumbag, and every phone call he makes is monitored. He's watched constantly, because he's the unit's number one badass and they are out to make his life miserable. Whenever they take him out of Holloway, he's a royal pain in the ass, so they don't take him out anymore. I don't see how he can be sending instructions to someone else without being seen. And they haven't had a patient leave there in over a year. I don't see how he's doing it.'

'I don't either,' Maggie agreed. 'But we better figure it out before someone else dies.'

Calvano could not resist second-guessing his own hunch. 'We could have it backwards,' he said. 'Maybe Parker has found a way to get out without anyone noticing. Maybe he killed the girl himself.'

'What's in it for him?' Maggie asked.

'I don't know,' Calvano admitted. 'Maybe he missed it? Did you hear back from the coroner yet? Is it for sure his signature?'

Maggie nodded. 'Doc called late this afternoon.' She sounded grim.

'What is it?' Calvano asked.

'He said that if it isn't the same man as before, they have something in common. They both really enjoy their work. Because after this guy strangled our girl, he did other things to her. The exact same things Parker did to the prior victims.'

'Things I don't want to know about,' Calvano said and he meant it. He was funny that way. For a guy on the job who had seen it all, he couldn't handle the details of what killers did to their victims, not if they were women.

'Definitely things you don't want to know,' Maggie agreed. 'Maybe she knew her killer? Picked him up at a bar?'

'Maybe, but her panel showed no evidence of alcohol or drugs in her system. She was clean.'

'Baby daddy?' Calvano suggested. He tended to head off in predictable directions when it came to an investigation, directions clearly colored by his own life.

'She was definitely not pregnant,' Maggie said. 'Doc said she may even have been a virgin, based on—'

'I don't want to know,' Calvano interrupted.

Maggie smiled at him tolerantly. 'We'll know a lot more when Doc is done.'

'So let's find her connection with Parker,' Calvano suggested. 'Find out who she is – get to know her and who her friends were – and how she ended up on that riverbank, right? Maybe we'll find a connection to Parker in there somewhere.'

Maggie nodded. 'You know, Adrian, pretty soon you won't need me at all.'

'I think we both know that's not true.'

Make that three of us.

NINE

The dead girl was named Darcy Swan and her family had not bothered to report her missing. Maggie learned of her identity when a stammering fifteen-year-old boy who bussed tables at the Freeway Diner called 911 to say that Darcy had failed to report for her shift and he just knew she'd never do a thing like that unless something bad had happened to her. When the dispatcher realized he was describing the girl found by the river, she alerted Maggie. Sometimes, a small town has its advantages.

Calls to both high school principals in town quickly yielded her photo and address. The dead girl was confirmed to be Darcy Swan and she did indeed live on the wrong side of the tracks, in a shabby rental house down the street from a sprawling Walmart that had taken over that end of Helltown. Maggie and Calvano volunteered to do the notification in hopes of finding out something useful to start their investigation with.

I hitched a ride over in the back of their car, the ultimate third wheel, shamelessly eavesdropping on their conversation. They had an OK partnership these days – especially considering

Calvano made up half of it – and I admit I was jealous. It should have been me riding shotgun.

The woman who answered the door at Darcy Swan's house was pushing fifty and proclaimed herself to be Darcy's grandmother. Like everyone else in Helltown would have been, she was too busy being suspicious of Maggie and Calvano to realize why they might be there. It was clear she had been drinking for hours. Before Maggie could explain why they were there, the old lady assumed that her granddaughter had been caught shoplifting and began ranting about the girl's shortcomings. The house was already filled with useless objects touted in the front aisles of drugstores every holiday season and I quite frankly could not think of what was left for Darcy to have shoplifted. But granny had a head of steam up and neither Maggie nor Calvano could get a word in as she embarked on a rant about the moral shortcomings of the younger generation. Obviously, she had no concept of what generation she was in: she wore acres of costume jewelry and her hair was teased high in a style considered all the rage back in the 1960s. Her tight black pants ended just above her ankles, and a pair of stiletto heels went nicely with the plunging neckline on her purple top, which didn't quite hide the matching push-up bra. She looked equally hoochie mama in a holiday portrait displayed on the mantle, a photo that made it plain that this was a family where high school girls had children who, in turn, grew up to be high school girls who had children of their own. Barely fifteen years separated the generations. The neighborhood was full of families just like them. I couldn't decide if it was sad or a relief that Darcy Swan had not been able to carry on the family tradition.

Maggie and Calvano could not get a word in and, after a while, stopped trying. They accepted the old lady's ceaseless complaining as a gift and Calvano began taking notes. They learned that Darcy attended the same high school my son Michael was assigned to and I wondered uneasily if my son and Darcy had been friends. Soon, the old dame launched into a well-practiced and unflattering description of both Darcy Swan and her mother. Despite the fact that they were her flesh and blood, both of them were proclaimed to be selfish, deluded, upstarts who didn't work hard enough to support the old lady and would learn in the end that there was nothing more to life than the fact that it was hard, and maybe then they'd understand why she couldn't work at the beauty parlor any more and would take better care of her.

I started to feel sorry for the woman. I knew that once she found out her granddaughter was dead, she would remember her bitter words and they would likely haunt her for a long time. There are some things that even the most selfish of people can't escape.

Maggie and Calvano finally gleaned that Darcy's mother worked at the new Walmart. Convinced her granddaughter had been up to no good, the old lady gave them meticulous directions to the deli section and asked that they convey a 'told you so' on her behalf. Maggie and Calvano left to break the news to Darcy's mother that her daughter was dead, but I'd had enough of Darcy's family for one day. Instead, I decided to take a look at the block where Darcy Swan had lived. Darcy had to have met her killer close to home, in school or at the diner. Her life had ended at those meager borders.

I took off on my own for a tour of Helltown. It had been a while since I'd walked its streets. I was startled to see a familiar face half a block down from Darcy's house. The young man who had visited my son Michael at Holloway was sitting in the dark on the open gate of a red truck parked in the driveway of another cheap mill house. His hands were trapped between his knees for warmth as he stared up at the sky. The stars were exceptionally bright and sprinkled like diamonds across the night horizon, a reminder that there was a whole universe out there beyond. I wondered if that realization helped the boy or only made him feel more trapped. He did not seem happy at all. He seemed as lost and depressed as my son, and for just a moment I had a vision of all the lost sons wandering in the darkness together, wondering when their turn might come.

A door slammed behind the boy and a deep voice bellowed for him to get his ass inside. The boy barely twitched as a stocky man in a wife-beater tee shirt and plaid boxer shorts appeared in the doorway, holding a beer can in one hand and a cigarette in the other. 'Your grandmother needs to be changed,' the man shouted, knowing his son was somewhere near in the darkness. 'I'll be damned if I'm going to do it.'

The door slammed shut behind him as he ducked back into a brightly lit living room, where the sounds of the television blared almost loudly enough to disguise the bleating of an old lady crying for help. The boy hopped down from the back of the truck and trudged inside, resigned to his fate.

This was the kid comforting my son?

I could only hope that Michael offered him comfort back.

TEN

Helltown depressed me. By morning, I was sorely in need of therapy. Not my own, of course. I had missed that boat while I was alive and there was nothing I could do about it now. But I could sit in on therapy sessions at Holloway, puzzling out the mysteries of the human soul and reassuring myself that I was not the only one who had lost his way in life.

I'd hoped to learn more about my son, even if it ended in another session consisting of reviewing my failures as a father, but Michael was in group therapy that morning and I could not tolerate being in the same room as a dozen awkward, depressed teens. Just seeing them slumped in their chairs, staring at the clock, staring at their feet, staring anywhere but at each other, made me feel so self-conscious that I had to leave them to the guidance of a tall man with glasses who had been handed the thankless task of trying to get them to open up.

With most of the other patients either in early-morning therapy or painting flowerpots or wandering quietly through the grounds, I decided to head over to the unit where Otis Parker lived to see if I could find out anything new. I came upon him having an argument with the red-haired orderly who had taunted Parker the day before during his interview with

Calvano. This time, Parker was unrestrained. He was standing in the center of the common room where he and his fellow inmates spent time in a futile attempt to socialize them and keep them from ripping each other's limbs off. Clearly, Parker had little to fear from the others – many of whom were so doped up that their greatest achievement of the day was probably not drooling on their own trousers. Most of them, however – even the most medicated among them – were alert enough to be watching the fight between Parker and the orderly like it was an Ali-Frazier rematch. As the two men squared off and shouted insults at each other, it became clear that Parker was too smart to resort to physical violence, given the other staff members heading their way. But he was comfortable threatening the orderly with everything this side of dismemberment.

The gist of the argument seemed to be that Parker was refusing to take his medication and the red-haired orderly was threatening him with an injection if he did not comply.

I wondered why Parker had let the fight get this far. He could have hidden the pills in his cheek and spit them out later. Patients did it so often that the mice at Holloway wandered around in a happy daze from scavenging the booty. The orderly, who was easily half of Parker's size, should have known that – but then he should have known better than to take on Parker in the first place. Both of them had clearly been waiting for an excuse to go at each other. While Parker stood rooted to his spot on the worn linoleum floor, the aide circled him like a prizefighter looking for a spot to jab.

'I'll pull your privileges, too,' he threatened Parker. 'Don't think I won't do it. I don't give a crap how much your lawyer earns an hour or how many times he threatens to sue. I'm sick of your bullshit, I'm sick of your bullying, and I'm sick of this act you pull every day. You're no crazier than I am. I've watched you when no one else is looking and I know you're a fake. Your ass belongs on death row with the rest of the losers waiting to die.'

It was one thing to taunt Parker with his authority. It was another to let Parker know outright that he didn't believe he belonged at Holloway. If I knew Otis Parker, the orderly had just made his workplace a very unsafe place to be.

'I'm on to you,' the red-haired orderly repeated, poking a finger in Parker's chest.

Parker let loose one of those crazy, high-pitched laughs of his, but the orderly continued to taunt him. 'I've seen you at the back fence,' he told Parker. 'Don't think I don't know what's going on.'

At this, Parker lunged for the orderly but four other staff members had arrived by then and they pulled Parker off. They led him away, casting glances at the red-haired orderly that made plain they had little patience for either his methods or his judgment.

I followed Parker, curious as to where they might take him to calm him down. But it turned out that he was scheduled for a session with his psychiatrist. He was taken to a spacious room where a short, tubby man awaited him, notebook in hand, his legs crossed precisely as he perched on the edge of a leather chair. He gestured for Parker to sit on the couch across from him.

Two of the orderlies forced Parker to sit and started to handcuff him to the legs of the leather couch.

'Is that really necessary?' the psychiatrist asked, casting a thin smile at Otis Parker as if to say, 'I'm on your side. Isn't it awful how backward these brutish men are?'

The psychiatrist had all the degrees in the world, but he was a fool.

'Yes, it's necessary,' one of the orderlies said. As if to make his point, he pulled on one of the chains that attached a couch leg to Parker's wrist, forcing Parker to wince.

The shrink glared at the orderly, but said nothing. Parker looked mildly interested in the disagreement between the two men. I knew he was filing the information away, just in case he could use it to his advantage later.

The two orderlies left the room and stationed themselves outside the door, in case something went awry. I wondered what this session was all about. Was it an attempt to rehabilitate Parker or a court-mandated session to assess whether or not Parker was any better than he had been when admitted?

I was not keen on getting closer to Parker's mind. I knew what I would find there. But I was interested in how much he had fooled the psychiatrist sitting across from him, and if he would be able to resist revealing his connection to Darcy Swan's murder.

I found out the answer to my first question when the psychiatrist put his notebook aside and leaned forward, clasping his hands together as he stared at Parker with what he thought was professional detachment but I decided was perilously close to admiration. The shrink was not a big man. In fact, he was barely five and a half feet tall and he was plump in that way people are when they've spent a lifetime unable to resist overeating. He could not take his eyes off Parker. I had seen that look before. People hated following the unwritten rules of their world each day and often secretly admired those who ignored them. Especially those who did it without apology. The psychiatrist had fallen for Otis Parker's charisma, mistaking an excess of testosterone for evidence that Parker was somehow a superior kind of human being worth saving.

He'd learn soon enough.

'What's this I hear about an altercation?' the shrink asked. 'Was it with the same orderly as before?'

Parker managed to look downright perplexed. His trademark shit-eating grin faded and he looked quite sad, as if he could not understand the injustices visited upon him. 'I do everything he asks,' Parker explained. 'But it's never good enough. The guy has some kind of complex about me. He thinks I'm faking it. Sometimes I don't even feel like going through with my therapy because of him. What's the use?'

Oh, he knew what buttons to push. The psychiatrist nearly hopped in his agitation. He could not, I noticed, stop staring at Parker's immense biceps nor refrain from glancing at Parker's narrow torso and powerful thighs. I wasn't sure it mattered at all what Parker said; the shrink was under the spell of Parker's sheer physical power. He was in no position to evaluate him objectively.

'You can't think that way,' the shrink told him. 'We've worked too hard to throw it all away. If you keep accepting your illness, and doing what I ask you to do, you'll have a chance at starting a new life one day.'

'But will that day ever come?' Parker asked. He flexed his arms and rubbed the tops of his thighs, shifting his weight from leg to leg. He knew exactly what he was doing. If he'd had a spotlight he couldn't have shined the psychiatrist on any more. 'First I get arrested for something I didn't even do, and then they say I'm crazy, and then they send me here with no release date in sight. I would've been better off going to prison. At least then I would have had a shot at getting out.'

He managed to pour such hopelessness into this series of preposterous statements that even I felt sorry for him, until I remembered that there had been overwhelming evidence that Parker was indeed the killer. So much evidence, in fact, that even I had been able to connect the dots at a time when I was rarely sober for more than an hour at a stretch and could hardly find my files, much less solve the cases in them.

'If I knew when I had a chance to get out of here,' Parker added slyly, 'it might give me a reason to work even harder getting over what's wrong with me.'

The shrink was staring at him thoughtfully. Even he, so enamored of Parker, had his doubts. 'I'm not likely to begin a conversation about your release from here for several years,' he explained to Parker. 'The things that are wrong with you are serious psychiatric disorders. We may never be able to change their power over your behavior. The best we can do may be simply to find the right mix of medications to help you control them. Whether or not I can let you out into the world under those circumstances is still uncertain. I want to be upfront with you. I want you to know that I will always tell you the truth.'

'But I'm in here for something I didn't do,' Parker insisted. 'I'm presumed to be violent because of something that someone else did. And now I've got the proof. The other patients are saying a girl was killed yesterday,' Parker said. He looked sorrowful with this loss of life. 'That she was killed in the same way as the girls I was accused of murdering.' He looked up at the psychiatrist, his eyes wide with hope. 'Doesn't that prove I wasn't the one who killed those other girls? It's the first ray of hope I've had in years.'

The psychiatrist looked confused. 'I hadn't heard about another murder,' he said cautiously. 'I'll have to look into it and see what I can find out.'

Parker nodded eagerly. 'Can you talk to my lawyer about it?' Parker asked. 'I don't think he is smart enough to understand without your help.'

'I can consult with your lawyer about your condition,' the psychiatrist said uneasily. 'Beyond that, I cannot get involved. After all, I may be called to testify at your next competency hearing.'

Parker leaned forward again, staring at the psychiatrist intently. He was really working it. 'I can pay for your time, if that's what you're worried about. I have a lot of people who believe in me, who know I'm not guilty. Your support would mean so much to them.'

Of course he had people convinced of his innocence. Even Charles Manson had his fan club. There were probably dozens of misguided women across the nation sending Otis Parker checks and transferring cash into his legal defense fund. If they had seen the same crime scene photos I had seen, they would have held on to their hard-earned dollars. And probably never gone outside their own front doors again, either.

The psychiatrist had seen the same photos, and whether or not he believed that Parker was innocent, he looked old enough to have been around the block a few times. Surely, he still had doubts, even if Parker had been spending months, maybe even years, trying to convince him otherwise?

'Let's talk about those groupies,' the psychiatrist said, reaching for his notebook again. 'How do they make you feel?'

'What do you mean?' Parker asked, leaning back and stretching his legs out so that his pants stretched tight against his groin.

Of the two of them, only one was good at reading people – and it sure as hell wasn't the shrink.

'How does the thought of being close to another person make you feel?' the psychiatrist asked primly. 'How do you feel when you think about being close to them, emotionally or physically?'

'How do I feel?' Parker repeated, his trademark grin

returning. 'I feel like slowly unbuttoning their blouses and ripping off their bras and running my hands up and down that firm sweet flesh above their ribs until I reach their breasts and then . . .' He began to recite a pornographic list of things he would happily do to the women who wrote to him if he ever had the chance.

His lust sounded real, but I was more inclined to believe the guard who had said Otis Parker didn't care about the women who sent him money, or what they could do for him physically. He just took their money and asked for more.

The psychiatrist listened carefully and made frequent notations, as if Parker's monologue was fascinating. But I thought it sounded like a late-night Cinemax re-run and I could see no value in this line of questioning other than to titillate them both.

The truth was that the shrink was no safer in Parker's presence than any of his prior victims had been. He was a fool to believe a word out of Parker's mouth.

ELEVEN

How Holloway feels often depends on the time of day. It can be a frightening place at night when the air is heavy with restless dreams and private realizations that life's opportunities have been squandered. In the mornings, there is a palpable air of release that the darkness is gone, tinged with the skepticism that the day ahead will bring anything but the same. By mid-morning, the mood has often changed again. Especially in the spring time, when many of the residents cannot help but notice that the sun is high in the sky and the air is fresh and the birds bounce along the brick walkways and perch on the statues that decorate the courtyard with resolute devotion. This benign mood can often last until dinner time, when the encroaching evening casts a pall over everyone's optimism. That's when this sort of jittery, wait-and-see attitude comes over everyone, patients and staff alike.

I prefer the daylight hours, when it is still possible to believe that not everyone who enters Holloway is doomed to remain inside its walls.

Especially when it comes to Olivia. I found her that afternoon in her usual spot, watching the fountain. She seemed unable to take her eyes away from the water and did not notice me. The little girl, Lily, had discovered an anthill on the great lawn. Under the watchful eye of a nurse's aide, who knew all too well that Lily's smaller stature in no way rendered her harmless, she was busy poking a stick down into the anthill and watching the tiny creatures scurry away in panic. Harold had more ambitious plans for the day. He was once again wearing his newsboy cap and had trundled over to the double fence marking the maximum security and was sending a steady stream of babbling nonsense toward the inmates playing basketball on the courts inside. His words gushed out in staccato bursts, making sense only to him. It seemed to be a mix between childhood memories and the plot of an insipid sitcom I had seen him watching a few nights before. As often happens with Harold's monologues, it started out interesting but soon descended into the mundane: 'Harold Babbitt sees the court of the Mountain King. It is filled with jesters who dance and sing. I see a killer, a baker, a candlestick maker, a jump-start faker and an innocence-taker.'

It was OK to accuse them of murder, but the inmates on the other side of the fence lacked any appreciation for Harold once he started attacking their athletic talents. One of them picked up the basketball and rocketed it toward the fence with ferocious strength. The ball slammed into the fence right in front of Harold's face with a terrifying clank, causing Harold to scream and jump surprisingly high for such a round little guy. He landed unsteadily and fell backwards over a bush before sprawling on the lawn like someone trying to make snow angels without the snow. The basketball players roared with laughter – but I noticed that only one was not paying attention, as his gaze was distracted by someone walking by. Otis Parker had found someone far more interesting than Harold to occupy his attention.

I followed his gaze. He was watching Olivia. A rage filled

me with such intensity I was taken aback by how very human
it made me feel. How dare Parker look at her that way? I felt
an overwhelming need to protect her. It was a new sensation.
I had always been the weak one in life. I had never been able
to protect her. But now that I felt the impulse, there was little
I could do. I was helpless to stop him as he made loud smacking
sounds and called out 'Hey, mama!' He grabbed his crotch
but Olivia ignored him, lost in her own world.

My wife Connie had seen the exchange. She wasn't used
to people like Otis Parker, but with one look at his face, she
got the message. She hurried away, determined to put as much
distance between her and the maximum security unit as
possible. I followed her to the juvenile wing where she asked
after Michael and was told that he was in therapy and she
would have to wait if she wanted to see him. The nurse added
that he had a visitor waiting already and gestured toward the
boy I had seen with Michael the day before. This time, he
was slumped in an orange plastic chair in the common room
where the teenagers gathered for television and group therapy.
He looked just like the other patients there for treatment: ill
at ease and unhappy. Connie joined the boy and seemed to
know him well. He smiled when she approached and it transformed his face. He was not a bad-looking kid. He just held
a lot inside and it showed on the outside. I knew how that
felt.

'How's it going, Adam?' Connie asked him. She took a seat
beside him and placed her pocketbook on her lap. Her legs
were pressed tightly together and she was balancing on the
tips of her toes, telling me that she had not come to grips with
the fact that her son was living in such a place, however
temporarily.

'I'm OK,' he mumbled. 'Mr Phillips let me leave a few
minutes early so I could stop by and see Michael before I
study. I have a big test tomorrow.'

'In that case, I'll wait while you see him. I have the afternoon off, so it's no big deal.'

Adam looked startled at this show of concern for his needs,
and I wondered if the kid had anyone in his life who ever
gave a damn about him. More likely, his life had always been

about putting fresh diapers on his grandmother while avoiding the drunk in his underwear who liked to bellow instead of conversing with his son. I'd been there myself and knew what it was like. The kid had a lot to get past each morning, just to get out of bed. Worse, he knew it. To have a friend in the mental hospital was just another step forward into the life of disappointment he was destined for.

They waited in silence after that, and I wondered if there was something even bigger weighing on the kid. He seemed distracted and lost in thought. Or maybe waiting to see a friend in a mental hospital was just too much to ask of a kid his age.

Connie noticed his mood, too. 'Are you OK?' she asked him.

Adam did not respond for a moment and I knew he was hiding something from her. 'Sure, Mrs F. I'm just worried about some school stuff.'

He was lying to Connie. I was sure of it.

'If you ever need anything, you know I'm here, right? You're always welcome at our house, or you can call me any time if you just need someone to talk to. It would just be between us. Not even Michael has to know.'

I thought for a moment Adam might start to cry at Connie's unexpected offer of help, but his exceptional self-control won out. He managed to say, 'I know. Thanks.'

I left them to their waiting and went to check on Michael. He was sitting with his therapist, Miranda, in a sunny corner room. Michael was sitting a few feet away from Miranda and staring at his feet. His self-consciousness was painful to watch. I knew it was wrong to eavesdrop on my son, and another part of me knew that if I listened long enough, I would only hear something else I didn't want to hear. But I had to know that my son was going to be OK. I had to know that he real-ized how many people loved him, and that he was there at Holloway because they loved him.

'He's, like, the only guy at school who bothers to listen when I talk,' Michael was telling Miranda. 'Most days, I go all day with him being the only one I talk to. Or, at least, the only one I talk to who actually hears what I'm saying. And I can tell the other kids are talking behind my back sometimes, but not Adam. I've seen him stick up for me and once he took a swing at this jerk for saying something bad about my father.'

'So he's your friend?' Miranda asked. 'He sounds like he's your friend to me.'

Michael shifted uneasily. 'Yeah, I guess. Don't you think it's kind of gay and all to be so close to another guy?'

Miranda's answer was immediate. 'No, I don't think it's kind of gay and all. I talk to a lot of people as part of my job and I find that the happiest of them have friends like the kind of friend you have in Adam.' She looked at him in silence for a moment. 'Michael, no one should go through life alone.'

'My father did,' he said.

'But your father did not go through life alone by choice,' Miranda explained. 'He just lost his way. When that happened, he left the ones who loved him behind. I don't think that he meant to, though.'

I was grateful to her, both for comforting my son and for putting into words a regret I had not been able to express. She was right. I had been lost and wandering for so much longer than the past year.

'Our time is up,' she told Michael. 'Do you want to stay longer today? I have the time.'

He shook his head. 'Adam is coming by to see me and my mom took the afternoon off to bug me.'

He and Miranda laughed.

'Tomorrow, then,' she told him. 'I'll be here for you.'

Michael nodded his thanks. When he left the room, he looked visibly lighter and his step seemed more confident. I guess sometimes all people need is for someone to listen.

Michael greeted Connie and his friend with some embarrassment, aware he had more visitors than most of the other kids in the unit. Michael had never been the kind of kid who wanted to be different.

Adam felt his discomfort. 'Come on, man,' he said. 'Let's get some fresh air.'

Michael cast an anxious glance at his mother.

'I'll be fine,' she assured him, waving them away. 'Cal's going to stop by. I'll spend some time with him.'

The two boys left the oppressive atmosphere of the unit

behind. I could feel his friend Adam's anxiousness radiating
off him. He had come bearing bad news.

'What is it?' Michael asked as they hurried down the steps.

'Wait until we get outside,' Adam mumbled. Whatever it
was, he was trying to put it off.

Michael's anxiousness grew as they walked over the lawn
that linked Holloway's units and created the illusion, if you
could ignore the security fences penning in the criminally
insane, that Holloway was nothing more than an expensive
resort.

Finally, Michael could take it no longer. He pulled up short
in the middle of the lawn and turned to his friend. 'Just tell
me,' he said.

'You know the girl they found by the river?'

I could feel the fear starting to bubble up in Michael. 'Yeah.
Everyone has heard by now. Everyone on the unit is saying
it's someone who was let out of Holloway too early, that she
killed herself.'

Adam shook his head. 'No, man. It wasn't anyone from
Holloway.' He hesitated. 'It was Darcy.'

'Darcy?' It was a single word, but in those two short
syllables, Michael managed to convey disbelief, instant devas-
tation and something akin to panic. I could feel the bottom
drop out of his world. I could feel him spiraling down into
the darkness. The girl had meant a lot to him. He swayed, as
if he were dizzy.

His friend reached out to catch him. 'Michael?' Adam's
voice rose. 'Are you OK? Can you hear me?' He looked
panicked, as if Michael's distress was too much for him to
deal with.

'I have to go back inside,' Michael mumbled, waving his
friend away. 'I need to be alone. I need to talk to someone.'
He hurried off before Adam could follow him. He left behind
a sense of words unsaid that was palpable in the air.

He was hiding something from Adam. I knew it – and I
think that Adam knew it, too. Adam stood, alone on the vast,
green lawn, and stared after my son, emotions racing through
him with such intensity that I could not pinpoint any one. I
felt confusion and jealousy and fear move through him as he

struggled with his thoughts, but his thoughts were interrupted when a familiar voice bellowed at him from across the lawn.

'Light a fire under it!' a gruff voice bellowed out. 'Move it now or you're walking.'

Adam's father stood at the main entrance to Holloway. Behind him, through the gate, I saw a red pickup truck idling at the curb.

Adam pulled his emotions back under control, something he did so well it was starting to frighten me. What would happen the day they all came out again? He turned his back on Michael and trudged resolutely toward his father.

I followed. I had found a connection between Darcy Swan and Holloway – and maybe even Otis Parker. I needed to know more about this boy. He was closer to my son than anyone else in the world. And I knew enough about kids to know that, where Adam went, so too would go my son.

TWELVE

B y the time we reached the truck, Adam's father was already at the wheel. His flannel shirt had grease stains on it and he wore a baseball cap pulled so low that you could not see his eyes. His jowls sagged and were peppered with gray stubble – it was a look I knew well. He was barely holding on until he could get to the bar and start drinking again. I felt a flicker of unease in my gut at the reminder of what I had been, but something else, too: the air around me grew heavy. Adam and his father were a doomed combination. It was as if the light contracted and shrank away from the truck that held them. There was an irreparable rift between them, one fatal to a father and son.

Adam hopped in beside his father and neither spoke. I did not like the feeling of apprehension that the two of them together inspired in me, but I wanted to know more. I climbed into the truck and found a spot directly behind the bench seat, where the smell of the father's boozy sweat and the lingering odor of his cigarettes wafted over me as he pulled away from the curb. To think that had once been me.

'What the hell's the matter with you?' the old man demanded of his son. 'You look like someone just shot your dog.'

Why had he gone there? I wondered. Somehow, I doubted that Adam had a happy pet ownership history.

'A rumor went around school today,' Adam mumbled, moving as far away as he could from his father. He rolled down his window and leaned out of it, seeking the refuge of cold air against his face as his father accelerated on to the highway.

The father actually sounded interested. 'What kind of rumor?' he asked.

'That the girl who got murdered yesterday was Darcy,' the boy said. 'Turns out it was true.' Unlike my son, Adam did not feel so much sad as resigned. As if he had always known that Darcy's life would end like this, that neither one of them would ever have a lick of good luck, not given where they had come from.

'Who the hell is Darcy?' his father asked.

'Seriously? She was only my girlfriend for a year.'

'You mean that tease from a few doors down?' his father asked. 'The one with the huge tits just like her mother? Just like her grandmother, too, come to think of it. I went to high school with the mother. She was a slut, if I recall.'

The thought of that creature terrorizing a high school with his greasy looks and ill-temper chilled me. Thank god I had not known him then.

'Her name was Darcy Swan,' Adam said and he managed to infuse every syllable with hatred so thick I was astonished the father did not pick up on it. 'And she wasn't a tease.'

The father pulled into the fast lane and shot past a series of cars, more interested in trying to beat a black Cougar than he was in trying to console his son. 'If it makes you feel any better,' he finally said, 'her life wasn't going to amount to much anyway.'

Adam propped his feet up on the dash and stared at his boots. He started to chew on a fingernail, noticed that he had already gnawed the cuticles down to the quick, and dropped them into his lap again. 'Yeah, dad, that makes me feel so much better.'

His sarcasm was wasted on the old man.

'How the hell is your friend doing anyway?' the father asked suddenly. I realized with distaste that he was talking about Michael.

Adam glanced over at his father, surprised that he had asked. 'He's OK. His mother is there a lot and he agreed to stay there for a couple more days, at least, to see if it makes him feel any better.' I knew just what the poor kid was thinking: it sucked to be in Holloway, but at least Michael had people who cared for him and who noticed what he was going through.

'His mother being that snooty blonde bitch that drops him off at the house sometimes?'

'Don't talk about her that way,' Adam said, taking the words right out of my mouth. 'She's done more for me than you ever did.'

'That still doesn't make her any less of a snooty bitch. Thinks she's better than us.'

Adam just shook his head. He wasn't going to take the bait.

His father slowed and turned off the highway on to a winding side road. The kid looked up in alarm. 'Where are we going? I've got homework. I have that big test tomorrow.'

'Relax. I'm just checking out a club the guys down at the bar turned me on to a few weeks ago. I'll only be a minute. You can stay in the truck and study if you need to.'

Yeah, because studying in the dark is so productive. He was truly Father of the Year.

They pulled up in front of a low-rent bar I'd never seen before, which was no surprise since places like this tended to flare up like cold sores in our town. They were usually fronts for laundering cash from drug dealing or illegal gambling operations and were popular with people from a few states up because they brought in a good cash flow. By the time the IRS got on to them, the doors would be padlocked and the owners long gone, having happily opened up shop somewhere else. This version was called *The Pussycat Lounge* and it was housed in a building that looked like it had once been a self-storage unit. They'd slapped a neon sign above the door, but the walls were corrugated metal and there were no windows to be seen. A real charming place to take your son.

His father hopped from the truck and slammed the door behind him without another word to Adam. He headed for the front door like a heat-seeking missile and I knew it was going to be a hell of a lot longer than a few minutes before he returned.

Adam knew it, too. He jumped from the truck and went to the rear bed, where he unearthed an enormous toolbox from under a small mountain of scrap metal and broken tiles, then rummaged around inside it until he produced a large flashlight. Back in the truck, he wound the seat belt strap around it to make a miniature lamp above his shoulder, pulled a book from his knapsack and began to concentrate on the questions in front of him.

I could feel his mind gradually settle, the agitation leaving him as he zeroed in on the complicated formulas that filled the page from top to bottom. He had an amazing ability to tune out the world around him. I was starting to think that was a very good thing indeed. Maybe it would get him out of this place one day.

THIRTEEN

I spent that night in Lily's room, watching her look out over the darkness of the great lawn. I often kept her company at night, in part because I was fascinated by the dark landscape that filled her mind. It did not seem fair that such a young child should have to carry the burden of those terrible sights.

Lily seemed particularly restless that night. She wore elastic pants and kept pulling the waistband out before letting go. It would make a snapping sound and a red line soon formed around her middle from her obsessive tugging at it. Her lower lip was red from where she had been scraping her top teeth against it for hours. I did not know if it was her illness or the medication that made her repeat the gestures over and over.

She stood at the window for hours and only she knew what she saw. The thought of her spending another sixty years like that was dizzying. I would have chosen even my otherworld existence over such a fate. Just standing with her was mind-numbing.

I was considering leaving to check on my son when Lily grew agitated and began to flap her hands up and down like a bird trying to fly. She looked around and seemed surprised to find herself alone in her room. She rushed to the door and flung it open so hard that it banged against the wall behind it. I followed her as she ran out into the hall and dashed to the far end, where a bored aide was leaning back in a chair, half-asleep, his feet propped up on the desk.

'A monster, a monster!' she cried, banging her fist on the desk.

The aide jumped up with a start, knocking over his chair. He looked panicked and then angry when he realized that it was just Lily. He fought to make his voice soothing. 'It's just a nightmare, little one,' he said. 'Did you take the medicine I gave you?'

'It's real,' Lilly insisted. 'I saw it. It was a big one.'

'Let me walk you back to your room,' the aide said soothingly, grabbing her shoulders and guiding her down the hall. She went unwillingly and he had to push her a few times. Lily could be like that. She was little, she was stubborn and she was sure of the things she saw. The aide locked the door of her room as he left. He did not want Lily disappearing on his watch: her escapes were legendary.

She resumed her vigil at the window and I stayed with her, unwilling to leave her in her distress. Her attention to the darkness never wavered. She stood staring out at the monsters only she could see until the sun finally rose over the horizon.

Sunrise changes everything and it was no exception that day. As the first rays cleared the hill behind Holloway and sent fingers of sunlight creeping across the lawn, I saw a crumpled shape slumped beside the brick of the courtyard fountain. The shape had barely registered as a human being when Harold's screaming began.

'Harold Babbitt sees a dead man!' he cried as he dashed across the lawn, making a beeline for his unit. 'Harold Babbitt sees a dead man!'

I knew Harold had been out walking, as he often did at daybreak, hoping to spot some of the rabbits that lived among the bushes on the edges of the lawn. He must have seen the same shape that caught my eye and marched over to investigate. He had wasted no time sounding the alarm, but Harold was always announcing his discoveries. No one paid attention at first.

Still shouting, 'Harold Babbitt sees a dead man,' he reached the long-term building, flung open its doors and began shouting bloody murder. Soon, a stream of nurses, aides and curious patients ran out to see if Harold had actually seen anything or was simply suffering another episode.

I beat them to the fountain. Harold Babbitt had indeed seen a dead man. I did not know his name, but I recognized his face – it was the red-haired orderly who had fought with Otis Parker the day before. He was sprawled across the brick walkway in front of the fountain, his legs bent at unnatural angles. His body had been propped on its side and his broken legs folded into place to make it look as if the aide was trying to run backwards.

Like an old-time cartoon. One someone my age or older would have seen.

Since I have begun my wandering life, I have borne silent witness at many a crime scene. Murders almost always leave behind a mixture of the same feelings – surprise, betrayal, fear, rage, and shock – albeit in different proportions each time. These emotions hang in the air and entwine around me in my twilight world until, gradually, they fade away, I think because the victim has moved on, taking the last vestiges of life with them. But I had never felt a crime scene quite like this one. I could sense urgency, a trace of love and then . . . nothing. Nothing at all.

I tried to put it all together. It was as if the orderly had gone from being here to not being here, all in a millisecond, with no time to struggle and no time to reflect on what he was leaving behind.

Yes, that was it. The red-haired orderly had not known the attack was coming. He had never even heard his killer approach. He had been hit from behind, his neck broken in an instant before he dropped like a stone to the courtyard below. The killer had lingered long enough to break his legs after death and to arrange them in their strangely mocking position. That odd touch had been clinical and, to the killer at least, necessary. But the killing itself had not been a murder of passion. It had been one of expediency. Someone had needed him gone – and I was certain it was either Otis Parker or his partner.

Then I wondered if the red-haired orderly had been Otis Parker's partner. Had he killed Darcy Swan and been killed by Parker in turn to keep him from betraying their connection?

No, I did not think so. There had been nothing between the orderly and Otis Parker but a mutual hatred. It had been pure and absolute. There were no secrets binding them. Besides, how could Parker have done it when he was locked up in the maximum security ward?

I decided to make absolute sure that Otis Parker was still confined to his unit. I found him fast asleep in his bed, his face as serene as a child's in innocent slumber. No nightmares tortured Otis Redman Parker. Quite the opposite. Otis Parker *was* the nightmare.

But I did not think it was a coincidence that the red-haired orderly lay dead a day after hassling Parker. No way in hell. But if Otis Parker had not killed him, then who was roaming the lawns and halls of Holloway, where my son now stayed? Who had killed the orderly?

By the time I got back to the courtyard, Holloway was in chaos. Patients had left their breakfasts sitting on the table as hysteria swept the hospital, drawing patients and staff alike to the fountain. Sirens in the distance only whipped the crowd into more of a frenzy. Harold was marching circles around the crowd, all the while shouting, 'Harold Babbitt saw a dead body.' No one tried to stop him. The staff had recognized the victim as one of their own, which meant they had bigger problems than trying to control Harold Babbitt

At the fountain, patients pushed and shoved each other, unable to control the physical impulses fueled by the excitement of a sudden break from their routine. The staff regained their composure and tried valiantly to control the patients, shooing the worst of them back to their wards. I saw with dismay that Michael was among the crowd of bright-eyed adolescents watching the scene with that peculiar detachment of the younger generation, children raised on YouTube videos of the most extreme nature. They had seen it all before from the safe perspective of a computer screen and, as a result, processed everything unpleasant as potentially faked or, at the very least, slightly unreal.

It was not until the police arrived that the crowd began to scatter. Most of the patients let themselves be herded back into the buildings of Holloway, but they were soon supplanted by the shouts of a dozen patients on the criminally insane unit who had been let out into the exercise yard and had noticed the fray. They rushed to the inner fence and wound their fingers around the wire so that they could shake it back and forth like monkeys at the zoo. Hooting and hollering, they shouted insults at the cops who arrived first at the scene.

Otis Parker was not among the crowd at the fence. I did not know if he remained sleeping soundly in his room or if he had been denied his exercise time because of the fight with the red-haired orderly the day before. Regardless, the inmates allowed outside were soon hustled back inside by a line of muscular aides, who were in no mood to indulge out-of-control behavior. They cleared the yard in less than five minutes, casting anxious glances back over their shoulders at the growing crowd of uniformed officers handling the crime scene. They had seen the green of the victim's clothing and they knew it had to be a staff member.

Maggie and Calvano arrived and reached the dead orderly just as I returned to the fountain. Maggie ducked under the yellow tape that had been draped around the scene and stared down at the body, calculating the posture, potential source of the wounds and the message the tableau was trying to send.

It was a ghoulish and disconcerting sight – and it was most certainly staged.

Maggie pressed her fingers against the dead man's flesh and calculated how long he had likely been dead.

'When?' Calvano whispered. He was kneeling beside her, inches from the body. Male victims he could handle.

'A few hours before dawn at the latest.' She rose and stared down at the body again. I could feel her piqued interest from where I stood behind a tree. I moved closer to the body and tried to gauge what she was feeling.

'This is a little freaky,' Calvano mumbled. 'Look at his legs.'

Maggie nodded.

'It's different from Darcy Swan,' Calvano pointed out.

'In some ways,' Maggie admitted. 'But there's still that need to stage the body, to create a pose. Maybe he does one thing for women and another for men?'

Calvano looked skeptical, but not for long. Maggie put him to work interviewing the first officers to respond to the scene, taking down their description of what they had encountered. Maggie started interviewing staff while she waited for the lab techs to arrive. She'd gone through four staff members by the time Calvano had finished with the pair of responding officers. He was dragging his feet, I knew, since the next step would be to get the names of patients who might possibly have interfered with the body or, less likely, committed the murder or seen something that could be useful. Calvano didn't like dealing with crazies, unless you counted the women crazy enough to go out with him. He was reluctant to dive into the dirty work that lay ahead and was looking for an excuse to put it off.

In a way, I understood. Facing the sorry army of lost beings who occupied Holloway would be like coming face-to-face with your own worst-case scenario. There was little more than a teaspoon of chemicals separating Calvano from the patients of Holloway and he knew it. No one liked that reminder.

For the first time, I noticed Olivia sitting alone on one of the park benches dotting the lawn, weeping quietly to herself. I do not think that death held any titillation for her.

'Can you see me?' I asked quietly as I took a seat beside her.

'Yes,' she said simply, staring across the grass at the fountain.

'Don't let anyone else know you can see me,' I warned her.

She did not ask me why, but she nodded. 'I saw him,' she said matter-of-factly.

'Who?'

'Vinny.'

'The man lying over there?' I asked.

'Yes. I saw him this morning. Just after dawn. He was standing in the hallway outside my door, waiting for me.'

'That's impossible,' I said. 'He'd been dead for hours. Trust me, I can tell.'

'I saw him,' she said stubbornly. 'I was surprised to see him because he had been transferred into the other unit weeks ago. But there he was, waiting in the hallway for me, standing there outside my door. Not saying anything. Just standing there and looking at me.'

'What did you do?' I asked, wondering what bond between them had made it possible for the dead orderly to linger behind long enough to tell her goodbye before he moved on.

'I smiled at him,' she said. 'He smiled back. But it was a sad smile. That wasn't like him. He was always trying to cheer me up.' She paused. 'Just as I was going to say something, he said to me, "I just wanted to know that you were going to be OK."'

Olivia stopped and stared at the ground.

'What is it?' I asked.

'I was going to thank him for caring about me when he was in my ward, for being my friend and helping me get through it, but a nurse came by and said I needed to take my medication. I was distracted by her and when I turned back around, he was gone. He was just gone.' She looked at me. 'I don't know where he went.'

'He went to a better place,' I said. 'That much I know.'

'But now I'll never get a chance to tell him how much it mattered to me that he was my friend.'

'He knows,' I promised her. 'He knows.'

FOURTEEN

By mid-morning the orderly's body was on its way to the morgue, but it would take Holloway days to recover. The patients were restless and agitated. Staff had imposed sign-in and sign-out procedures for even the most competent of patients. And the maximum security unit, in particular, was in chaos. Maggie had heard about Otis Parker's altercation with the orderly from several staff members. Over a dozen uniformed officers were searching every inch of the building for evidence of how Otis Parker could have escaped undetected. It took them into the evening and, in the end, they came up empty. There was no indication that Otis Parker could have had anything to do with it.

Parker spent the hours while they searched lying on his bed, hands folded under his head, exuding a sense of satisfaction that remained undented by either the angry threats from other patients, who were pissed off at being confined, or the gruff treatment by the officers searching his room. If Parker had a way out of the unit, he was absolutely confident the cops would never find it.

Word soon leaked about the orderly's murder. Families hurried to Holloway to accuse the administration of failing to keep their loved ones safe. I noticed that very few offered to take them home, however.

Connie was among the anxious who came to Holloway when they heard the news. I am ashamed to say that I felt a stab of satisfaction when her fiancé Cal rushed past her as she hurried toward Michael's building. He looked flustered and worried, and managed only a feeble wave before he dashed toward a grim-looking older man and woman with their lawyer in tow. Connie looked after him, perplexed, before heading upstairs to see our son.

Michael had joined his ward-mates in the common room. They were watching a twenty-four-hour news station, waiting

for information on Darcy Swan's murder and more about the
murder they had stumbled on by the fountain. The news anchors
were hyperventilating over both deaths. A few of the teenagers
on the ward had known Darcy and, from what I could tell,
although poor, she had been a good kid. Michael listened to
their comments without saying a word, though I knew he had
known the dead girl. I could tell he felt scorn for the kids who
were trying to elevate their status by bragging about how well
they had known Darcy. But I feared he held back about his
own relationship with her for a darker reason. I could feel his
anger rising at some of his ward-mates for not understanding
that Darcy's death was not entertainment, but real.

When Connie arrived, Michael was embarrassed to see her,
despite the fact that she was far from the only anxious parent
there. He pulled her away from the crowd, muttering under his
breath, 'I told you not to come. I'm fine. You're smothering me.'

No mere accusation of smothering was going to stop Connie.
'I'm not so sure it's a good idea for you to stay here,' Connie
said. 'I think it's better you come home with me.'

'I'm going to be fine,' Michael told her, patting her arm
in the same way, I suspect, he had once reassured her that I
was going to be OK. I had asked a lot of my son and I felt
ashamed at seeing how it had shaped his relationship with
his mother.

'You mean you want to stay here?' Connie asked, surprised.

Michael tried to look casual, but I could tell he didn't just
want to stay at Holloway; part of him felt he *needed* to stay.
'I may as well finish what I started. Isn't that what you always
say to me? Besides, I just have a lot going on in my head. I
have people I can talk to here.'

Connie stared at him without saying a word and I knew she
had taken his words, in part, as a rebuff – why could he not
talk to her about his problems? She was willing to listen.

'I'm just starting to figure things out,' Michael tried to
explain, with a maturity that I had not known he had. 'I like
my therapist. She's really nice. And I don't feel stressed out
or confused in here. I don't have a lot of stuff hanging over
my head or some mental list of all the things I didn't do.'

That last comment was like an arrow through my heart.

That was the way I had felt my entire life, as if I had a long list of obligations I had failed to fulfill hanging over my head each morning, pressing me down further and further into the earth before I'd taken my first step of the day. I was proud of my son for rejecting the same kind of life. I was proud of him for wanting to take better care of himself.

'But I'm worried about you,' Connie said. 'That dead girl went to your school. Did you know her?'

'I knew who she was,' he said. 'But a lot of kids did. I'm sure whatever happened to her had nothing to do with school or with me. You don't have to worry about that.'

He was lying. Once again, he was leaving something out – something that had to do with Darcy Swan.

'I don't know, Michael,' Connie said, shaking her head. She could be stubborn when it came to family matters. Six generations of supreme confidence about what is good for the family will do that to you. She had Sicily running through her veins. 'That orderly was murdered not even fifty yards from where we're standing. What the hell am I supposed to think about that?'

'I'll be fine in here,' Michael argued. 'That guy was probably selling drugs or something and got in with the wrong people. I'm barely going outside. It's just for another week. I want to finish what I started.'

Michael seldom took a stand about anything, he was the kind of kid who, until now, had just sort of drifted along with whatever his family or friends were doing. That he was taking a stand now meant it was truly important to him that he stay. Connie looked resigned. 'At least let me come back later today and bring you some noodles and sauce,' she negotiated. *Now that was pure Connie: food cured everything.* 'I'm making Grandma Nester's recipe. It's been cooking on the stove all day.'

Michael was growing up, but he was still a fourteen-year-old boy. His face lit up. 'Bring enough for Adam, too,' he told his mother. 'He's going to stop by before his shift.'

'Adam is too young to be working,' Connie said. 'How can he keep his grades up?'

'Adam can do anything,' Michael assured her. 'You'd be surprised.'

Anything? The thought did not reassure me in the least.

FIFTEEN

News coverage about the two murders told me that it would not be long before our police commander, Gonzales, stuck his nose into the investigation. Sure enough, I found Maggie back at the station, making a case to Gonzales that the two murders were likely related. She knew how to appeal to him – figure out why your theory would give him the best possible media exposure and then sell the idea to him. Gonzales was obsessed with the press and so skilled at politics that he was destined to be mayor, if not governor, one day. But for now, he used his shrewd, if self-centered, instincts to decide which cases received the spotlight and which cases were concealed from public view, either because they reflected badly on the department or because they would cause panic if word got out.

The murders of Darcy Swan and the red-haired orderly had the potential for both.

'You have a good theory, Gunn, but I am not convinced that the cases are related,' Gonzales was telling her. He always called Maggie by her last name – an indication not only of his respect for her, but also to put distance between them since, in private, he had been her unofficial uncle since she was a child.

Calvano was with them, sitting in one of the narrow leather chairs Gonzales reserved for people he doesn't like. I'd been in those chairs too often to remember. The leather stuck to your body and triggered a humiliating farting sound when you stood up. Gonzales so loathed Calvano that not only had he ordered Calvano to sit in the worst of them, he was now refusing to look at him at all. Calvano had no choice but to sit there looking like a well-dressed office plant, clearly aware that he was redundant. I almost felt sorry for the guy.

'I can't find a direct connection yet,' Maggie said to the commander. 'But there is one and I intend to find it. The girl was killed in the exact same way as Otis Parker's prior victims, even down to a lot of details we did not release to the press at the time the original murders were committed.' She gave Gonzales 'the look' – the look that meant, 'You know? The details about the mutilation you refused to release to the public because you knew it would cause the entire town to rise up against the police force if we didn't find the perpetrator immediately?'

Gonzales needed no interpreter. He went right to the heart of the matter, at least so far as he was concerned. 'Gunn,' he warned her, 'I better not hear a single word about those details in the media now. Do you understand me?'

Maggie looked utterly innocent in that infuriating way she had of being able to control her emotions far better than her opponents. I admired this ability of hers greatly. It was like telling them to go stick it where the sun didn't shine without ever actually saying a word.

'Do I at least get to keep trying to convince you?' she asked cheekily. She got away with it because her father Colin had been a mentor to Gonzales during his meteoric rise up through the ranks. On top of that, what Gonzales loved more than anything else was competence and Maggie had that in spades.

Gonzales sighed. Maggie's greatest strength – and her greatest fault – was unsurpassed stubbornness. 'Go ahead, convince me.'

'Every one of Parker's prior victims was desecrated in the same way,' she began. 'And they were all strangled, then left in an outdoor location, always in an area where their upper bodies were higher than their lower so that they appeared to be crawling for help.'

'If I recall correctly, we missed that signature ten years ago,' Gonzales said. He did not add, 'which is not surprising, given that Fahey and Bonaventure could barely find a toilet by then, much less a clue.'

'Darcy Swan was arranged in exactly the same way, and she had a crude brand burned into her torso that matched the one Parker left on his prior victims.'

'I concede the similarities,' Gonzales said. 'But it only makes me wonder if we got the right guy to begin with. Are you absolutely convinced that Otis Parker is guilty of the earlier murders?'

I wanted to groan. The Otis Redman Parker conviction remained pretty much the only bright spot in an otherwise wretched career and it was my one hope for being thought even marginally competent when I was alive. Now even that was being taken from me.

Once again, Maggie came to my rescue. 'Absolutely,' she said. 'Without a doubt in my mind, without a shred of hesitation, I would swear on my mother's grave that Otis Parker is guilty of those earlier murders.'

Wow – swear on her mother's grave? Maggie had adored her mother and still mourned her passing, though it had happened four years ago. I was not worthy of such an oath.

Gonzales conceded the point with a nod and Maggie continued. 'In my mind, given that the arrangement of the body and the brand were withheld from the media, those two details alone establish that Parker had something to do with the killing of Darcy Swan. I don't know how he's doing it, or who is doing it for him, but there is a connection.'

'Could he be getting out of his unit somehow?' Gonzales asked.

Calvano felt the need to prove he was still breathing. 'No, sir, we've had over two dozen men search his unit twice now. We've gone over his records and the sign-in and sign-out procedures. He's not getting out of that ward.'

Gonzales looked at Calvano as if he was something nasty on the bottom of his shoe, but he seemed to accept his assurances. 'Is it possible that the murdered orderly was working with Otis Parker? Or that he was the go-between linking Parker and a follower?'

'Vincent D'Amato,' Calvano said suddenly.

Maggie and Gonzales stared at him.

'The dead orderly's name is Vincent D'Amato,' Calvano explained. 'I went to school with his older brother. They grew up a few doors down from me.'

Gonzales had the decency to look vaguely ashamed at Calvano's veiled rebuke.

'Is it possible that *Vincent D'Amato* worked with Parker in

some capacity and helped cause Darcy Swan's murder?'
Gonzales asked.

'It's possible,' Maggie conceded.

'What do you know about Darcy Swan so far?' Gonzales
asked.

'Her name, her address and the fact that she stayed out of
trouble at school. She seems to have been one of those kids
who showed up, never made waves, had a handful of friends,
but that was about all, and barely registered with the teachers.
We're going to question the mother again in a few hours. She
was too broken up to answer any of our questions the first
time around. We'll know more then.'

Judging from her tone of voice, I knew that Maggie did not
like the mother. If she was anything at all like Darcy Swan's
grandmother, I totally understood.

'Tell me about the murder this morning,' Gonzales asked.
He glanced at Calvano. 'Vincent D'Amato, I mean. It was
nowhere near Parker's unit, right? It was outside the fence
surrounding the building where he's being held?'

'It was outside *both* fences surrounding his unit,' Maggie
explained. 'When they added on the unit fifteen years ago,
which they had to do to stay afloat as a private institution, the
trustees were concerned about the safety of the other patients.
So they put a lot of money into security and checkpoints. I'm
not seeing how Parker could get out. The murder itself took
place in the center of a huge lawn that connects the long-term
and short-term units. Anyone who is allowed out on the grounds
– and that's pretty much anybody, except for the inmates on
Parker's ward, or some of the more troubled civilian patients
who are kept in locked wards – would have access to the lawn.
Vincent D'Amato was found in a courtyard built in the center
of it, next to a fountain.'

'The fountain shows a bunch of naked cherubs and stuff,'
Calvano interrupted. 'The water squirts out of their . . .'
Calvano hesitated. 'Well, you know, it squirts out of their
genitals, if that seems relevant.'

Maggie and Gonzales stared at him as if he were daft.
Maggie put Calvano out of his misery by continuing quickly.
'When I first saw the body,' she explained, 'my mind went

straight to Otis Parker. I know that's not enough to say there's a definite connection, but hear me out. It was the way the body was staged. It was the fact that the body was staged at all. Granted, the orderly's murder was quicker than Darcy Swan's and it lacked the attention to detail, shall we say, of Otis Parker's prior killings, but it's the same mindset at work. I promise you that. It's as if the killer is creating a panel from a comic book.'

'What do you know about Vincent D'Amato?' Gonzales asked.

'He had a pretty good work record until about nine months ago,' Calvano explained. He flipped open his beloved notebook and consulted his notes. 'There was nothing on his record before that, except for a few concerns that he sometimes got too close with some of the female patients.' He looked up at Gonzales. 'No accusations or charges, just a few supervisor notes. But about nine months ago, he started missing a lot of work and taking them as sick days. Co-workers suspected he was taking drugs, and it turned out they were right.'

'What kind of drugs?' Gonzales asked.

'Drugs to treat lupus,' Gonzales explained. 'Everyone thought he was on smack or oxycodone or some other kind of downer, but it turns out the guy was diagnosed with lupus and he was in some pretty heavy-duty physical pain. After a while, his treatment seemed to work and he got the pain under control and his work record stabilized a little. But, concerns about him getting too close to female patients came up again and so they transferred him out of the long-term unit about a month ago and put him in the hardcore unit. No women there.'

'Which would have put him in daily contact with Otis Parker,' Gonzales pointed out.

'That's true, sir,' Maggie said. 'But there was instant animosity between the two, according to all other staff members, and I am talking about from day one. I don't think it was an act. I think the two men hated each other. It's possible they were working together, but I think it's more likely that Vincent D'Amato found something out about Otis Parker and was killed because of it.'

'Tell me more about how Vincent D'Amato's body was staged,' Gonzales asked. I knew he was just fishing for a good story he could tell his golfing buddies at the country club.

Maggie shifted uneasily in her chair. 'You know that Road Runner cartoon? And the way Wiley Coyote looks after he zooms off the edge of a cliff and lands on the canyon floor below? That's how D'Amato looked.' She looked a little embarrassed. I had never thought of Maggie being young enough to watch cartoons.

'And . . .' Gonzales encouraged her, certain there had to be more to the theory than that.

Calvano did his best to save her. 'And Otis Parker has a Road Runner tattoo on his ass,' he said, trying his best to look dignified.

Maggie gave him a look that would have scorched leather, inspiring Calvano to hold both hands up in an exasperated gesture. 'What? The guy has a Road Runner tattoo on his ass. I've seen photos of it. It looks like the Road Runner is racing right out of his—'

'I get the picture,' Gonzales interrupted. 'And all I can say is God help us all if this is what we have to go on.' He looked at them in silence for a moment, with that way he had of making you feel like you were the most embarrassing, useless link in the entire department. Maggie wasn't used to that look from him and squirmed uncomfortably in her chair. On the other hand, it bounced right off Calvano like he was coated in Teflon.

Gonzales reached a decision. 'I want the two of you to concentrate on solving the Darcy Swan murder, period. I'm going to put a separate team on Vincent D'Amato and see what they come up with. I don't want the assumption that they are connected to drive the investigation and I see no evidence that they are connected. Once you find out who killed the girl, I want you to go back and take a look at the murders that put Otis Parker away and make absolutely sure that he was guilty. I do not want anyone else to know that this is what you're doing. You are to report to me and me alone on it, got it?'

Maggie was disappointed, but she was also a professional.

'We won't let you down,' she managed to say as she rose to go. Calvano followed her lead, although he did not have a skirt to smooth down the way that Maggie did.

At least not yet.

SIXTEEN

'You had to mention that tattoo on his ass,' Maggie said to Calvano.

'You're the one who brought up Wiley Coyote,' he said defensively. 'I was just trying to help. Besides, I got to use the word "ass" right to his face.'

Maggie looked pissed, but after about fifteen seconds of silence, they both began to laugh. 'Did you see the look on his face?' she asked. They laughed even harder.

It was one of those moments when a partnership crystallizes into something you know is going to endure. I was jealous I wasn't a part of it and, yet, grateful I had been a witness to it.

They were on their way to question Belinda Swan, Darcy's mother. Apparently, she had been so upset at the news of her daughter's death, that she had barely been able to march straight into the manager's office, demand a week of family leave, cause a scene about Walmart's lack of insurance for funeral expenses, and then negotiated to be paid early for the next month, even though her paycheck was unlikely to put much of a dent in Darcy's funeral home bill. She had then marched over to the women's clothing section, selected a ruffled black dress with a plunging neckline, picked up a pair of matching black heels with sequins from the shoe department and walked right out the front door without paying for either item. No one tried to stop her. The manager had just shrugged and returned to his office, leaving Maggie and Calvano to watch her drive away. She was already dialing people on her cell phone. To her, the tragedy was not about her daughter. The tragedy was all about her.

Maggie and Calvano discussed the strange scene on the way

over to her house for a second interview. They did not seem
to have much love for Belinda Swan, though neither thought
that she'd had anything to do with her daughter's death.

What happened next would not change their poor opinion
of her. When Maggie and Calvano arrived at her house,
Darcy's mother was sitting in her living room sucking down
a beer while waiting for a news anchor to arrive to interview
her about the tragic death of her daughter. She seemed giddy
at the prospect of being on TV. I could feel any sympathy
that Maggie or Calvano had for her evaporate. Me? I'd never
felt any sympathy for her in the first place. I'd met many
versions of Belinda Swan before, and I am ashamed to say
that I had never been particularly sympathetic to any of them.
She was overweight from too much booze and constant junk
food and her brassy hair was far too harsh for her ruddy face.
She was dressed in clothes both too short and too tight, and
her heavy make-up only made her look more desperate. I
wondered what she saw when she looked in the mirror each
day. Did she see a woman beaten down by life or did she
still see a pretty high school girl who'd once had hopes of a
better life one day?

Many women just like Belinda Swan had come into the
station house when I was alive to complain that their live-in
boyfriend had stolen their car, or given them a black eye, or
raided their bank accounts. I wanted to feel sorry for them, I
really did. But after a few trips out to their homes, and dropped
charges of assault, and being turned on by complainant and
abusers alike, the truth was that I stopped caring. I began to
think of them as hamsters on the most unfortunate of wheels,
repeating a cycle over and over without any real thought as
to why they were doing it at all.

I felt the same way about Belinda Swan, at least at first.
She was defensive about being caught drinking and belligerent
when Maggie asked her if they could sit and talk for a few
minutes. 'Only if you got the cash,' she said defiantly, raising
the can of Budweiser to her lips. 'I'm out of Darcy's paycheck
now and we needed that money. If anyone talks to me, they
have to pay.'

I had a sudden fantasy of Maggie pulling out her gun and

shooting the can of Budweiser right out of Belinda Swan's hand, then maybe plugging her in the ass for good measure. But that was never going to happen and, besides, Calvano spared Maggie the trouble of putting her in her place. He smiled at Belinda Swan and sat a little bit too close to her on the couch. She immediately turned toward him and assessed him. He was several rungs up the ladder from her league and passed with flying colors. It appeared that Adrian Calvano was good for something.

'We just want to ask you a few questions about your daughter and her friends,' Calvano explained. He leaned in even closer. 'You deserve justice. She deserves justice. We want to make sure that her story has a final chapter. You know how the media loves a good ending.'

The reminder that she could milk more money out of her daughter's murder if it were solved softened Belinda Swan up. She looked at her watch, but said, 'OK. But make it quick. That skinny Channel Five bitch with the blonde hair is arriving in ten minutes.'

A door slammed in the back of the house, startling Maggie and Calvano, but it was only the grandmother. She ambled out of the back hallway dressed to the nines, hair teased high and make-up troweled on. Clearly, both women planned to be on the news that night.

'Don't even think about it,' Belinda Swan warned her mother. 'I'm the one they want to interview.'

I felt a flash of impatience at their self-centeredness. They had lost a child, and from what I had overheard from the kids on Michael's ward, Darcy Swan had been trying as hard as she could to rise above her circumstances. She was going to school, she was paying attention in class, she was trying to find something she was good at it and she was working a job after school on top of it all. She deserved better than what these two women had to offer her memory. But I also felt bad for the two women before me, if only because the bed they had made would be a tough one to lie in going forward. Judging from their hair, their make-up and their attire, their entire lives revolved around attracting the attention of men. Neither one realized that they had long since grown invisible to the male species. They would keep trying to regain their glory, to no avail, until the day they died.

Calvano dealt with the stand-off by patting the cushion on the other side of him and inviting the grandmother to sit. She perched next to him and crossed her legs conspicuously – I had to give it to her, they were damn fine legs for a grand-mother – then promised her daughter that she would just sit quietly in a chair once the newscaster arrived unless a question was specifically asked of her.

Had Maggie and Calvano not been there, I have no doubt Belinda Swan would have taken her mother to the mat. As it was, she agreed somewhat ungraciously and once again told Maggie to make it quick.

Maggie and Calvano led the two women through a series of questions. It soon became apparent that neither one of them knew a damn thing about Darcy's life. They lied about it, too, inventing details, I was sure, because they were vaguely aware that they should be ashamed of knowing so little about her. No, they told Maggie and Calvano, Darcy had never known Otis Parker and, they assured them, neither had either one of them. They seemed titillated by the thought of knowing a notorious killer, but were smart enough to realize that he could not have killed Darcy since everyone knew he was locked up in Holloway. They did not know the names of Darcy's friends, nor even the names of her teachers, and while they were sure she had boyfriends – all the women in their family always had plenty of boyfriends, they assured Maggie and Calvano – they didn't know their names or how long they had lasted nor if Darcy had anyone special in her life. They knew Darcy brought home at least $30 in tips per night when she worked at the diner, since the girl had given them $100 a week for room and board ever since the two older women had locked Darcy out of the house once, when she failed to give them the full amount, 'to teach her a lesson in responsibility.'

Nice – charging your teenage daughter to live in her own home and then throwing her out on the street when she couldn't cough up the cash. My burgeoning sympathy for them disap-peared. I had visions of them going up like torches, their hairspray fueling a mighty conflagration that would startle even the most seasoned residents of Hell.

They weren't even sure what kind of grades Darcy had made, but the mother bragged proudly that no disciplinary notes had ever been sent home with the girl. No doubt. The school officials probably didn't even know Belinda Swan existed, or if they did, they knew that Darcy had been far more responsible that her mother.

Maggie and Calvano left hurriedly once the interview was over, anxious to leave the house before the TV crew arrived. They knew Gonzales was serious about his orders to keep things out of the press, and Maggie had learned that the only way to keep Calvano out of trouble was to keep him out of sight.

SEVENTEEN

I knew Maggie was furious at the two older Swan women for their selfishness. I sat in the back seat, enjoying the crackles of energy Maggie gave off when she was mad. She was like a pinwheel spinning off droplets of life as she whirled.

In her anger, she drove too fast toward their next stop, and sent Calvano banging against the dashboard more than once when she had to stomp on her brakes to keep from ramming the car in front of her. About the fourth time this happened, Calvano turned to her and demanded to know where the hell they were heading in such a hurry.

'To get you a tetanus shot,' she said, keeping a straight face. 'I don't know how you could sit that close to those two women.'

'Sometimes you just have to take one for the team.'

And I was part of that team, I told myself, even if they didn't know it.

We were heading toward Holloway and I knew what it was probably all about – the time had come for Maggie to meet Otis Parker for herself. She was ready.

Otis Parker was brought into the interview room by one of

the same orderlies who had guarded him during Calvano's first interview. The dead orderly, Vincent D'Amato, had been replaced by a new guy who was easily as tall and muscled as Parker. Like Parker, he was stone-cold white and his head was shaved. It gleamed beneath the room's fluorescent lights. He had numerous gold studs and hoops in his ears and colorful tats decorated both of his truly massive arms. I spotted an angel tattoo, a dolphin leaping from blue waters, a bright yellow sun and a rose-framed heart with 'Mother' etched across it in flowery script. I had never seen such happy tattoos in my life. But the new orderly's most distinguishing feature was a red beard that dangled in a series of six small braids from his chin. A tiny brass bell tinkled at the end of each braid. He looked like a modern-day pirate dressed in hospital scrubs.

Something told me that Otis Parker had met his match.

The new orderly didn't ask Parker to sit. Instead, he shoved Parker into place and strapped his feet tightly against the legs of the metal chair while the other orderly shackled Parker to the arms of it.

'Is that necessary?' Maggie asked.

'Yes,' the new orderly said and tightened the straps. He was a man of few words.

'You are built like a brick shithouse, mamma,' Parker said to Maggie. 'Come back alone and I'll show you what a real man can do to you.'

The new orderly moved quickly. He slapped his palm hard against Parker's ear. It made a sound like a gunshot. Parker flinched in pain. It had been a well-aimed blow. The other orderly looked startled, but said nothing. They both suspected Otis Parker had orchestrated Vincent D'Amato's murder and they were going to get their revenge any way they could. Parker had killed one of their own.

Maggie took it all in her stride. She was used to scumbags and while she preferred to take care of such situations herself, she knew she might need both of the orderlies in the hour ahead. She was happy to let them take the initiative.

'She was a sweet soft thing unsullied by others,' Parker said suddenly. He smiled at Maggie, awaiting her reaction. 'Those

high school girls always are, at least if you get them young
enough.'

'So you're admitting that you knew Darcy Swan?' Maggie
asked mildly.

Parker back-pedalled immediately. 'Naw, man. I've just
known a million girls like her,' Parker boasted. 'They're always
looking for a firm hand and I provide one.' He sat back and
smiled just as the white orderly bounced another hard blow
off his ear.

'There's your firm hand,' the orderly said, then lapsed back
into a watchful silence as if nothing had happened.

Parker had slumped to one side. I could feel the anger rising
in him like boiling water but he sat up straight again if it were
no big deal. He did not want to give the other man his due.

Honestly, I appreciated the orderly's violent chivalry. Maggie
deserved more than the filth that spewed from Parker's mouth.
I was pretty sure that the orderly felt the same way and planned
to slap the crap out of Parker each time anything approaching
an obscenity escaped his lips.

'Thank you,' Maggie murmured faintly and it was hard to
tell if she was talking to Parker or the orderly. 'You know who
I meant when I asked you about Darcy Swan. How is it that
you knew I was talking about her?'

'Hey, I'm not an idiot. I watch the news. I saw her photos
and I know her kind. Darcy Swan was just another piece of
white trash and she deserved to be taken out with the rest of
the garbage.' Parker smiled. 'Whoever did that to her deserves
a medal for helping to clean up the streets.'

His attempts to shock Maggie would do little good. She
had dealt with worse than Parker. 'She sounds just like your
type,' Maggie said mildly. The orderlies snickered – and Parker
did not like that one bit.

'My type? You know, I've never been able to decide what
I like best,' Parker shot back. 'Brunettes, blondes or redheads?
It's tough to decide. Especially when they all seem to like
me.' He stared at Maggie's brown hair like a connoisseur
trying to decide what brand and year of wine to buy. 'It's a
shame you keep yours cut so short. Though I suppose I could
make an exception.' His gaze lingered on Maggie's legs, but

that did not fluster her either and that seemed to anger Parker. 'Of course, I don't like them to be cold bitches, either. At least not at first,' he added. His peculiar high giggle followed and just like that it was on the wall behind him – the flicker of something dark and terrible, of wings unfolding.

Just as quickly, it was gone.

'But I've been inside for a while, so I think I'll go for a blonde instead,' Parker said with a smile. 'First chance I get, of course.'

'That'll be in about six hundred years,' Maggie assured him.

The air around Parker vibrated with something dark and angry.

Maggie saw that Parker was rattled and tried to throw him off further by changing the subject. 'I understand that you and Vincent D'Amato were close.'

Her sarcasm was wasted on Parker. 'Not close enough for me to have killed him,' Parker answered. 'Though I'd like to thank whoever did the job for me.'

This time, the white orderly bounced a punch off of Parker's midsection, causing him to double over in pain. The orderly stood back up and calmly folded his hands in front of him, like he was in a choir waiting to sing. No one said anything. The silence was broken only by Parker's wheezing as he attempted to regain his breath. When he finally straightened back up, I could see his dark shadow on the wall behind, twisting and craning, its long neck stretching outward as if it were trying to get at the orderly.

With supreme effort, Parker regained control. The shadow disappeared.

'Vincent D'Amato was a punk,' Parker said defiantly – but he could not keep his eyes from shifting to look at the new orderly. He wanted to see it coming this time. 'He was one of those punks who gets a little authority and then has to lord it over you because he knows he's a loser and a worm. I hated the guy, but you can't pin his murder on me. I was locked up in here.'

'Did you ask someone else to murder him for you?' Maggie asked.

'How would I do that?' Parker answered. 'I haven't had a

visitor in over a year and I can count the phone calls I've made on both hands, all of them to my lawyer. You can check the records if you like.'

Now, *that* was interesting – Parker spoke of this record of isolation as if he had deliberately built it, as if he had known he would need to bring it up one day.

'Yes, I see that you have had no visitors for nearly a year and no requests for visitors, either.' Maggie looked down at a sheet of paper in front of her. 'Not a lot of fans in your corner?'

'I have plenty of people who would come see me,' Parker said, smirking. 'I have women all over America sending me money and begging me to let them come here so they can suck my—' The white orderly cocked his right arm and Parker shut his mouth abruptly. 'I tell them not to come. I tell them I'll be out of here soon enough.' He grinned. 'They can't wait for me to be on the outside.'

They were the only ones, I thought to myself, and they'd change their minds soon enough if it ever actually happened.

'You have no family?' Maggie asked.

'My family's dead,' Parker asked. 'Good riddance to them.'

More likely, he was dead to them. My guess was that there were probably plenty of members of his family alive trying to escape into the anonymous sea of Parkers who did not have serial killers hanging from their family tree.

'Are you particularly close to another inmate?' Maggie asked. I knew she was trying to figure out if Parker was sending orders to someone through another patient, but Parker, predictably, took her meaning to be sexual.

'I'm not a fag, if that's what you mean,' Parker said, a smile growing over his face. 'Want me to prove it?'

The white orderly moved toward Parker, but a look from Maggie stilled him. 'I can easily find out from other people,' Maggie explained. 'I'm just giving you a chance to cooperate.'

'Cooperate in what?' Parker asked back. 'What exactly is it you're here about? No, wait – scratch that. What I really meant to say was that I want my lawyer because it sounds an awful lot to me like you're investigating a murder.'

'Two murders, actually.' Maggie's voice was calm, almost sweet. 'And it sounds an awful lot to me like you miss the attention from being the center of a murder investigation. Locked away in here with all the other crazies, just another patient like they are, just as forgotten as they are . . .' She shook her head. 'I'm guessing that must be pretty hard for you. You seem to really need attention and validation from other people.'

This time, the shadow bloomed across the wall behind him with an almost radiant intensity: dark jagged wings spread wide and instantly disappeared as, with monumental effort, Parker fought his true nature.

I stared at the wall behind him until, with fear, I realized that Parker was staring straight at me. *He could see me.* He looked momentarily startled, opened his mouth as if to ask who I was, then abruptly shut it again.

I thought I knew what had happened. Whatever power fed him, it had recognized me as its enemy. It had recognized that it had enemies beyond those who walked the earth in human form. And though it was not rational, though I feared few things in my afterworld, a feeling of overwhelming dread overcame me. I was, quite simply, terrified to be in its presence.

The room had grown quiet. The orderlies were looking at one another, having never known Parker to pass on the opportunity to run his mouth. They did not trust his silence. Parker seemed to have forgotten what it was Maggie had asked. He just stared beyond Maggie and Calvano to where I sat, unsure of what to do.

'Well then,' Maggie said, rising. 'We'll be in touch soon.'

Parker regained his composure. 'Next time you want to see me, go through my lawyer. He has a few surprises for you.'

Maggie stared Parker straight in the eye. 'Don't even try it,' she said. 'You are not getting out of here. Not in your lifetime and not in my lifetime. Believe me when I say, I will never let it rest.'

The white orderly was smiling at Maggie with admiration. I had a sudden vision of him throwing Maggie over his shoulder and taking her far away to a pirate ship where she would dress like a wench, and bring him jugs of rum as they sailed the high seas together. What was it about the orderly that made my mind want to wander into such fanciful territory? There was something odd, yet almost jolly, about him, as if he thought it a great, good joke to be here among us.

Maggie was ready to call it a day. She had known she would get nothing useful out of Parker. That had not been the purpose of her visit. She simply wanted to get a feel for the man, and how crazy, or how dangerous, he might be.

'Is he always shackled like that?' Maggie asked the orderlies as she chanced a glance with Calvano and gathered her things to go. 'Even when he's with the general population?'

'Not yet,' the white orderly answered. 'But we're working on it.'

EIGHTEEN

Maggie and Calvano left Holloway, intending to get a few hours of sleep. But there was something about Otis Parker that always made me want to check on my son, just to make sure he was safe.

The moment I entered Michael's ward, I could smell Connie's sauce. She made it the old school way, with beef and veal and pork, bathed in red wine and cooked all day in a rich tomato sauce. She had set out plates on the table in the common room, and had brought enough to give out samples to anyone who asked. She was the mother of two teenage boys: she knew what joy the simple act of being cooked for could bring to a young person – and that some of the kids on the ward had never experienced that joy.

A vivid memory came to me of one of Michael's birthdays when he was young. I remembered Connie bending over the birthday cake, cutting slice after slice for the boys running and shrieking around her, being careful to give each child an icing flower so that everyone got the same portion. Now, she was ladling out noodles and sauce with the same precision, taking pride in the way the teenagers before her transformed from suspicious and angry to younger, more buoyant versions of themselves.

Michael did not touch his at first and I suspected it was because he was waiting for his friend Adam to join them. A few minutes into this rare communal meal, Adam appeared in the doorway and Michael instantly relaxed. His friend meant a lot to him.

Connie made Michael and Adam sit at a table and served them like a waitress in a family restaurant. Once they were all set, she announced that she needed to get home to see to Michael's brother. She probably didn't. Sean was a pretty independent little cuss, but Connie was smart enough to know that the last thing Michael wanted was his mother fussing over him while the other kids watched.

The evening sky had grown dark and I followed her out to the front lawn, acutely aware that the safety of Holloway had been shattered by Vincent D'Amato's death. Despite the orderly's murder, my friend Olivia sat at her customary spot in front of the fountain staring at the tumbling waters. The crime scene tape had already been removed, a testament to the soothing power that the fountain had over many of the patients. It had been important to reopen the spot.

Connie noticed Olivia sitting on the bench and went over to her, taking a tentative seat at the other end. 'You must really need to be alone if you're sitting out here in the dark,' Connie said. 'I'm sure you must know what happened here earlier today. Is it safe for you to be out here alone like this?' Her voice was kind and without rebuke.

Olivia glanced at Connie, but did not recognize her from their earlier encounter by the fountain. I was not surprised. Olivia lived in her own private world. 'I don't think they know I'm gone,' Olivia admitted. 'I just slipped out. I had to.'

I hid behind the fountain to watch. I realized that I was looking upon two of the most important women in my strange world, yet neither one of them knew it.

Olivia glanced at Connie again, comforted by her silence. 'Sometimes I wonder if I'm ever going to get out of here,' she told Connie. 'Sometimes I wonder if I will ever have the strength to do it.'

'I know,' Connie agreed. 'There are mornings when I wonder how I'm going to get out of bed, when I think of all the things that are expected of me, and how many people need me, and how much must be done to take care of them. And then I think of all the things I once thought I would do and now know I'm never going to do. Sometimes I wish I could go away to someplace quiet and let it all pass, until I have a clean slate and can start over.'

'You have a family?' Olivia asked.

'Two boys,' Connie said. 'And last month I told a man I would marry him.' She said no more, but Olivia could read between the lines.

'And now you're not so sure?' she asked.

Connie nodded. 'My husband has been dead a little over a year.' She hesitated. 'I won't lie – it was a hard marriage. I was usually the only person in it. He did a lot of things to destroy himself. He did a lot of things that destroyed *us*, although I like to think he did not mean to do them, rather that he did not understand what he was doing to me.'

I thought my heart would break.

Olivia was nodding. 'It's hard to see someone you love destroy themselves,' she agreed. 'I had a husband like that too, you know. He was brilliant, everyone said he was, but he always walked away right before he was about to finish something. It didn't matter whether it was painting a room, building a bird house, planting a garden or, worst of all, committing to a career. All he had to do was turn in his doctoral thesis, but he never could finish revising it. It was never good enough for him, never defensible enough, and the more I tried to persuade him to get it done so we could move on with our lives, the more he felt it needed changing.'

'What happened?' Connie asked.

'We had a child together.' Olivia's voice faded. 'But it all sort of fell apart.' She was silent and seemed to draw into herself. Connie did not press her for details.

'Why are you sitting here?' she asked Olivia. 'So close to where that man was killed?'

'I just wanted to remember him for a few moments,' Olivia said. 'He was my friend. His name was Vinny. He played the bass guitar and had a rabbit named Stu and an old motorcycle he was restoring.'

Connie's face told Olivia what she suspected and Olivia hurried to reassure her. 'Not that kind of a friend,' she said. 'Vinny would never have hit on me. He just liked to look after me. He was a very kind person, even when he wasn't feeling well and that was often. He was sick, but he never complained about it. He was always too busy asking how you were. All the patients loved him and I think the supervisor was jealous of that. She said she was going to report him for being too close to the patients, but he would never have done what she was implying. He got transferred to another unit, but he used to see me sitting here on his way to and from his building and he'd always stop to talk. About a week ago, he told me he didn't think it was safe for me to be alone so much.'

'What did he mean by that?' Connie asked, knowing he could have meant it in any number of ways.

Olivia stared at the spot where Vincent D'Amato had died. 'He said there were too many unpredictable people here at Holloway, and I was too beautiful to be safe, and that there were bad men in the world who could never be kept behind enough fences. He even used to sit under those trees over there when he got off work, reading, and he wouldn't leave until I went inside and he knew that I was safe.' She hesitated, unsure of whether to say what she was about to say. 'I'm afraid maybe he got killed because of me. That he was coming over here to check on me and make sure I was safe when someone killed him.'

She looked up at Connie, unsure of whether she could trust her but badly needing to tell someone. 'I was here last night,' Olivia said. 'I couldn't sleep. I needed to sit by the water for a while. That's all. I thought the sound of it might calm me. I was only outside for fifteen minutes and then I went back in. What if he got killed keeping someone away from me?'

Connie was silent. They stared at one another and I knew that Connie was trying, without success, to gauge how much of what Olivia had said was true and how much was imagined guilt from a troubled mind. 'I'm so sorry about your friend,' she finally said.

'People around me always die,' Olivia whispered. 'It's me. I'm not safe.'

'Will you do me a favor?' Connie asked her in a voice as kind as any I had ever heard. My wife was like that. She had the gift of being able to understand a person's sorrows and she often took the sadness on willingly in order to give the other person a break. It was one of the things I had loved most about her when we first met.

Olivia was looking at her suspiciously. 'What kind of favor?' she asked.

'My son is in that building,' Connie pointed to the short-term unit. 'He's in the adolescent ward. I just brought him a home-cooked meal.' She smiled. 'He's embarrassed to be babied by his mother, so I had to leave. But I'm worried about him. I'm worried about him being here, and I'm worried about the reasons why he had to come here in the first place.' To my astonishment, Connie started to cry. Olivia waited while Connie struggled to regain her composure. If there was anything Olivia understood, it was tears.

'I was a terrible mother,' Connie said. 'I spent so much time worrying about his father and then hating his father for the way he left us. I didn't pay enough attention to my son and, suddenly, here we are, in this place, and he said to me earlier today that he'd rather stay here than come home with me. I've been a terrible mother.'

'You should be glad he wants to stay here,' Olivia said fiercely. 'It means he cares enough about himself to want to make his life better. You should be glad.'

Connie looked startled. 'I guess you're right,' she said.

'What did you want me to do for you?' Olivia asked. Something about Connie's tears had evened things between them. I'd never heard Olivia sound so strong before.

'I can't stop worrying about him. He's my son,' Connie explained. 'Do you have children?'

'I did,' was all Olivia said.

Connie's face fell as she realized why Olivia was probably

at Holloway. 'I'm so sorry,' she said and her tears returned as she thought about what Olivia must be suffering.

Olivia moved closer and patted Connie on the back. 'It was a while ago,' she told Connie. 'I'm going to be OK.'

Connie tried to stifle their tears, dabbing her eyes and sniffling in that way she had that made her sound like a little girl. 'I'm a mess,' she admitted and Olivia laughed.

'Promise me you'll go back inside now?' Connie asked. 'I'm worried about my son and I just can't take worrying about you on top of that.'

That Connie would worry about a stranger did not seem odd to either one of these women. I had a rare glimpse into their world, a world where you did not question who you cared for or why, you just took on the burden and did.

'I promise,' Olivia said. She stood. 'It's getting a little chilly anyway.' She held out her hand, it was pale and slender and the gesture itself was incredibly graceful. 'My name is Olivia,' she told Connie.

'I'm Connie,' my wife said. 'Thank you so much for understanding.'

Olivia smiled her goodbye and hurried back down the path, toward the bright lights of the entrance to the long-term unit. I followed her until she reached the safety of the building. I imagined her hurrying up the steps and taking a right into the common room.

I glanced up, waiting for her shadow to pass in front of the window – and that was when I saw Lily, the little girl with monsters who lived in her head. Lily was staring out the window and there was something about her posture that ignited fear deep in my core. She looked terrified. Not of me, though. She was staring at a spot on the lawn where a stand of trees curved in and partially hid the heavily enclosed maximum security unit from the view of the other buildings.

I followed her gaze and saw nothing, but my sense of dread increased. I knew now that Lily's monsters were real. At least some of them.

I can almost always feel evil when it is near. I believe that the nature of my strange existence gives me that gift, in part because the plane I wander in is evil's battlefield, the point at which it enters the hearts and minds of humans, the point at which it can be driven out by those who pay attention.

I could feel the presence of evil now.

Connie was walking down the brick path that led across the lawn to the pedestrian bridge linking Holloway with the parking garage across the street.

I had to choose. I could follow Connie, although there was nothing I could do to protect her. Or I could find out who lurked in the trees and find out what I was up against.

I hurried toward the thicket and my feeling of dread grew stronger the closer I got. Bartlett pear trees had been planted a number of years before in an effort to mask the unit for the criminally insane from the families of the less violent patients.

The wooded area was no bigger than the width and length of a basketball court, but enough trees had grown up, with bushes and vines linking them, to create a thick undergrowth that the groundskeepers protected in order to provide homes for the rabbits that delighted residents like Harold Babbitt. Birds flew out of the trees with a flurry of flapping wings at my approach, aware somehow of my existence.

Beyond the undergrowth lay a grove shrouded in permanent dusk. Its floor of leaves had been tramped down by human traffic and was littered with candy bar wrappers, juice boxes and the tiny paper cups staff used to dispense medication. This was probably a trysting spot for patients who'd found love at Holloway. But they had not been the ones who had scared Lily and left a haze of darkness behind them. I could feel it surrounding me: evil of an uncertain nature, as if it were not yet sure of its power. There was a deep hunger there, too, lingering, and I think that was what frightened me the most. Evil alone can simply exist, maybe even bide its time for centuries. But an evil fueled by hunger was dangerous. It would look for and find happiness to feed on. I feared whoever had been in the tiny clearing and what they might do next.

Up ahead, near the front gate, the main path curved to the left where it led to the parking deck overpass. There was no one manning the front gate. There never was after seven p.m. You had to buzz and wait for an orderly to hurry down from one of the units, unlock the heavy metal gate and check your credentials before letting you in. There should have been someone stationed there after the events of the day, and the fact that the guardhouse was dark, and that there would be no way to call for help if something happened, told me that Holloway's administrators were still clinging to the hope that Vincent D'Amato's murder had been an isolated incident brought on by his own actions.

I thought I saw a movement in the guardhouse, a shifting of the shadows cast by the street light a few feet down the sidewalk. Connie, oblivious to anything but reaching her car, turned away from the brightly lit main entrance toward the stairs that would take her over the road into the parking garage. Her shoes made a clacking sound as she hurried up the steps to the pedestrian bridge. A gate barred the entrance to the overpass, but Cal had given Connie an electronic entry card like those given to the staff to make it easier for her to visit Michael after hours. She unlocked the gate and hesitated. In front of her, the overpass tunnel seemed uncharacteristically dark. There should have been lights on to guide staff coming off the late shift. Someone had turned the lights off, and I wondered how – and why. Connie hesitated, unsure of what to do. She had to reach her car to get home, but the tunnel made her uneasy, especially after the events of the day.

She looked behind her, checking the path. Seeing no one, she pulled out her cell phone and held the brightly lit screen out in front of her like a candle. It didn't help much, but it gave her courage as she stepped into the darkness. I hurried toward her, determined that she not be alone. She was already a quarter of the way over the arching walkway by the time I arrived. I was just in time to see the shadow of the man careening toward her and hear the heavy clump of his shoes. Connie gasped and stepped back, shutting her cell phone so that she'd be hidden by the darkness. It did no good. The man headed straight for her. Connie gave a scream and turned toward the entrance, ready to run. The man reached out and grabbed her arm.

'Connie?'

It was Cal, her fiancé. He held a flashlight and cast the light across Connie. She was standing flat against the sides of the overpass, looking terrified.

'It's me, Connie. It's Cal.'

Connie did not move from her spot. 'What the hell are you doing out here in the darkness?' she said. 'You scared the crap out of me.'

'I had a report that the lights were off in the overpass,' he said. 'That's just what we need, someone to trip and hurt themselves and sue Holloway. There are still family members leaving and they have to be able to get their cars. I can't figure out how it happened. It looks like somebody flipped the fuse and then pried off the switch. I can't find the damn switch. I'm not a maintenance man, for Christ sakes, I'm just an administrator.'

He stopped, aware of how strident he sounded. I think it was the first time he had ever appeared less than in complete control to Connie. I could sense he felt ashamed, but I could have told him that Connie was used to flaws in her men. That he would probably be even more attractive to her now.

'Can you walk me to my car?' Connie asked him. 'I am now officially creeped out.'

He agreed immediately, then took her arm and started guiding her through the darkness, his flashlight beam leading the way. I tried to get a sense of how he felt. I wondered if he had been the one I sensed in the clearing. But the overpass was filled with the sadness, fear and anger that lingered from the presence of distraught family members. It was impossible to separate out what came from him, or from Connie, and what had been left behind by others.

They reached the other side of the overpass and the bright lights of the parking garage. Connie's car was only a few spots down the row. Cal, as usual, held the door open for her. I could tell Connie was angry at him for ignoring her all day in favor of other, bigger problems. Though she understood how difficult his day had been, he had failed to understand how very much she feared for Michael so long as he stayed at Holloway. She started to get into the front seat but stopped abruptly – and I knew what was coming next. She was going to tell him, to his face, how she felt. Connie was good about that. It had done no good with me, of course, as there was nothing I had loved better than standing there while she listed all my failings and shortcomings. God help me, I think I had enjoyed it. It had felt good to have someone else validate my low opinion of myself.

How Cal would take it, I did not know.

I decided not to stay and find out.

I headed back to Holloway, determined to search out the cause of the darkness that I had felt lingering in that clearing. But as I emerged from the overpass entrance into Holloway again, I stepped into a haze of wanton lust and evil so thick it almost made me gag.

Whoever had been in that clearing had been right behind me – and right behind Connie. What he had wanted from her was unspeakable.

I looked around but saw no one. I searched the grounds, I searched the grove, I even checked on Otis Parker. He was still locked in his room, still ranting at what his lawyer would do once word got through to him that he was being confined without cause.

I now had proof of two important facts: whoever had followed Connie had not been Otis Parker. And Vincent D'Amato had not been Parker's partner. Which meant that, whoever had killed Darcy Swan for Otis Parker was alive and well – and had access to Holloway.

NINETEEN

A thousand nights or more I had failed my son, but I would not fail him that night. There was no reason to think that Otis Parker's partner would come after Michael, but I was not willing to take that chance. He meant too much to me and, though I had little to give him, what I had was his. I would watch over him for as long as it took to find out who – or what – was roving the grounds of Holloway, seeking victims.

Through the long hours of the night, I stood guard as my son slept. Michael looked years younger without the worries of his waking hours weighing down on him. My love for him was so overwhelming that I felt a physical ache where my heart used to be. How can people say that heartache isn't real? Or deny the fact that its pain is proof that we exist beyond the confines of our physical bodies? I felt it that night for my son: the fear of loss that comes with love; the panic that it might be taken from me.

The sun finally rose, and with it came an overcast spring day, the kind that reminds you that winter is still lurking in the wings. Though no one else at Holloway was out and about yet, Maggie and Calvano were waiting by the front gate for the morning guard to appear, coffee cups in hand as they stomped their feet and rubbed their arms to get warm in the cold morning air. Both looked as if they had managed a few hours of sleep and were equally determined to get back to work. It was amazing how much Calvano had changed since his time with Maggie. All he had needed was someone to show him the way.

'You did tell them we'd be here first thing in the morning?' Maggie asked Calvano.

He nodded and sipped at his coffee. I'd pegged him for a latte man and was glad to see he knew better than to flaunt a five dollar coffee in front of another cop.

'You can handle this on your own, right?' Maggie asked. She looked longingly at their car. 'I want to head over to the diner while you run employees through the system. That would save us some time.'

'Go, go,' Calvano assured her, waving her away.

Their partnership was starting to click. Calvano was going to track all the employees that Parker could have come in contact with at Holloway, and Maggie would start filling in the blanks of Darcy Swan's life by driving out to the diner where she had worked after school each day. It wasn't much of a choice – I hitched a ride with Maggie.

The Freeway Diner was a battered silver train car propped up on cinder blocks on the edge of town. Ugly concrete additions had been built around it at some forgotten point in time. I knew the place well because it had the best poor man's coffee in town. I used to go there to sober up before reporting to work on my worst days. 'Coffee,' I'd tell the waitress, 'And keep it coming.' I'd add four teaspoons of sugar to each cup and sip until I could stomach scrambled eggs and donuts on the side, hoping the combination of caffeine, sugar and protein would get me through enough hours to convince myself, if not my co-workers, that I could make it through another day.

As I followed Maggie inside the diner, I suddenly remembered that I had last been there the day that I died. I'd broken with my traditional hangover habits that morning and ordered pancakes instead. Halfway through, I'd felt nauseous from mixing Scotch and beer the night before and walked away, never knowing that the half stack of pancakes left behind would forever represent my last meal, or that the wad of dough and syrup in my belly would be the last thing I ever ate and ended up carefully weighed on the coroner's scales. It felt odd to be back, as if I were visiting another world.

It was early on a Saturday morning and the only customers in the diner were retirees living in the cheap apartments adjacent to a shopping strip a quarter mile away. They sat together at their booths, nursing their coffees, knowing to the dime what they could afford to spend on breakfast out. I'd probably have ended up just like them had I lived: making the most of free coffee refills and slowly eating my scrambled eggs and toast special to make the moment last.

Darcy Swan had been one of the teenage waitresses manning the front tables, to bring more customers in the door. Like the other young girls working there, she had probably told herself every day that she would never be one of the worn-down middle-aged women who stood out back taking turns sneaking smokes and wishing that they could just enjoy the damn cigarette inside the diner like in the good old days.

I sat behind a trio of old men, where I could vicariously enjoy their coffee and eavesdrop on their conversation, while Maggie waited to see the busboy who had reported Darcy Swan missing the day after her body was discovered.

The old men were swapping medical horror stories. I'd never even had the chance to talk about my prostate and creaky knees and heartburn after eating tacos. *Had I finally found a silver lining to my untimely death?* They were arguing about whether diabetes was a big deal at their age, when a pimply-faced boy with an immense bush of wild curly hair that hung down to his shoulders took a seat across the booth from Maggie. He looked like nothing so much as a sheepdog who had yet to be shorn. He had an unnaturally low voice for his age and was embarrassed by it. He looked down at his hands and answered Maggie's questions with monosyllables, forcing her to drag every detail out of him. Yes, he had known Darcy Swan from school. She had been at the diner for more than a year, which was six months longer than he had been working there. She had been the nicest of the waitresses, at least according to him, and had been the most generous in sharing tips. She had asked him about his progress as a guitar player nearly every day. She had not laughed at him like the other waitresses often did.

I realized that the boy had seen Darcy Swan as no one else in her life had seen her. To him, she had been a kind and sophisticated woman, one he had loved from afar. She would always stay that way to him now, and perhaps there was something beautiful in that.

Maggie pressed him hard on who had been in the diner the night that Darcy disappeared. Was anyone acting peculiar? Have there been any fights, had Darcy broken up any disagreements? Had she had any trouble with customers?

No, the boy insisted, it had been a slow night, the same as any other night, really, with the booths filling up with regulars, and a couple of long-haul truckers here and there, and maybe a lost tourist or two. As always, a few carloads of drunken college kids had arrived late that night to order cheeseburgers medium rare and take full advantage of free refills on their sodas as they attempted to mop up all the alcohol in their system before weaving down the highway back to campus.

No, he said, the college kids had liked Darcy, no one gave her a hard time. Everyone had liked Darcy. He remembered that she had been dropped off at work that night by another waitress who would stop by her house and give her a ride to work when she needed one. Darcy had an old Toyota that was always having trouble and he was pretty sure it had broken down earlier that day. He did not know how she had gotten home after her shift. The only unusual thing that he could recall was that Darcy had wanted to clock out an hour early and, since it was slow, the cook – who was also the diner's owner – let her leave.

'Why did she want to leave early?' Maggie asked the boy.

He shrugged. It had not occurred to him, nor did it occur to him now, that she must have wanted to leave early for a reason – a reason that might have led to her death.

'What do you know about her personal life?' Maggie said. 'Did she have a boyfriend?'

The kid looked momentarily startled. The thought of Darcy having a boyfriend had never occurred to him. He had been too busy casting himself in that role. 'I don't think so,' he stammered. 'If she did, I never saw her with him. Maybe the other waitresses would know.'

The more they talked about Darcy, the more the kid started to realize that she was gone and that his dream of being with her one day was dead. His voice cracked as he fought back tears and he looked around to see if anyone had noticed. Maggie took pity on him and brought the questioning to a close.

'Is there anything else you can tell me about her?' she asked him. 'Even if it's just personal details, like what she wanted to do with her life. I'm really having trouble getting a sense of who she was.'

The boy wanted to help Maggie and he had started to believe that she truly cared about Darcy as he did. 'I know she was thinking about getting a new job,' he offered. 'About a week ago, some jerk came in and left her a fifty cent tip on a twenty dollar tab. Darcy gave it to me and said that I should keep it, that she was sick of crappy tips and dirty old men. She said that if men were going to stare at her and grab her ass and be pigs about it, that she ought to be getting paid a whole lot more for it.'

Maggie looked a little startled at this news. What had Darcy Swan been thinking? There were way too many options for young girls in our town that led to nothing but misery and, inevitably, danger. Surely Darcy had known better than to consider any of those?

The kid knew nothing more of use and Maggie sent him on his way. She spent the rest of the morning questioning the other waitresses: about whether Darcy did, indeed, have a boyfriend; if she had had any favorites among the regulars at the diner; if anyone had seen her leave the night she disappeared; had she mentioned any trouble at all with anyone in the weeks leading up to her murder; had she talked to them about getting a new job?

In the end, Maggie got nothing to help her other than that Darcy had once had a boyfriend who would pick her up in his red truck after work and give her a ride home. No one quite knew why they had broken up, but they thought it probably had something to do with Darcy's mother. All the troubles in Darcy's life usually had to do with her mother, most felt. Some of the waitresses thought Darcy's mother had probably put the moves on the boyfriend and scared him away. Others thought Darcy's mother had been so jealous of her daughter that she had forbidden Darcy to date at all.

It was hard to tell if their speculation about Darcy's mother was real or a by-product of their feelings about her. They had all seen Belinda Swan on the airwaves milking her daughter's death for all it was worth – and they all seem to despise her for it.

Finally, one waitress offered that recently Darcy had been upset about something that had to do with her old boyfriend, but would not talk about it. Under patient questioning from Maggie, the waitress offered that she thought maybe Darcy's old boyfriend was stalking her.

It wasn't much for Maggie to go on. The staff had pretty much confirmed what she already knew: for a kid from the wrong side of the tracks, Darcy Swan had been trying to do her best. She worked hard in school, she worked hard at the diner, she had believed that if she worked hard enough she could make something of her life. She had died before she got that chance.

Maggie finally threw in the towel and left her card with the cashier, extracting a promise from the staff to call her if they remembered anything at all that might be of value to her.

I longed to order a coffee and jelly doughnuts to go. Alas,

I was denied the second-hand pleasure of either when Maggie ordered hot tea – lemon, no sugar – and turned down the offer of anything with calories in it.

Damn, girl.

I was forced to admit that, had I lived, we would have been most unsuitable partners.

TWENTY

I t took Maggie less than half an hour to learn what I already learned by eavesdropping on my son and his friend: the identity of Darcy Swan's old boyfriend. A phone call to the high school principal triggered a phone call to the student body president, who in turn remembered that his first name had been 'Adam.' She put Maggie on hold while she checked her list of Facebook friends – over three thousand of them, she said proudly – and came back a moment later with the news that his full name was Adam Mullins.

Personally, I thought Maggie was lucky his name had not been Zeke. That would've taken all day.

Maggie called the principal back, obtained the kid's address and soon we were heading back to Helltown, windows rolled down so that the cold spring air rushed over us. I felt as alive as I had ever felt when I was actually, well, alive. It was good to be back in the field.

By now, the street was familiar to me: a block of rundown mill houses, rental properties all, perched on small patches of dirt where the grass waged an ever-losing battle with rusty lawn chairs, discarded garden tools, dented tricycles and other junk. No one ever worried about having their stuff stolen. These houses were slim pickings. Thieves looked elsewhere for their bounty.

There was a minor traffic jam in front of Darcy's house, caused by a couple of news vans and the morbidly curious who just wanted to drive by and see where the dead girl had lived. I caught a glimpse of Darcy's mother on the doorstep

of her home, dressed to the leopard print nines, being interviewed by the media. She was going to ride that gravy train
for as far as it would take her.

In the daylight, it was clear that my son's friend put more
care into his yard than any of his neighbors. Adam was, in
fact, pushing a mower back and forth across a front yard that
had a respectable lawn of newly green grass. He mowed
that lawn with the same contained seriousness he displayed
in every other aspect of his life. This poor kid wasn't much
of a kid.

Maggie had a dilemma to consider. Adam Mullins was a
minor and she could not legally question him as a suspect
without a parent present. In fact, Gonzales was so cautious on
this point that – in order to mollify voters who didn't care
what he did to other people's kids, but who were damned and
determined to cover the asses of their own – he had directed
that no minors be questioned at all without a parent or guardian
present. This had crippled the ability of the squad to pursue
drug cases completely and led to elaborate fantasies of teenage
gangs attacking the commander, or stealing his car and all
manner of nonsense until his deputies had come down hard
on the ranks and made it plain he was absolutely serious about
the policy. Maggie knew the drill as well as anyone, but she
was not good at delayed gratification. I could feel her mulling
over the implications of questioning Adam Mullins alone and,
predictably, could not stop herself.

As she pulled up in front of his house, eyes watched her
from behind the curtains and blinds of the other houses on
the block. I knew the drill well – this was like reality TV, only
better, as neighbors pegged Maggie for a cop and wondered
who had violated their parole or who finally bounced enough
bad checks to warrant jail time. A back door slammed nearby
as someone with a guilty conscience took flight. Probably
some deadbeat late on his child support. I hoped he would
trip and break an arm.

Adam Mullins saw Maggie coming and switched off the
lawnmower. He was a smart kid and knew why she was there.
His face betrayed nothing about what he might feel at finding
a detective on his doorstep. Even when Maggie was inches

from him, he simply waited for her to speak which, trust me, was not something that many teenagers could do.

'I wanted to ask you some questions about Darcy Swan,' Maggie said, showing him her badge. 'I know you used to be her boyfriend. You're not a suspect. I just need you to help me figure out who she had in her life.'

She had solved her dilemma by making it plain that he was not a suspect.

The boy still said nothing. He just opened the front door wide and followed Maggie through it. I brought up the rear. The living room wasn't very big, but it was surprisingly clean. It had to be the kid who was keeping it that way. From what I had seen the night I hitched a ride in his truck, Adam's old man, with his unshaven chin and greasy shirts, was not exactly Mr Clean.

'Who is it?' a tremulous voice called out from a back room. 'Is that you, Adam?'

'Just me and a friend, Grandma,' the boy called back. 'I'll be in to check on you in a moment.'

Adam moved a stack of school books off the couch to make room for Maggie. He sat across from her in a tattered recliner with sunken-in cushions – proof that his father pretty much lived in front of the widescreen television bolted to the far wall.

'What do you want to know?' he said. I had to give the kid credit, he tried to keep the traces of resentment from showing up in his tone. I'd noticed, but Maggie might not. Darcy Swan had broken up with him, I suspected, and the thought of it still bothered him. I knew first-hand that the thought of what-might-have-been can do that to you.

'Well, first of all,' Maggie said, 'I'm sorry about your friend. It was a lousy way to die. She seemed like a really good person and she didn't deserve to die that way.'

Adam looked startled. 'Thanks,' he mumbled. He did not know what to make of Maggie.

'How long did you know her?' Maggie asked casually, trying to put the boy at ease.

'I knew her my whole life,' Adam said. 'We've been in the same classes since we were in first grade together.'

'She lived just a few doors down, right?' Maggie asked, though she knew the answer. She'd noticed how tightly wound the boy was and was trying to find a way in.

Adam nodded. 'She's lived in a couple of houses in the neighborhood. They had to move around a little after her dad walked out on them. But she's been in the same one for a couple of years now. It's pretty easy to tell which one. Reporters have been camped out there since it happened.' He hesitated. 'Her mother keeps giving interviews and stuff.' A flash of anger had showed in his face. Maggie noticed.

'What is it?' Maggie asked. 'I can tell something bothers you.'

'It's just that Darcy's mother never really gave a shit about her, and now she's crying for the cameras and making it sound like they did everything together and she's lost her best friend and stuff like that. But when Darcy was alive, all her mother really did was make her do all the work around the house and then pay rent on top of that, and give her a hard time about bringing friends over to the house, not that anyone wanted to go over there.'

'Why not?' Maggie asked.

The boy turned red. My guess was that Belinda Swan liked to put the moves on any or all of Darcy's friends who were male. God, what if the grandmother had joined in, too? No wonder Darcy had not replaced Adam with a new boyfriend.

'She was just really friendly,' the boy mumbled. 'She liked to hug you a lot and . . .' His voice trailed off. He looked so miserable that Maggie helped him along.

'Can you tell me more about Darcy and her mother. How did Darcy feel about her?'

'She hated her mother. Darcy said that most of the time she didn't give a crap about Darcy, unless she was asking for rent money. But every now and then, she'd get really strict with Darcy, usually in front of one of her scummy boyfriends. She tried to tell Darcy what to do just to prove she was a good mother or something.'

'Did they fight a lot?' Maggie asked.

'She didn't have anything to do with Darcy's death, if that's what you mean. Her mother was kind of . . .' He searched for the right words. 'She kept trying to be Darcy's friend instead of her mother, and she always tried too hard to act like she was as young as us, but she was OK. So long as you avoided her when she'd had too much to drink, she could actually be kind of nice. She was really proud of Darcy. She'd never have done anything to hurt her.' He stared directly at Maggie for the first time, as if she might challenge this belief. He had a confidence and intelligence in his gaze that most kids his age lacked.

'Did you see her after Darcy died?' Maggie asked. 'Did she have a boyfriend with her?' Maggie was just fishing, but it wasn't a bad guess – in Helltown, when you put together an ageing woman, her booze-hound boyfriend and a young daughter, you almost always had the makings of trouble.

'She came down here after Darcy was killed,' he said. 'She was really upset. She just wanted someone to talk to about it. She was crying and asking why things like this always happen to her.' He shifted uncomfortably. 'I couldn't figure out a way to get rid of her, actually. She brought a whole bottle of vodka with her, so when my dad came home, she and him stayed up drinking together. In the morning, she was gone.'

'She came here the night after Darcy's body was found?' Maggie asked.

He nodded. 'I saw her the next day, outside of her house, talking to some reporters. I think my dad clued her into the fact that she could make money off of Darcy's death.' His voice was bitter; he blamed his father for most of the things wrong in his world, I realized. And, perhaps, rightly so.

'Adam?' his grandmother called out from the back of the house. 'Are you there?'

'I'm here,' he called back. I had the feeling this went on every few minutes whenever he was home.

'Do you need to check on her?' Maggie asked.

'She'll be OK for a few minutes,' he said. 'Is there anything else you want to ask?'

'Was Darcy's mother the reason the two of you broke up?' Maggie asked.

The boy shook his head. 'No, she really liked me. She knew

I got good grades and had a job. Darcy and me breaking up was just one of those things.'

Maggie leaned toward him. 'Look, I know it's hard for you to talk about this. People say you were together for a long time, maybe even months.' She looked at him for confirmation and he nodded. 'Maybe you could just go into a little more detail about why the two of you broke up?'

The kid was no fool. 'You think there was someone else, don't you?' he said. When Maggie did not answer, he continued. 'I don't think she had another boyfriend after me. If Darcy had wanted a boyfriend, she would've chosen me. We were together almost a year, but one day she just told me that we couldn't be together any more. She said that having a boyfriend and getting married and telling yourself that life was all about having a man was what had gotten her mother and grandmother into trouble. She said she wanted more for her life. I tried to explain that keeping her back was the last thing I wanted to do, that I would be there for her no matter what she decided to do with her life, but she just said she wasn't ready to get involved with anyone. She wanted to concentrate on school and her art and stuff like that. She said she just wasn't ready . . .' For the first time, he looked uncomfortable. He was trying to say something, but I couldn't figure out what.

I hoped that Maggie had a better take on it. I knew it probably had something to do with sex. At his age, what were the chances it didn't?

'Did you have a close relationship before that?' Maggie asked gently.

'What do you mean?'

'Did you spend a lot of time together? Did you hang out at her house a lot? Did she hang out here a lot? Spend the night?'

The boy looked embarrassed. 'She liked to hang out here with me. We would do our homework together and watch TV. Even with Grandma asking for help all the time, it's still quieter here at my house than over at her house. My dad owns his own business, so he's gone a lot. At her house, her grandmother is always watching TV with the volume turned up really loud. So we liked to hang out here and sometimes she would make me and Grandma a sandwich or something, if we had anything to eat in the house. I used to stop by the grocery store and pick up stuff to make sure we had supplies.' He sounded wistful at the loss of this simple pleasure. 'But then my dad would usually come home and ruin things. He's an asshole. He would start yelling for a beer or asking where his sandwich was and why didn't Darcy like him enough to have a sandwich waiting for him. Darcy would always leave soon after he got home, not that I blame her. I'd have left, too, if I'd had anywhere to go.'

'Look,' Maggie said. 'I really hate to ask you this, but where is your mother? It doesn't seem like she lives here.'

The kid was still just a kid. Whatever had happened to Adam's mother, it had been bad and it showed in his face. 'She died six years ago.'

He did not explain and Maggie did not press him further. He was shutting down enough as it was. I could tell that she felt sorry for him. Like Darcy Swan he, too, had deserved a better life than the one he had been given.

'Did you and Darcy stay friends after you broke up?' She asked, steering the conversation back to safer ground.

He nodded. 'Yes. I mean, as much as we could. She started working at the diner a lot more, she was saving up to get out of here as soon as she could, but she still had to come up with the rent money in the meantime. And . . .' He looked miserable, but had the courage to continue. 'It hurt a lot to be around her at first, so it's only in the last couple of months that we've been able to really be friends again. But she talked to me, if that's what you mean.'

'Are you absolutely sure she did not have a new boyfriend?' Maggie asked him. 'I know it's not something that you want to think about, but it could be really, really important. It could lead us to who might have killed her.'

The kid thought hard. A whole kaleidoscope of emotions crossed his face as he wrestled with each possibility. In the end, he stuck to his belief that Darcy could not have had another boyfriend. 'I really think I would have known about it,' he explained to Maggie. 'I mean, I know all of her friends, and even when we weren't talking much, I could keep up with what she was doing on Facebook. I could see when she came and went from her house, and it really didn't seem like she did much more than go to school and work at the diner.'

'Do you think you could do me a favor?' Maggie asked him. 'Do you think you could go through her list of Facebook friends and tell me if there are any names you don't recognize?'

I could only hope that Darcy had not had as many friends as the mega-achieving student council president did or else the kid would have his hands full.

'Sure, I can do that,' Adam said. 'She wasn't really in to all that online stuff. She could never get on the computer at home because her mom was always hogging it for online dating and stuff. Darcy used her cell phone for posting updates and she didn't really like to spend time online. I only have a couple hundred friends and I think she has even less.'

'It would help me a lot if you could do that,' Maggie said. For the first time, she pulled out a notepad and made a comment to herself in it, probably to check the whereabouts of Darcy Swan's cell phone. It had not been found with her body, her mother had not mentioned a phone and Maggie had probably assumed Darcy could not afford one.

'I can look at her Facebook friends right now,' Adam offered. 'I'll just need a couple of minutes.'

Before Maggie could reply, the sound of a truck motor startled the boy. He looked out the side window and then at Maggie, knowing that trouble was coming. His father was home and Adam was smart enough to know how he might react to finding the police there. He leapt up from the recliner nervously.

Maggie instantly understood. 'It's OK,' she told him, rising. 'I'll take care of it. I'll make sure he knows that this was just routine questioning.'

Adam's father came charging through the back door with the unselfconscious focus of someone who does not realize he has company. He had the refrigerator door open and was reaching for a beer before he realized that his son was not alone. He took one look at Maggie and pegged her for what she was: law enforcement. He did not look happy to see her.

'What's he done?' he asked belligerently. He stared at Adam with a warning in his eyes.

Nice. Good to see a father with such faith in his son. He reminded me of my old man.

'He hasn't done anything. I'm going door-to-door in the neighborhood asking people if they knew Darcy Swan or her mother.' Maggie kept her voice casual, but I could tell it took effort.

Adam's father belched and popped open his beer. He had drained half of it before he spoke again. 'My kid's got nothing to say to you. He barely knew the girl.'

'And yet they were boyfriend and girlfriend for almost a year,' Maggie answered mildly. She shot a warning glance at Adam, begging him to let her handle it.

'Dumbass,' the older Mullins shot at his son. 'Don't know why you're bothering,' he taunted Maggie. 'Her mother's making a fortune on the kid's death. It's the best thing that ever happened to that family of gold-diggers.'

'*Dad!*' Adam was appalled at his father's comment. 'You know she was really upset about Darcy. You sat here and listened to her talk about it for hours.'

The old man settled down in his recliner and put his feet up, holding his beer can out as he debated whether or not to ask his son to bring him another cold one. I could almost feel the weight of the can in my hand. I had done the same thing a thousand or more times in my lifetime – gauging how much beer I had left, always wanting more.

'You thought we were talking all that time?' Mr Mullins leered. 'Let's just say me and Darcy's mother went way back. Like mother, like daughter.'

'Perhaps you would like to talk about your relationship to Darcy Swan for the record?' Maggie said sharply, hoping to keep Adam from going off at his father.

The old man got the message. 'I was just talking crap,' he said, holding up a palm like Maggie was getting ready to come at him swinging. I could only imagine the legions of females who had been presented with that hand and how much they had wanted to slap the smirk off his face in response to it. I know I had the same impulse, although I thought he deserved a series of punches more.

'Darcy was a good kid, and me and her mother go way back,' Adam's father said. He slurped at his beer. 'We went to high school together. She's OK. She's just another old broad desperate to hook someone to support her fat ass, but she didn't deserve what happened to her daughter.'

Wow, the kid had truly been right: his old man was an asshole.

Maggie let it go. She'd been baited by plenty of men before. There was something about Maggie's position of authority that just seemed to piss them off. She wasn't going to waste her time on this loser. 'I'm just collecting background information on Darcy,' Maggie said calmly. 'I may stop by again. But I think I better get going. I have a lot of people to talk to.'

'Yeah, maybe you better,' Adam's father said. 'Sounds to me like you guys don't know your ass from a hole in the ground when it comes to who killed her.'

Maggie ignored him. She stuck out her hand at the boy instead and Adam, after a startled moment, shook it. 'Thanks for your help, Adam,' she said. 'I really appreciate it. Good luck with your studies. I hope you keep up the good work. I heard really good things about you from your principal. He says you're really going to go far in life. I wish you the best.'

She left without a word to the father, and I knew her encouragement to Adam had been her parting shot. 'Your kid is so much better than you,' she had wanted the old man to know. 'One day he will leave you in his dust.'

Adam's father got the message all right – but he was the kind of guy who likes to take his anger out on those who were weaker than him. Maggie had barely left the house when he moved with a quickness that startled me. He was out of the recliner and in his son's face before Adam could react. He slapped his kid across the face and sent him reeling into a wall.

'I catch you talking to the cops ever again about anything,' he threatened Adam, 'and I will beat you within an inch of your life for sheer stupidity. You think the cops give a shit about people like us? You think they want to do anything but blame us for their problems and put us behind bars so they can say "case closed" and call it a day? You are a living, walking, breathing patsy and don't you ever forget it. You are garbage in their eyes. They only pretend to be your friend so you'll do something stupid like give them enough rope to hang you with. I don't ever want to see you talking to that bitch again.'

'Adam?' His grandmother's voice floated out from the back of the house. 'Adam, honey? Are you OK? Are you alone?'

Adam was leaning against the wall, his hand resting on his cheek where his father's blow had left a red imprint. I don't know how he did it, I really don't, but the kid had monumental self-control.

'I'm OK, Grandma,' he said. 'I'm coming in to check on you before I go to the library.'

He stood there for a moment, staring at his father, before he walked calmly from the room. His actions spoke louder than any words ever could.

Adam was letting his old man know that he was of absolutely no importance to him and that all the violence in the world would not change that fact.

TWENTY-ONE

I returned to Holloway to find that a guard had been posted at the front entrance and was checking the credentials of all visitors against a list. My guess was that the press had tried to infiltrate the grounds in the wake of Vincent D'Amato's murder and that no one wanted the spotlight of publicity shone on either Holloway or the residents who lived there.

I saw Morty, the beat cop I had known when I was alive, checking in with a bouquet of yellow roses in his hands, on his way to see the woman he visited each week. The guard started to give him a hard time about not being related to her, but a nurse coming in for her shift saw the situation unfold and intervened. She took Morty by the elbow and guided him around the guard, with a warning glance that told the kid he was not to argue.

A few visitors later, Adam Mullins showed, backpack in hand, and handing it over to the guard to be searched. The guard rooted around in it, handed it back to him and accepted Adam's lie that he was there to see his brother.

Or maybe it wasn't so much of a lie. I followed him back to the juvenile unit, where Michael and his peers were being shooed away from the television set by a harried-looking nurse. Her grim expression told me that she had not liked whatever the newscaster had just announced. And no wonder: I caught a glimpse of a well-dressed man with graying blonde hair being interviewed right before she clicked off the image. The news scroll beneath his name said it all: Otis Parker's lawyer had requested a competency hearing, citing his years of treatment and the recent murders by unknown parties as proof that he was not a mad killer as everyone thought. He wanted Parker released from Holloway as soon as possible.

It was inconceivable that Parker might one day be set free to prey on the world again, but I had seen enough of the law to know that his freedom was a definite possibility. If that happened, no one was safe.

Michael spotted his friend Adam at the entrance to the ward and shook off the attentions of a girl who had been trolling for his friendship all week. He and Adam greeted each other in that awkward way of teenage boys who don't want to shake hands like their fathers or hug like their mothers. They leaned forward and touched shoulders while thumping each other on the back then drew away, embarrassed by their affection for one another.

'How's it going?' Michael asked his friend, and I realized that Adam was one of the few people who could distract Michael from his own troubles.

Adam shrugged and glanced around to see if they were being overheard. Michael understood and led him out of the unit on to the grounds. I followed, filled with fear that Adam might reveal things to Michael he had refused to say to Maggie. I prayed for my son's sake that Adam was not involved in Darcy Swan's murder.

They reached the courtyard where the orderly's body had been discovered. My friend Olivia was there, sitting on her bench, staring at the cascading water. Harold Babbitt was there, too, marching in deliberate circles around the fountain, lifting his feet and then placing them down precisely so that he rolled all the way down on his heel and finally to his toes, paused and repeated the motion again. There was an aide sitting next to a man in a wheelchair a few hundred yards away, keeping an eye on Harold – along with half a dozen other long-term patients who were working out their excess energy from the events of the past few days. The aide was overwhelmed and worried about Harold. No one wanted him to go porpoising over the edge of the fountain and shatter his head on one of the cherubs. It was always a fine line they walked, as carefully as Harold now walked his, to allow him some freedom while still protecting him from his own mad impulses.

'What's the matter with that dude?' Adam asked Michael, eyeing Harold with apprehension.

'Beats me,' Michael said. 'But I think he's lived here forever. It's kind of sad.' He glanced up at Adam and I realized that one of his fears was that he might be following in Harold's footsteps.

Adam understood that, too. 'Don't worry, I won't let them do that to you,' he said to Michael, and laughed. It was good to see the smile on my son's face.

They reached an empty bench far away from the others and sat, side-by-side, letting the sun warm their faces. After a moment of comfortable silence, Michael spoke. 'I feel pretty good,' he said. 'That lady Miranda is pretty cool. She just listens and she never tries to tell me what to do, and I always feel like she understands what I mean.'

'Wish I had someone like that to talk to,' Adam admitted. 'The cops came to see me about Darcy. It was a lady cop and my dad embarrassed me. He was really rude to her.'

Something in his voice caused Michael to glance over at him. He saw the bruise below Adam's eye. 'He do that to you?' he asked, sounding as if he had asked the question many times before.

Adam nodded. 'I can't wait to get out of there,' he said.

'I've been saving up my money. As soon as I have enough, I want to get my own apartment. Mr Phillips says he'll help me. I got an "A" on my essay and he wants to recommend me for this writing camp next summer. I get to go to Philadelphia and everything. He says he'll help me with the train fare and make sure that my father doesn't stop me.'

'Phillips is pretty cool,' Michael admitted. 'At least to you. I guess if I was as good as you are in his class, he'd like me too.' It was Michael's way of complimenting his friend and I was glad that Adam had the chance to shine at something.

'I've been working on a new story,' Adam said. He pulled a composition book from his knapsack and opened it. 'It's pretty good, I think. I'm going to show it to Mr Phillips.'

'What's it about?' I think Michael was glad to have the excuse to talk about something besides himself and his depression.

'It's about this kid whose mother dies. Everyone thinks that it's suicide, but he knows the truth. He knows that his father killed his mother.'

'How does he know that?' Michael asked slowly. He had sensed the story meant more than just an assignment to Adam.

Adam shook it off, shrugging as if he had not quite decided. 'I think he knows because he saw it happen. But he was too young to really remember, and it was only later that he realized what he had seen. Maybe something else happened to remind him and suddenly it all came rushing back.' He looked up at Michael. 'Do you think that's believable?'

'I believe it,' Michael said softly.

Who – or what – were they really talking about? I had a feeling that both Michael and Adam knew. There were secrets that they shared with no one but each other.

I was so deep in my thoughts, wondering if my son could possibly be involved in Darcy Swan's murder, that at first I did not notice the arrival of Lily. She had crept up quietly to the two boys. The orderly who usually looked after her when she was allowed to leave the unit had turned his back on her to shout something at the harried aide. Lily stood in front of Michael and Adam, her strangely disfigured teddy bear tucked under her arm so that it dangled down and its ghastly red-rimmed eyes gaped at the boys. Lily's face, as always, was that of an angel. Her eyes were wide and dark in a pale, heart-shaped face.

'What are you looking at?' Michael asked her nervously. He had heard the stories about Lily, I guessed, and he knew that, at least in her case, looks truly were deceptive. He glanced sideways at Adam in warning.

But Adam did not know Lily. He probably thought she was a patient's little sister. He patted her teddy bear on its head. 'What's his name?' he asked Lily.

'Magoo,' she said and held it out for Adam to take.

Adam held the bear up and examined the holes where Lily had gouged its eyes out and rimmed them with red magic marker. 'Dude looks like he's been through a lot,' Adam said to Lily. 'What happened to him?'

'The monster got him,' Lilly explained. 'The monster gets everyone. I think he's coming for you.'

Adam looked startled. He handed the bear back. 'Why do you say that?'

'I've seen him coming for you,' she said. 'I've seen him following you around.'

Michael stood up abruptly. It was bad enough he had to be at Holloway, he did not like to be reminded of how bad off some of the other patients were. 'Come on,' he told Adam. 'Let's go. I want you to meet this girl I met. She's pretty cool. She knew Darcy. She says Darcy really liked you a lot, man. She'll tell you all about it.'

Adam rose, looking down at Lily, unsure of what to do. Lily looked up at Adam and took his hand. 'I want to go with you,' she said.

Adam looked startled but did not draw away. 'Why?' he asked her.

'I'm afraid. The monster wants to get me, too.'

Adam looked at Michael. 'Let's just walk her back to her building,' he said to Michael. 'What can it hurt?'

'I got her,' a man's voice interrupted. The orderly was hurrying toward Lily. 'Her parents are going to be here any minute for a visit anyway.' The orderly took Lily by the hand and pulled her away, casting a look of apology over his shoulder at Michael and Adam.

'That was weird,' Adam said as he fell in step beside Michael and they headed toward the short-term unit. 'Not to mention a little bit creepy.'

'You have no idea,' Michael said, shaking his head. 'You have no idea at all.'

TWENTY-TWO

It had taken days for Calvano to run the names of Holloway's employees through law enforcement databases. This search had uncovered a myriad of transgressions, including marijuana possession, drunk and disorderly and a couple of DWIs – but nothing substantial on anyone, and certainly not anything that would indicate a Holloway staff member had the capacity for torture and violence that Darcy Swan's murder indicated. Calvano had dutifully presented Cal with the list of employees who had criminal records, but Cal had quietly stuffed the list in the trash after reading through the violations. I guess he had enough problems keeping staff as it was.

Maggie had done an equally thorough job of tracking Darcy's life. But neither she nor Calvano could find a connection between Darcy Swan, Holloway and Otis Parker.

Maggie was frustrated. She had resorted to spreadsheets and long conversations around the table with the other detectives investigating the recent murders, which meant that she was losing faith in her theory that the murders of Darcy Swan and Vincent D'Amato were connected. Maggie did not like asking for help from others. When she did, it meant she was at a dead end.

'We could show photos of all Holloway employees to the waitresses at the diner where Darcy Swan worked,' Calvano suggested during an otherwise unproductive case conference. I'd joined them as an unseen participant and had determined two things over the course of the hour-long meeting: one, I didn't like most of the other detectives any more than I had

when I was alive; and, two, it was true that the oldest among
them, Freddy the Mooch, was indeed responsible for eating
seventy-five percent of the donuts. I'd always suspected as
much and this particular theory of mine, and Freddie's
resulting nickname, was the one permanent mark I made
during my career on the force that remained a part of department lore.

The other detectives, who didn't like each other much
more than I had liked them, groaned at Calvano's suggestion
that they show Holloway employee photos to Darcy's
co-workers – this was both a civil rights hurdle and a monumental task. Even if you started with the theory that Darcy's
murderer had to be male, it was still a lot of photos to show.
Holloway had to employ over a hundred men alone.

But Maggie was desperate enough to go for it. She sent
Calvano back to Holloway to beg for the administration's help
in providing copies of employee photo badges. I tagged along
so that I could see what exactly Cal, my wife Connie's fiancé,
did at Holloway – and what Holloway was doing to protect
the patients and staff from further violence.

Cal had a huge office. I guess that made him a big cheese.
He looked less harried than he had right after Vincent
D'Amato's murder, but he was still fielding one phone call
after the other and had a huge stack of messages aligned
precisely in front of him. As fast as he returned a call, his
secretary added more messages to the file. From what I could
tell, he was indeed the head of human resources at Holloway
and was having to deal not only with a public relations nightmare but also with a steady stream of staff coming into his
office to ask if they were safe or if the police had found Vincent
D'Amato's killer yet.

It occurred to me that with all the focus on patient safety,
everyone seemed to have forgotten that it was a *staff* member
who had been killed.

Except for the rest of the staff, that is.

Cal was good at what he did. He never lost his patience,
he was tactful and yet ruthlessly efficient, and he seemed
understanding of staff concerns, at least on the surface. But
as I stood there watching, I could see him start to slump under

the relentless pressure of holding everything together. I could never have tolerated interacting with so many people in a single day. I'd been barely able to deal with myself.

Calvano arrived within the hour to request access to Holloway's employee photos. Cal's answer was immediate and to the point: it would take a court order before he would comply. Calvano took the news without arguing and left.

I followed him out and wandered through Holloway's grounds, heartened to see how quickly the patients had returned to their version of normal. I guess when your reality is filled with unpredictability, it doesn't take much to bounce back from an invasion of police and yellow crime scene tape. Patients sat on benches and lay on the grass, faces turned to the sky, basking in the promise of the coming spring. It made me miss my corporeal body. To feel the warmth of the sun on my skin again seemed a truly divine gift. It was a small pleasure, but I missed it.

Otis Parker had no interest in the weather. I found him deep in a meeting with his psychiatrist and his lawyer. Although no orderlies were present this time, the small room seemed crowded and it smelled of fear. The plump shrink was sweating more than usual and his admiration of Parker had paled next to his dislike of Parker's lawyer.

The lawyer looked like every other one of the beefy-faced, overfed legal shills who practiced law in my town. His blond hair had started to gray and his weathered face bore testimony to too many nights eating steak and drinking booze, and too many weekends fishing with his buddies off the coast. He must've been more ambitious than most lawyers, however, to have taken on Parker's case. It was bad publicity, but it was worldwide publicity. Representing Otis Parker meant no turning back – from here on out, he would probably spend the rest of his career defending national scumbags. His mother would be so proud.

I guess the lawyer thought putting up with Parker was worth it. Or maybe he just needed the money, since his suit cost at least three times as much as the one the psychiatrist wore. This fact did not seem lost on the shrink. But I don't think it was their difference in economic standing that apparently irritated the psychiatrist. I think it was the way that Otis Parker blatantly admired his lawyer over his doctor.

I wondered if Parker was pitting his shrink against his lawyer on purpose so that he could keep control of both. He was smart enough to know such a strategy was possible. No, it was more likely instinct that led him to do this, rather than a deliberate decision. Parker was like a tiger. He did not waste time pondering situations, he just went for the kill.

Parker was not restrained for the meeting. Either the orderlies had figured it would be no great loss if either one of Parker's advisers was sacrificed, or the lawyer had insisted Parker be allowed to consult with him free of handcuffs. The orderlies had been forced to leave because of Parker's right to consult in private, but no one could banish me.

The three of them took up all the space at the small table in the center of the dingy meeting room. I had no desire to be near Parker. I chose a spot against the wall where I could see him clearly. I wondered if he had brought his dark shadow in with him. And if it returned, would Parker be able to glimpse me again?

I smiled, realizing that it would do him no good to point me out. Who would believe a crazy man? Parker had painted himself into a corner. Seeing me would only prove he belonged at Holloway. That's the rub when you convince other people you're crazy. Trying to prove you're not crazy anymore can be harder than you think.

However successful Parker may have thought he was at fooling his shrink, it was soon clear that the psychiatrist did not intend to testify that Parker should be set free pending his request for a new trial. He did not consider Parker well enough to be deemed competent and he announced outright to the lawyer that he felt Parker was still a danger to the public.

This was tantamount to saying he thought Parker was guilty of the earlier murders. The little guy had courage after all.

The shrink said this shortly after I entered the room. His whole body was rigid with fear when he said it. And no wonder. Parker was glaring at him as if he was contemplating ripping off the guy's head and breathing fire down his neck.

The psychiatrist cast a nervous glance at Parker and inched

his chair away from his patient and looked longingly at the door. I knew from the lawyer's face that he, too, was regretting their decision not to restrain Parker.

'Are you certain?' the lawyer asked Parker's doctor, breaking the awkward silence. 'Do you need more time to examine him before you decide?'

The shrink shook his head in a barely perceptible gesture. I almost feel sorry for the little guy. He was an idiot, but to stand up for his convictions with Parker sitting inches away proved he had a backbone. It also meant that the psychiatrist knew that releasing Parker posed a direct and immediate threat to the safety of the public. He had not been fooled on that score.

The lawyer knew when a witness could not be bought. Resigned that they would not be able to change the psychiatrist's mind, he defused the situation. 'I'll get back to you,' he told the doctor. 'I'll let you know if we want to call you at the hearing or not.'

'You do realize that I am essentially a government contractor?' the doctor said. 'That I could well be called by opposing counsel to testify?'

Otis Parker shifted in his chair and his face flushed a deep red. The air in the room grew thick. I felt a fluttering in my chest as if something hungry and terrible had roosted there. Whatever lived in Otis Parker wanted out.

'I'm sure we can find plenty of people willing to testify that Mr Parker has made incredible strides in his treatment,' the lawyer said calmly. 'Combine that with the fact that he was railroaded for crimes he did not commit and I think we can find a panel sympathetic to his cause.'

The look of alarm that flickered over the shrink's face mirrored what I was feeling. Surely no one would sic Parker on the world? And yet, it was now a possibility.

The psychiatrist rose, going out of his way to stay as far away from Otis Parker as possible. 'Good luck,' he muttered as he knocked too loudly at the door to the hallway. The click of the lock soon after confirmed that staff were standing right outside the room, waiting to come to the visitors' aid, if needed.

The huge orderly with the braided beard stuck his head into

the room, his face cheerful as he asked, almost playfully, 'Everything OK in here?' He beamed at Parker and then smiled at the lawyer. 'Play nice, now,' the orderly said as he held the door open for the psychiatrist and locked it again.

Boy, did he know how to get Parker's goat. I could feel the hatred raging inside Parker. I hoped the orderly was prepared to put some serious money where his mouth was when the time came.

'So you think we can get some other doctor to testify I'm fine?' Parker asked, once the shrink had scurried from the room.

'Pay them enough and I can get you five doctors to testify you're fine,' the lawyer promised. He stared at Parker, gauging his mood. 'Of course, the testimony of paid witnesses is not going to carry as much weight as that of the psychiatrist who actually treats you. You understand that, right?'

Parker gazed at his lawyer with a look so dispassionate, it was more terrifying than his glare. 'Meaning what?'

'Meaning, it's definitely a problem,' the lawyer said slowly. He was underestimating Parker's intelligence, and I knew he was grossly underestimating Parker's desire to be free. 'You told me that he would not be a problem. You said you had his full support.'

'He won't be a problem for long,' Parker predicted.

His lawyer shifted uneasily in his chair. Parker had sounded supremely confident.

'What's that supposed to mean?' the lawyer asked, though he sounded as if he did not really want to know the answer.

'It means, leave the doctor to me. You take care of the judge, and I'll take care of the psychiatrist.'

His lawyer looked uneasy. 'By that, I presume you mean that you feel confident you will be able to change his mind about whether or not you should be released from here?'

Parker nodded eagerly. 'Sure, that's right. That's exactly what I meant.'

And though he was grinning broadly and looked relaxed, the wall behind him filled with the shape of his terrible, dark essence. I could feel the air in the room vibrate with anticipation and hunger.

Whatever Otis Parker had in mind, I knew that it was ugly.

TWENTY-THREE

Never underestimate the love of a mother for her child. That night, when I went to stand watch over my son, I discovered Connie sleeping on the sofa in the common room. A nurse was covering her with a blanket when I arrived. I knew Connie and I understood that, reassurances or not, she needed to be near Michael. If Michael was not going to come home, then she would come to Michael.

I lingered for a while, watching her sleep. She was getting older and, yet, she looked so much younger than she had when I had been alive. I was ashamed of what her responsibility for me had done to her and I was glad she had a second chance without me to drag her down.

I, too, needed to make the most of my second chance. I decided to leave Michael in the care of his mother and to spend the night watching Otis Redman Parker. His confidence that the psychiatrist would not be a problem nagged at me. He had been so sure, so absolutely convinced that the way was clear for his release. He knew something that the rest of us didn't. I needed to find out what it was.

When I arrived, he was in the shower room taking one of his famously long and fastidious showers. He could not abide being anything but scrupulously clean, as if the filth he harbored inside had to be kept from showing on the outside at any cost. Spying on Otis Parker naked was not my idea of a good time, so I waited until he had been returned to his room to assume my vigil. I was not looking forward to the hours that lay ahead. Otis Parker's thoughts filled me with a nearly unbearable sadness at all times and, sometimes, with a horror that transcended any I had felt while alive. He looked like a man, and yet I always had this feeling that little more than a tissue-thin barrier separated me – and, indeed, the world – from unspeakable viciousness that waited within him.

I honestly did not know if I could make it through a whole night near him. But I knew I had to try.

I sat on the floor of his room, as far away from him as I could possibly get, praying for my soul. The room held little more than a steel bed bolted to the linoleum floor and he kept the window shut. Before long, the room had filled with his body heat and the smell of his acrid sweat. Both sensations were unpleasant, but neither one as unpleasant as his thoughts.

Parker lay on his back, on top of the bleached sheets and thin blanket, at home in his austere surroundings. He had spent years in foster homes and orphanages as a child and he was comfortable in the institutionalized environment of Holloway. He had thrived in prison, too, rising quickly to rule whatever wing he landed in during his many incarcerations. His complete self-interest and his brutality served him well in dangerous, confined environments.

That made Parker no different from thousands of other men, of course. But what did set him apart were the dark thoughts that he stored in his memory and took out each evening to lovingly relive, extracting every jolt of gratification he could from the memories of what he had done. I was forced to relive every violation of flesh with him again and again that night.

As he relived each murder, a feeling of heavy darkness filled the room, as if the room was a receptacle filling with his victim's despair. I could sense a change in Parker as every moment of this nightly ritual of his passed. He fell further and further away from where he was until his breathing grew more rapid and then dropped off abruptly into an unconscious state. His pulse slowed and the air in the room turned cold.

The further away he felt from wakefulness, the more I fell into anguish. All the sadness I had ever fought off in my life washed over me in waves. I was reminded of every hurt that I had suffered, every pain I had inflicted, every regret I had never faced. I wanted to weep. I wanted to throw myself from the window and pray for a body that might break upon the fall to save me from myself. All hope, all joy, all of the love I had learned to find in my afterlife was taken from me in those hours. I felt myself falling into darkness.

A scratch at Parker's door saved me. I heard the peephole being drawn back and saw a bright-blue eye peer through it into Parker's room. I felt a sudden lifting of my despair and, unable to resist, I followed that blue eye into the hallway, leaving Parker to his strange, solitary state of half slumber. Outside Parker's room, the orderly with the braided beard seemed to be standing his own watch by the door. He had to be on his second straight shift, and yet he seemed determined to keep Parker under his watch. He would check on other patients, scribble notes in files, sometimes confirm a dose on the computer, but he always returned periodically to stand outside Parker's door, listening carefully.

Unfortunately, the other orderlies were less conscientious about Otis Parker and this one could not work every shift. Parker would have more freedom when he was gone.

There was something intensely compelling about this particular orderly, though. He triggered feelings I had never experienced before. As I watched him perform his night-time rituals, I felt the world around me fall away as I entered an even deeper plane of consciousness. I felt filled with a heavy, almost magnetic tingling. That was when I noticed them: strange, albescent figures, little more than white shapes at first, that glowed in the artificial twilight of the hallway, perambulating up and down the unit floor, as if following the bearded orderly on his rounds.

I calmed my mind and the figures came into sharper focus. I saw a man dressed in blue jeans with a scraggly beard, long hair, beaded headband and vacant eyes. I saw a woman who wore a turn-of-the-century dress and clutched a lace handkerchief in one hand. I saw an old man whose well-worn linen pants, handmade shoes and oddly shaped hat had come from another era, followed by a man in a dapper top hat who wore spats and carried a cane.

The dead were all around me.

The lost souls who had lived and then died behind Holloway's stone walls still roamed its buildings and its gardens, just as those patients who still lived there roamed them aimlessly. They were all seeking the same things, I knew: peace, a way out of Holloway, and a home they had yet to find.

Why did they feel compelled to follow the bearded orderly? I did not know. All I knew was that, all through the night, they came and they went, figures that were there, and yet not really there – the people of Holloway.

TWENTY-FOUR

B y morning, despite my vigil of the night before, Otis Parker's psychiatrist was dead. His body was discovered by a downstairs neighbor after she noticed water dripping through her ceiling. The puddle staining her carpet was pink and she insisted that the super investigate. The poor man complied, only to suffer a heart attack when he discovered the source of the leak. Paramedics had to take the super to the emergency room. There was no point in taking the shrink anywhere. The psychiatrist had been stuffed in his bathtub either before or after he was beaten so badly the medical examiner could only harvest three usable fingerprints to confirm his identification.

I saw – and felt – the aftermath of his brutal death first-hand. I had been enjoying the morning sun with Colin Gunn, Maggie's father, keeping him company while he listened to his ever-present police band radio. I liked to sit on his couch and pretend we were friends while he had his morning coffee. Sometimes he even talked to me, though he could not see me, and at other times he talked to his dead wife as well. He had just said, 'Fahey, if you're skulking about this fine morning, you better get your ass out there and keep an eye on my girl,' when the dispatcher on duty issued a special call for Maggie and Calvano to report to an address immediately.

I knew it had to be related to the case they were working on, so I beat them to the scene. When I first entered the apartment, I could feel a void in the air, the kind of emptiness left behind when a living being leaves the earth, and the living left behind have not yet filled in the gap. Then I stepped into a patch of lingering pain and felt an undercurrent of humiliation mixed with sadness. I knew then whose apartment it must be. Otis Parker had taken care of 'his problem.' His psychiatrist was dead. I could feel what his last few seconds of life had been like. He had been both terrified and ashamed, as if he blamed himself for his own death and felt that he had once again failed somehow. He had not fought back, I could feel that clearly. He had frozen up, paralysed by his own physical inadequacies, and accepted the terrible, terrible beating and the painful death that followed as his due. He had gone out, not with a bang, but truly with a whimper, his last image that of a memory from childhood: a hiding spot beneath thick overhanging vines, where he could read his beloved books in secret, safe from the teasing attacks of other children, a small Styrofoam cooler full of drinks and snacks by his side.

Now, only traces of the psychiatrist's life force and his battered body remained – a body that was barely recognizable as human. Photos of a younger, happier version of Parker's psychiatrist were scattered throughout the apartment, to tell the responding officers who lived there. No one would have recognized him in the mountain of flesh and blood and bone heaped in the bathtub otherwise. He looked even smaller in death, the violence done to his body reducing him to something less than human. I could not even tell whether he lay face up or face down in the tub.

As I stood over what was left of his body, one of the responding officers ran from the room covering his mouth. This, I thought to myself, is where evil lives. I could feel it around me just looking at his body. I, too, wanted to run, but I forced myself to stay. He deserved to have someone with him.

But no one deserved what had been done to the shrink and I felt ashamed of how I had judged him, how I had made fun of his size and his secret desires. Maybe he was just another poor bastard trying to get through life, just another traveler struggling to understand what it meant to do the right thing. If he had unconsciously turned to studying the human mind in an effort to understand himself a little bit better, then so be it. He had also tried to help other people along the way. It didn't seem fair that his life had ended in such an undignified frenzy of violence. My guess was that he had been stripped naked and forced into the bathtub before being beaten to death, which meant he had found neither the mental nor the physical strength to fight back. He had simply complied. What humiliation he must have felt at the end. His diminutive stature had failed him. His mental superiority had failed him. He had lost out to brute strength.

But whose?

The staging of his death was curious. Killing him in the bathtub had certainly been a tidy choice, but what kind of killer exults in brutality while clinging to neatness? I suspected he had been left in the bathtub for a different reason. Congealed blood and bits of tissue had quickly clogged the drain, causing a small but persistent leak from the faucet to eventually fill the tub until it overflowed. I wondered if the leak had been deliberate, if the faucet had been left turned on so that the body would be discovered more quickly and not left for days as might have happened otherwise.

I thought about it some more.

Parker wanted out of Holloway as quickly as possible. The psychiatrist had stood in his way. Now he was dead and no longer an obstacle. He would never testify against Parker's release now in a competency hearing. The hearing would move forward without him.

Parker's follower was at it again. And whoever he was, I feared that he had enjoyed the task. The psychiatrist had been destroyed beyond the point of death, as if the person inflicting the damage was extracting revenge on more than just one man and had unleashed his rage at the entire world on a single victim.

I did not think one death would be enough to diffuse that rage. I knew that this death was a beginning.

I felt and saw all of these things within minutes of arriving at the crime scene. When I heard Maggie and Calvano coming through the door, I knew that they would understand it, too. This had been more than a murder.

This was a message and, regardless of whose hand it had been written in, it was a message signed by Otis Redman Parker.

TWENTY-FIVE

I f Maggie and Calvano had been the only ones to believe that Otis Parker was somehow involved in Darcy Swan's and Vincent D'Amato's murders, the psychiatrist's brutal death changed all that. Within twenty-four hours of the shrink's death, media outlets nationally were full of speculation that all three murders were somehow connected. While most of them focused on the fact that two Holloway staff members had been killed, they struggled to find a connection to Darcy Swan. But then a local television station with an alert news anchor who had been on the job for over a decade – and who remembered Otis Parker and what he was capable of all too well – noticed the resemblance of Darcy Swan's murder to those Parker had been suspected of before being sent to Holloway. They reported on the connection as fact and the theory spread nationwide within hours.

Whether Commander Gonzales liked it or not, the public agreed that Otis Parker was somehow behind everything. Whether that theory would hold any sway with the panel convening to reconsider his commitment was anyone's guess. Parker tried to tip the scales in his favor by having his lawyer release a statement saying that Parker was deeply saddened by the tragic loss of lives and in no way connected to any of the murders. As an innocent man, he maintained, he prayed that other people would consider the facts and acknowledged that it had been impossible for him to have anything to do with any of the murders. 'I have been unjustly accused,' he maintained. 'I ask that good people everywhere take steps to make sure it does not happen again.'

Now, that took balls. Otis Parker even using the word 'pray' was like a fox trying to cluck like a chicken.

The publicity catapulted Holloway into turmoil. Though the latest murder had not occurred on hospital grounds, the connection to Holloway was inescapable. Staff members failed to show for work, terrified they would be next. One by one, families arrived to take patients home.

Connie arrived for Michael as soon as the psychiatrist's death hit local news outlets. She didn't bother with paperwork or calling ahead. She simply showed up, threw all of Michael's clothing into a duffel bag and led him out the door. Michael was too confused and too scared by the crazy rumors sweeping through the juvenile ward to protest.

Cal saw her marching across the lawn with Michael in tow and reversed course to try and reason with her. The look she gave him stopped him before he got close enough to speak. He saw her face, turned on his heels and hurried after another distraught family instead.

How had I missed appreciating Connie's strength when I was alive?

By the following afternoon, almost all of the short-term patients had been pulled out of Holloway. Next door, in the long-term unit, not all of the patients were that lucky. Some had no families to rescue them, others had no place to go. Among these: Lily, the young girl whose parents had no choice but to leave her there because of what she would do to their other child. Harold Babbitt stayed, too. He would, I suspected, be at Holloway until the day he died. But, unlike the others, Harold was perfectly content to be at Holloway. He did not want to be anywhere else. He entertained himself well into the evening hours the day of the exodus by keeping watch out the windows of his unit shouting 'Harold Babbitt sees someone leaving! Harold Babbitt sees someone leaving!' over and over again.

The little dude would have made one hell of a border crossing guard.

Olivia, too, was left behind, whether by necessity or choice I did not know. I thought of the young daughter she had lost and of the way she spoke of her husband, and I wondered if she had anyone left to go home to. Whether she stayed or not didn't seem to make a difference to her. She spent most of the day after the shrink's death sitting on her bench by the fountain watching the other patients leave. I drifted by in late afternoon, inflicted with the same agitation and indecision that everyone around me was suffering from, and she gave me a half wave. I waved back automatically – and then realized that Olivia being able to see me was not a good sign. It meant she was inching closer to my world.

I went to her and sat at the other end of her bench. 'There are a lot of people leaving us today,' I said.

She watched an old woman leading a profoundly retarded middle-aged man down the walkway. 'Everyone is afraid,' she said. 'That little girl Lily is walking around telling everyone that there are dark angels coming out of the ground to get us. I think she likes scaring people. I want to get out of here. I want to go home. But there's no one that I can call to come and get me.'

I did not know what to say to that. 'Maybe it's a good sign that you want to go home,' I offered. 'Maybe that's the first step to getting out of here. Did you tell your doctor that?'

'My doctor is dead,' Olivia told me. 'He's dead, just like everyone else I ever cared for. A nurse told me this morning when he didn't show up for our appointment. She made me take extra pills because she thought I would be upset. But I'm not upset, not really.' She hesitated. 'He never really liked me, you know. Sometimes when I talked to him, I knew he wasn't listening to me.' She looked at me, seeking absolution. 'It's terrible of me, isn't it? I should feel sad he's gone. I should feel bad that he's dead. But I feel nothing. I'm getting used to death.'

Her eyes widened as she considered me more closely. 'Are *you* death?' she asked.

I was startled. I did not know what to say. That I was dead, but not death?

'It doesn't matter,' Olivia said. She stared at the fountain, transfixed by the water that tumbled over the stone figures and pooled at its base. 'Death follows me and always will.'

I could not think of anything that I could say. The moments stretched out. 'Don't you think they will give you someone new to talk to?' I finally said. 'Surely they will assign you a new psychiatrist. Maybe they'll be better than he was?'

'Maybe,' she agreed. 'Maybe.'

She turned her attention back to the fountain, as if I were not there at all. I was used to feeling invisible and moved on.

I spotted Maggie in the distance, showing her badge to one of the guards at the overpass entrance that led to the parking deck. Holloway's administrators had gotten serious about security and there were now two guards posted at the bottom of the steps. They had printouts of all patient names and their next of kin. A line had formed that stretched across the walkway as people waited to be admitted to the grounds.

Maggie was on a mission. As soon as the guards let her through, she took off at a near run. I followed her to the administrative building and straight to the corner office where Connie's fiancé, Cal, worked. Maggie did not stop to ask the receptionist permission before she opened his door, her badge held up high in front of her so that it would be the first thing he saw.

Cal was handing a stack of files over to Miranda, the therapist treating my son. Cal looked as if he had aged ten years overnight. He was startled at Maggie's abrupt entrance, so startled that he said nothing and simply stared.

Maggie knew Miranda and nodded an apology at her. 'Sorry,' Maggie said, backing out of the room. 'I'll wait outside until you're done.'

'It won't take long,' Miranda called after her.

I stayed to see what they were up to.

They were trying to find a way to salvage the treatment of patients affected by the death of Parker's psychiatrist. How like Parker, I thought, to order a man's life taken because it was expedient for him, and to not give a thought to the many struggling people left behind who now had to confront the abrupt death of the one person in the world they had come to trust, on top of everything else they faced.

'I need you to take more,' Cal was begging Miranda. He held several patient files in his hands. 'Just until we can get a psychiatrist on staff.'

Miranda took the files and paged through them, putting the first two in her lap but tossing the other one back on Cal's desk. 'Not that one,' she said firmly.

'Someone has to represent our interests at his hearing,' he said to her. 'Please, Miranda – just this once.'

Miranda shook her head. 'First of all, I'm not a psychiatrist and his lawyer would take me apart on the stand. Every reason why I chose not to be one will be ripped apart, my credibility will be destroyed and, I feel certain, my self-confidence will go with it.'

'Can you not just do it temporarily? How about if I bring in someone from the outside and you bring them up to speed on Parker? You take them through what Alan was working on with Parker. I know he talked to you about him and I'll give you access to his files. You could just give the new hire your impressions.'

Miranda was quiet for a moment, deciding how she would phrase what she was about to say. In the end, she kept it simple. 'Cal, the best way I can say it is this: every day, I deal with adults so fragile they may not make it through the week, and every day I deal with teenagers who cannot see the future because they are overwhelmed by the present. It is a precarious balance and sometimes I am the only one keeping them here. Do you understand?'

'I understand,' he said. 'Really, Miranda, I do. I am more grateful than I can say for what you're doing for Michael. I look on him like a son.'

Hey, that's my son, buddy, not yours.

'I know that you are grateful and that you care about Michael,' she said sincerely. 'That's why you'll understand when I tell you that I do not want Otis Parker in my life, in any way, shape, form or period of time. I suspect Parker is very adept at finding what you believe is lacking in your own persona and using that to own you somehow. I will not be owned by him. I will not allow his depravity to occupy a single moment of my life, nor will I allow the evil he embodies to become a part of my patients' lives – and it will, if I start to see him. You cannot be around evil without it clinging to you. Believe me when I say that I know.' Her face was sad and I realized I knew nothing about her, not where she came from nor why she worked so hard on behalf of others. 'Cal, you must do everything you can to keep Parker from being freed. You must find someone who will fight to keep him inside and who is capable of telling the courts what he is. Otis Parker cannot be allowed to go free.'

Cal looked frightened. 'I can't change your mind?'

Miranda rose. 'Not in a million years.' She took her new patient files and left the room, nodding to Maggie in passing. I wondered how much Maggie had overheard of their conversation while she waited outside.

Maggie entered Cal's office looking more sympathetic than she had the first time around. 'Rough day?' she asked.

Cal nodded. He looked exhausted.

'Cheer up, then. I may be the only one in this entire state having a worse day than you. As I am sure you know, the general consensus seems to be that Otis Parker is behind the killings and that he has an accomplice working with him. If we don't find out who the accomplice is, this town is going to explode in fear and panic. People will start turning against each other and if, on top of all that, Otis Parker goes free . . .' She shook her head, unwilling to contemplate that outcome.

Cal ran his hands through his hair and sighed wearily. I wondered if he had slept the night before. 'What do you want me to do about it?'

'My partner says that you've asked for a court order before you'll let us have the employee photos,' Maggie explained. 'We don't have that time. I need them now. I need to find out if Darcy Swan knew anyone who worked here. I need those photos.'

Cal had been defeated by the violence that had penetrated his sanctuary, and he was weary from putting out fires for days. The conversation with Miranda had shaken him and he no longer cared about the legalities. 'Take them,' he said. 'I'll call Security and ask them to give you a disk with everyone's photos on it. We keep them on file in case someone loses their employee badge. But there will be a lot of them. We have around two hundred people working here at Holloway, and that's not even including the outside contractors.'

'How many are outside contractors?' Maggie knew they'd be harder to track down.

'Another fifty or so, maybe more. It's become more cost-effective to hire specialists from the outside for a lot of services,' he explained. 'For example, we don't need a full-time physical therapist, so we contract with an outside agency to send someone over a few times a week. Same thing goes for the physical plant. We keep a grounds maintenance crew on staff and a handyman, but that's about it. If we need an electrician or a plumber or roofer or what have you, we hire someone from the outside. Obviously, we don't have outside contractor photos on file. After this, however, I wager to say that we will.'

'Who would have a list of outside contractors?'

'Accounting could give you a list of any of the businesses we've used this past year. Some of them, like the electricians and plumbers, might be one-man shops, so it will be easy to track down who actually worked here. Others are larger companies and you'll have to ask them who clocked in at Holloway. But they should have records, since they have to bill us for their services by the hour.'

Maggie already had her cell phone out and was dialing Calvano. 'Can you set that up immediately?' she asked.

Cal looked startled. 'Of course. I'll make the call now.'

TWENTY-SIX

Otis Parker was once again a celebrity. In the days that followed the psychiatrist's death, even the most disconnected among the maximum security patients knew that something was going on involving Parker and that he had somehow gamed the system. Some high-fived him, others gave him admiring glances and still more whispered their private theories that he would soon be out of Holloway. Parker basked in it all. He had transformed from being a bully to being admired. He shook other inmates' hands, he patted them on the back and he cracked jokes as he swaggered across the exercise yard.

Otis Parker was absolutely confident that freedom was days away. His competency hearing had been fast-tracked and would be held by the end of the week.

I don't think I've ever hated anyone more.

The party did not last long. By late afternoon on the day that Parker's hearing was supposed to take place, word reached Holloway that it had been postponed. The hearing had not been able to go forward because Parker's lawyer hadn't shown up with the necessary paperwork and no one had been able to reach him.

'Looks like you've been stood up,' the orderly with the braided beard told Parker, pleased at bringing him bad news. The orderly's tiny bells tinkled and his gold teeth twinkled merrily when he smiled.

Parker had been pacing the hallways, waiting to be transported to his hearing where, I am sure, he fully expected the next step in his plan to go smoothly. He stopped at this news and squared off with the orderly, certain that he was lying.

'Man, I'm telling you the truth,' the orderly said cheerfully. 'Your lawyer did not show and he is now MIA. Did you have him bumped off, too?'

Parker's temper lived in him like an animal that came to life when it did not get its way. It rose in him now, even changing the color of his eyes from dark green to nearly black. His shoulders twitched and his hands jerked as if he longed to rip something, anything, apart – be it a table or a human being.

A small group of inmates had gathered to watch the confrontation, but they scurried away with the unerring instinct of rats as they sensed Parker's mood swing.

'Steady there, Parker,' the orderly warned. 'Two more points and it's solitary for a week.'

This pronouncement had an immediate effect on Parker. As quickly as the anger had flared, it subsided and was replaced with an eerie calm. 'He'll show,' Parker predicted. 'He's getting paid too much to back out now.'

'Maybe he's afraid?' the orderly suggested. There was a taunt in his voice. 'Odd, isn't it, how people around you keep showing up dead? Maybe your lawyer man decided he'd rather not be the next one?'

'He'll show,' Parker predicted with a confident smile. 'With what he's being paid, believe me, he'll turn up.'

I wished I could be as sure. But people close to Otis Parker did have an odd way of ending up dead.

I went in search of Parker's lawyer.

I'd known a lot of lawyers in my time and I figured that Parker was probably right: with that much money on the line, there was a good chance his lawyer would show up in front of the hearing panel sooner or later, pleading for Parker's release. He was probably there right now, apologizing for being late, proper paperwork in hand, ready to bullshit his way into a hearing the next day.

I was wrong.

I found Parker's lawyer sitting on a bench by the large pond that anchors the center of the park beside the courthouse and municipal offices. The day had turned cold and cloudy in that capricious way of spring and he was staring out over the gray waters of the pond. His briefcase was tucked between his legs and I wondered how long he had been sitting there. There was something about his posture that made me wonder if I had misjudged him. I wondered if he had tried to go to the hearing, been unable to follow through and wandered instead to this bench, where he had sought refuge from his own conscience . . . and then been too paralysed to leave his refuge behind.

Surely he had to know how angry Otis Parker would be at him for not showing up at the hearing. Surely he knew of the role Parker had played in the psychiatrist's death.

Yes, I could feel anxiousness and fear radiating off the lawyer as he contemplated Parker's wrath. But beneath this fear, I felt an undercurrent of something even darker – hopelessness perhaps. He was torn between duty and conscience.

He did not want to be representing Otis Parker; the death of the psychiatrist had shaken him badly. Whatever rationale he had come up with in order to take Parker's money, however badly he may have needed that money, whatever internal illusions he had created to convince himself that Parker was innocent – those reasons were all gone now. He was trapped between what he had once believed, what he had tried to convince himself he believed in and what he now knew in his heart to be true: Otis Parker was a monster.

His despair was absolute. Maybe Parker's lawyer had once believed in justice. Maybe he had once believed that in representing the criminally insane, he was making sure that everyone had their day in court. But now? I could feel terror and disillusionment beating in his chest, fueling an insurmountable uncertainty over what he should do next. He could not defend Parker – at least not with good conscience – nor help him seek release. But neither could he drop his client; he'd never get a client to trust him again, at least not one with enough money to choose his own lawyer.

It was a terrible dilemma. The best he had been able to do was dress, get as close to the hearing room as the park and then sit on a bench, frozen with indecision, watching the wind ripple across the water.

That was when I realized that Otis Parker lived to destroy people. Some, he destroyed with exuberant violence. Others, like his lawyer, were destroyed moment by moment just by being in Parker's proximity. Miranda had been right when she turned down the chance to be Parker's therapist: just being close to evil changed you. It was a law of physics, not morality. Otis Parker was proof.

I tried to reach the lawyer somehow, I even tried to access his memories, hoping to give him solace or strength. But fear had made him impenetrable. He would have to struggle with his decision alone.

TWENTY-SEVEN

I returned to Holloway to find its acres of lawn deserted. Holloway had become a ghost town. The irony was not lost on me

The short-term unit had been converted into a staging area for the detectives poring over patient and employee records, trying to find someone who connected the victims. It looked as if the entire force was involved in one way or the other, although Maggie and Calvano were nowhere to be seen.

Next door in the long-term unit, the remaining patients were being carefully watched by extra staff. This new layer of precaution had triggered the paranoid tendencies of many,

Harold Babbitt among them. He was marching up and down his hallway chanting, 'Harold Babbitt does not appreciate Her Majesty's secret spies who move among us in their gaudy plumage like jesters hoping for the chance to dance for the once and future King. Yeah, baby. Yeah, baby. Yeah.' His marching was more frantic than usual and I feared it would not be long before he launched himself at a wall with such ferocity that not even his protective helmet could stave off the damage.

My imaginary family was falling to pieces. Olivia sat in a near catatonic state in the common room, oblivious to everything around her. As for Lily, she was nowhere to be seen.

Only the maximum security unit still operated in a semblance of normalcy. The violent and the insane patients housed within its walls fed on the chaos caused by the murders. They seemed as giddy with anticipation as spectators at a gladiator match who, having tasted blood, were now in the mood for death.

Extra guards had been brought in from the prison a county over, allowing most of the inmates to be let outside to exercise in an effort to calm them. Otis Parker was among them. But while the other inmates played basketball, jostling and shoving each other, Parker stood at the far end of the exercise yard, staring out over the valley spread below the hospital. He was calculating something, but I could not pinpoint what – the incline? Escape? Or was he waiting for someone other than his lawyer to arrive?

Reassured that Parker was still safely imprisoned, I returned to the long-term unit and discovered that Olivia had actually been waiting, filled with anxiety, to talk to her new therapist. She was sitting in a private room with my son's therapist, Miranda, listening to her explain in an infinitely sympathetic way how very glad she was to have been given the chance to get to know Olivia, how she had seen her often when visiting Holloway and wondered why she was there.

Miranda knew, of course, why Olivia was there. But she wanted to hear Olivia's version. I felt Olivia's responding to her. There was something about Miranda that invited others to open up and share the secrets that burdened their hearts. I had seen it happen to suspects at the station, and with my son

Michael here at Holloway, and I saw it happen again that afternoon from my hidden spot in a corner of the room.

What I saw was a miracle.

There, in the midst of murder and madness, while detectives swarmed Holloway and criminals played basketball nearby, and the town below was busy double-checking the locks on their windows and doors, my lovely, lost Olivia found her way to salvation.

Under Miranda's gentle probing, she revealed her terrible secret: she had lost her husband and child in a car accident after insisting that her husband take the child out for a drive to calm her. Trapped in a too small apartment by thunderstorms and darkness, Olivia had found she could not endure the crying any longer and begged her husband to take the child away.

'She was just starting to get her teeth, you see,' she explained to Miranda as she laced her fingers together, then unlaced them, and laced them together again. 'She had two little teeth on the bottom just starting to poke out. They were like tiny pearls. They were so beautiful.' Her voice broke and she could not go on.

Miranda had said little, but she knew more than Olivia herself did about that night. 'You lived with your husband and daughter in that apartment?' Miranda asked her softly. 'Is that right? I read in your file that you lived on the first floor, near a garden area. Your neighbor said you loved to work in the garden.'

Olivia nodded. 'Yes. Emily liked to sit next to me and jab her plastic shovel into the dirt. Everything I did, she watched. She liked to pretend she was me.'

'Are you aware that your neighbor could hear much of what was said in your apartment?' Miranda asked. I wondered where she was going with this knowledge.

Olivia nodded again. 'It was embarrassing sometimes. When Jeff and I fought, I always felt like we were fighting in front of an audience.'

'She gave a statement the night of the accident,' Miranda explained, tapping her finger on the folder that held Olivia's patient information. 'There's a copy of the police report in your patient files.'

'Why is that important?' Olivia asked anxiously. In her world, news was never good.

'It's important because she says, very clearly, that it was your husband's idea to take your daughter for a ride that night,' Miranda explained. 'She says that he insisted a car ride would soothe your daughter, but that you were afraid the bad weather made the trip too dangerous. You wanted him to stay. He protested, insisting that your daughter loved the sound of the rain on the car roof and that he knew a quiet road where there would be no other traffic to fear. He said that you needed a break and that he would bring you ice cream when he returned. Your neighbor was quite clear about what was said. Apparently, your conversation took place right outside her door. And they did find a carton of ice cream in the front seat of your husband's car. The police asked you about it. Do you remember any of that?'

Olivia did not answer. She was seeing that evening in a different way for the first time since it had happened. I could feel something in Olivia coalesce and crumble as she clung to the proof of that carton of ice cream. Something heavy and dark inside her broke into infinitesimal pieces and fell away.

Miranda waited out her silence.

'What do you mean?' Olivia finally asked. She sounded fearful of the answer.

'I mean that it wasn't your fault,' Miranda explained gently. 'It was your husband's choice to take your daughter for a drive that night.'

'But I remember it so clearly,' Olivia said. 'I practically threw him out of the house.'

Miranda shook her head. 'I know that's what you think happened,' she said. 'But your neighbor is very specific. The important thing is that you probably remember it the way you do for a reason, and we need to find out what that reason is. If we can figure out why it is that you feel so guilty about Emily's death, then . . .' She smiled. 'Well, it would be a start.'

Olivia could not take it all in. She was unable to respond. But I felt a light inside her start to grow, erasing the darkness she had carried around for so long. Miranda was right. It was a beginning of sorts – and it meant that something good, however small, had come out of what was happening at Holloway.

The psychiatrist's death had brought Miranda and Olivia together, and because of that, there was a chance that Olivia could escape the prison her mind had imposed upon her.

From darkness shall come the light.

It seemed to me a kind of miracle, the kind that made me believe there was a purpose to my still being here on this earthly plane. Something bigger than me, bigger even than Otis Parker, was guiding us toward the light and, in the end, making the terrible things that human beings could do to one another better. Not perfect but, somehow, better.

TWENTY-EIGHT

I wanted to see my real family. In the weeks following my death, I had often stood across the street from my old house wondering if they mourned me – or if they secretly felt a sense of relief. Eventually I had wearied of self-torture and moved on.

This time was different. This time it wasn't about me. I had seen Connie march my son out of Holloway, I had felt Otis Parker's power, and I needed to know that they were safe.

They were gathered around the dining-room table, celebrating Michael's return home. It had been several months since I had seen my youngest son, Sean. He was starkly older, as if my passing had released him to grow up. Sean's disposition had come from Connie; he would never suffer the dark bouts that I had passed on to Michael. But despite our differences in temperament, Sean looked remarkably like me physically. He was now nearly as tall as his older brother, but lanky and healthy, an athlete full of energy and life as he sat at the kitchen table with his mother and brother, making it clear through his jokes that he loved Michael and welcomed him home.

I was surprised to see a fourth face at the table: Michael's friend, Adam Mullins, who had been such a stalwart friend while my son was at Holloway. Adam teased both my sons so expertly, it was clear that he was considered by all to be part of their family.

Connie had made veal chops and the smell of my once favorite dish was irresistible. I perched on a rickety antique chair passed down from Connie's great-grandmother and took in the sounds and smells of my family breaking bread together. I had been banned from the chair while alive for fear I would reduce it to matchsticks, and enjoyed the joke I now played on my wife. There's not much else to enjoy when you're dead.

Michael seemed brighter somehow, as if his spirit had been tarnished and now glowed with a new shine. His stay at Holloway, although cut short, had still done him a world of good. He had the promise of future therapy sessions with Miranda to get him through any dark days that might come and I could feel a determination in him to stay strong. He was giddy at being home and had a new appreciation for the care that Connie gave him after hearing the horror stories of the other kids on his ward. The smile he gave his mother, so rarely bestowed in the past year, made it plain that he was not the same boy who had entered Holloway ten days before.

I wonder how much having a friend like Adam had to do with Michael's recovery. I had not had many friends while growing up. My own father had been too violent and unpredictable to risk bringing someone else into the secret life of our broken family. Yet Adam Mullins was growing up in a similar situation and he had found a way to be a good friend to my son.

They, of course, talked of nothing but the murders at dinner, despite Connie's best attempts at introducing new topics. The mention of Darcy's name triggered the same ritual each time: either Michael or his friend Adam would say softly, as if to himself, 'Man, I can't believe she's really gone,' and the other would nod their solemn agreement. But, like the kids they were, they also sought refuge from their sadness in enthusiastic speculation about who the killer – or his next victims – might be.

My youngest son Sean wanted to dwell on the possibility that his future stepfather, Cal, might be next in the unknown killer's sights. Connie looked scandalized and frightened each time he brought it up, and Michael finally kicked his brother under the table, inspiring Sean to return to the safer topic of the murder of strangers. Connie did not want to talk about such things at all; she wanted to forget the uncertainties that existed outside the safe home she had created for our sons. But the world was not going to let her forget. Just after dessert, the insistent buzz of the doorbell signaled that the world was coming to them.

Connie knew at once that the news was not good.

She folded her napkin and, without a word to the boys, walked to the foyer and looked out the front door. Maggie and Calvano stood on the doorstep, *my doorstep*, their faces frozen in that expressionless way every detective I have ever known had been taught to adopt when trying not to give anything away.

My spirits faltered. Was Michael involved in this somehow? Why else would Maggie and Calvano be here personally when there was so much else for them to be doing?

Connie had not been a cop's daughter, and then a cop's wife, without learning something about cops. She suspected the same things I did. She opened the door slowly, her mouth set in a determined line that signaled to Maggie and Calvano that they had better have a full grasp of Michael's constitutional rights before they even thought about setting a big toe inside her house.

Maggie recognized Connie as someone not to tangle with and, I like to think, wanted to show her respect as my widow. 'We're here to talk to Adam Mullins,' Maggie said quickly. 'His father said he would be here.'

'You can't talk to him without a parent present,' Connie shot back. 'He's a minor.'

'His father has signed a waiver,' Maggie explained. 'He's agreed to let us bring him in for questioning.'

You couldn't take the Italian out of Connie if you tried. The thought of someone caring so little about their own child that they would not bother to be present at a police interrogation pissed her off royally. She lit into Maggie and Calvano with both barrels blazing.

'His father may have signed that waiver,' she lectured them, 'but I'd like to know what Adam wants to do. And if he doesn't want to talk to you, he's not going to talk to you.'

She stared at Maggie with a fierce confidence she had inherited from her mother. Calvano took an instinctive step backward when he saw the look and Maggie took a very deep breath before she replied.

'If Adam wants you to be present during the questioning,' Maggie said, 'it's OK with us.' She cast a glance at Calvano, who was clearly so terrified of Connie that he was likely to agree to anything she said.

'Don't I know you?' Connie asked Calvano suddenly. He shook his head rapidly and she peered at him suspiciously, but let it drop.

Yeah, she knew him all right. She had smacked him in the face once in front of four dozen other people for grabbing her ass at a Christmas party three years ago. It was a good thing for Calvano she didn't remember him or he'd have gotten a fresh earful about it now.

'I'll see what Adam says,' Connie said, her voice tight. She was not about to be mollified easily. She left Maggie and Calvano standing on the doorstep, but returned a moment later with Adam Mullins in tow. She gestured for them to come in, pointing grimly to the living room, which she kept impeccably clean in case of disasters like neighbors dropping by unexpectedly – or the police showing up on your doorstep.

It was a living room just like every other living room in our town, no worse off and no fancier than the rest. Maggie and Calvano relaxed in the familiarity of their surroundings. They'd both grown up in living rooms just like this one. Not even the plastic mudguard on the bottom of the couch threw them. They sat down, side-by-side, as if Connie was getting ready to interrogate them, instead of the other way around.

Adam sat uneasily on the edge of an armchair, where Connie could shoot him significant glances that the kid had no hope of ever interpreting. I had been at the receiving end of Connie's unspoken signals and, trust me, it was a loser's game.

It was her home and so it was her right: Connie decided to take charge. 'Why are you here?' she challenged them.

Maggie never missed a beat. She had grown up among women just like Connie. 'We are questioning anyone with a connection to Holloway who also has a connection to Darcy Swan,' she explained. 'It's in connection with Darcy's murder. Since Adam is her ex-boyfriend, I need to talk to him.' Maggie's voice faltered as she spotted Sean and Michael spying on them from the hallway. 'He's been at Holloway often visiting your son this past week, so that puts him in the group for questioning.'

'It's OK,' Adam interrupted suddenly. The adults looked startled at his confidence. 'I spoke to her before,' he told Connie. 'I have something for her.' He retrieved his knapsack from the front hall and rummaged in it for a moment, pulling out some folded sheets of paper and handing them over to Maggie. 'This is the list of Darcy's Facebook friends,' he explained. 'There's only a couple I don't know and I think they might be from some online games she played a long time ago. I marked them for you.'

Calvano looked suspicious, but Maggie took the papers with a nod of thanks. 'I appreciate that,' she said. 'I thought you had forgotten.'

Adam sat down across from her again and looked more dignified than any of them. 'I told you I wanted to help you,' he said. 'I want whoever did this to Darcy to be caught.'

It was hard to read what Maggie thought of the boy. 'Do you have any idea where her cell phone might be?' she asked him. 'Apparently, it's a disposable one. She doesn't appear to have an account with any of the carriers in this area, and we have no evidence that it's been used since her . . .' Maggie's voice faltered.

Adam saved her from continuing. 'She always used prepaid phones,' he explained. 'And hid them from her mother, because she would take them and use up all the minutes. Did you ask her mother about it? Maybe she's been using it?'

'We haven't been able to get in touch with her mother for the last few days,' Maggie said. 'She's not returning our calls.'

'Probably too busy giving media interviews about how

horrible it is for her that Darcy was killed,' Michael interrupted angrily from the hallway.

Connie looked like she was getting ready to tear Michael a new one for interrupting, but Maggie was nonplussed. 'Can I ask you some more questions today?' she asked Adam.

Connie interrupted. 'If you ask him anything that I feel is inappropriate,' she warned her, 'I'm going to tell him not to answer you. Understand?'

Maggie had decided not to take on Connie. 'Understood,' she said.

'I told you everything I knew when you came by my house the other day,' Adam said. I wondered if Maggie was as impressed as I was that Adam looked her directly in the eye when he talked to her. 'You have to remember what my father is like. You know the kind of person he is. If I talk to you, he's not going to like it. He just said it was OK because he can't be bothered to put down his beer long enough to drive to the station to be with me.'

Maggie's eyes moved to the bruise on Adam's cheek, correctly guessing when it had been inflicted.

'Look,' she said more kindly. 'We just need your help. Whoever killed Darcy has a connection to Holloway. I can't tell you why we think that, or how we know it, but trust me. It's true. I don't think you had anything to do with her death, but you were the only person we've heard of so far who really knew her well. You might be the only one who can lead us to her killer. Who can help us figure out what her connection to Holloway was.'

I think even Connie believed Maggie was sincere and was ready to let Adam talk more freely. But, as usual, Calvano missed the undercurrents in the room and displayed all the tact of a rogue elephant in the middle of a rampage. 'Your father says you're having a lot of trouble at school,' Calvano said to Adam in a challenging voice. 'What's all that about?'

'That's not true!' Michael interrupted. The comment made him angry enough to drop the pretense of hiding. He entered the living room and was indignant. 'Adam does great in school. He's won a whole lot of writing contests and he gets really good grades. He even tutors me in English.'

'Then why is he a year older than you but in the same grade?' Calvano asked. I did not like the fact that Calvano had done enough background work on my son to know he and Adam were in the same grade. And then it occurred to me that both Maggie and Calvano had to know that Michael, too, was one of the few people in town who had ties to both Darcy and Holloway.

I wondered if they had really come to talk to Adam after all.

I wasn't the only one who was suddenly more suspicious of their motives. Calvano moved straight to the top spot of Connie's shitlist with his last comment.

'Adam lost an academic year when his mother died,' she said with poisonous contempt. I'd had that voice leveled at me more than once and it was impossible to ignore. 'Soon after that, his grandmother became ill and it was left to Adam to make the arrangements for her care. Thanks to him, she gets home health care aides but Adam still does a lot of the work himself. Please tell me you've done your homework and you know the background? You must know how his mother died and how traumatic it was for him.'

Clearly, Calvano had not. The best he could do to salvage his dignity was stay silent.

Maggie tried to regain control over the questioning. 'We have looked into his background,' she hurriedly said. 'My partner is only asking because we've heard rumors that what happened to Darcy is somehow connected to a bigger plot at her high school. It's been suggested that she knew about some upcoming violence and was killed to keep her silent.'

'That's ridiculous,' Adam said. 'First of all, Darcy only stayed at school long enough to take the least number of classes she needed to graduate. She'd be the last person to know what was going on. I already told you, her mother was a real jerk and made her give her money each week for rent, so Darcy had to work all the hours she could. She was trying to save up enough money to get out of this dump. All she wanted was to be able to go to a new town and start over. But it was hard with her mother always asking for rent money.'

Connie looked scandalized at this.

'Besides, if there was some kind of big plot at school, I'd know about it,' Adam insisted, not realizing how it sounded. 'People are always shooting off at the mouth, acting like big shots, bragging about having guns. It's never true.'

Connie did not like what she was hearing. She stood up and her tone was abrupt. 'I'm not sure where you're going with this,' she said. 'But this interview is over. Adam had nothing to do with Darcy's death, and he certainly would not have anything to do with some plot at his school. You should know better than to believe rumors.' She aimed her gaze at Calvano, having decided to give Maggie a pass this time around.

Maggie's face was unreadable as she rose and extended a hand to Adam. The kid shook it limply, unsure of what to do.

'I apologize for our intrusion on your family dinner,' Maggie said to Connie. 'I think this can wait for another day.'

Calvano was smart enough to let Maggie call the shots. He made a big show of stowing his notebook away in his breast pocket and followed her out the door.

As the door shut behind him, I could tell by the look on Connie's face that she was every bit as worried as I was at what she had heard. How much was Adam involved? And how well did she really know him?

Worse, how much did Michael know?

TWENTY-NINE

'Is it just me, or did we look like complete idiots just now?' Maggie asked Calvano as soon as they were alone in their squad car. Or at least thought they were alone. I was enjoying my usual bird's-eye view of their partnership from the perp seat.

'Connie Fahey will do that to you every time,' Calvano mumbled. 'She comes from a long line of ball busters. It's genetic.'

'You're going to have to do better than that, Adrian,' Maggie

said. 'You did pull the jacket on the death of the kid's mother,
right? You were supposed to check any and all police reports.
Deep background, remember?'

'Sure, I pulled it,' Calvano said. 'I just haven't gotten around
to reading it.'

Maggie stared at him with something close to disgust, threw
the car into gear and sped toward the station. She did not
have to say a word. When they arrived, she kept the car idling
by the front door while Calvano headed straight to the fourth
floor. It took him a couple of minutes to locate the right file,
but at least he brought it back to Maggie with just enough
humility to mollify her.

Adam's mother had been named Charlotte Mullins. Maggie
flipped through the file, quickly reading the notes. When she
was done, she tossed it on to the back seat where the file
landed beside me, falling open to reveal a horrific photograph
of a woman sprawled across a bed, killed by what was clearly
a shotgun wound.

Damn. I was already dead, but that didn't mean I was
immune to the horrors of death. I moved as far away from the
file as I could get while Maggie sped through the streets like
an Italian taxi driver on crack.

'Where the hell are we going?' Calvano asked. 'And would
it be OK if we got there alive?'

'To see my father,' Maggie said as she missed the bumper
of a bus by inches. 'He was on the scene when the kid's mother
died.'

'You think it's connected?' Calvano asked.

'I have no idea,' Maggie admitted. 'Which is starting to be
a familiar feeling.'

'You know Gonzales has it in for the kid, right?' Calvano
told her. 'He's pitched about the media jumping on the Otis
Parker bandwagon and he's determined to prove them wrong.
Some of the guys told me they're working on the theory
that the Mullins kid is a drug dealer and was getting his
supplies from the orderly who got offed. The theory is that
Darcy Swan found out and was killed because of it, or maybe
she was in on it with him and something went wrong. They
think maybe the shrink found out his prescription pads had

been stolen or something. You've got to admit it all fits together.'

'Yeah, but where does Otis Parker fit into that theory?' Maggie asked.

Calvano looked uncomfortable. 'They're still not buying that he's involved. They're saying the kid admired him, so he copied him to throw people off and that's the connection.'

'Copied him down to the very last detail?' Maggie said. 'Even the ones not released?'

'You know we have bad leaks. One of the guys thinks that the details of Parker's signature leaked and got picked up on the Internet somehow and we just never found out. The kid is an online genius, apparently. It would be easy for him to find the details.'

'And we know this how?'

'The father's been talking to a couple of the other teams about it. The old man knows more about what his son's been up to than the kid thinks. That kid is hiding something.'

I felt panic flicker in Maggie at this news. I couldn't tell if it was because she didn't share everyone's enthusiasm for Adam Mullins as a suspect, or because she feared what would happen should Gonzales find out that she had questioned him without a parent's permission early in the case. If the kid turned out to be the killer, and his defense lawyer found out, it could screw up the entire case.

No wonder Maggie wanted her father's help.

Colin Gunn was an old man in a wheelchair, but he had once been a legendary detective. He lived in a stone house a few miles from the station. He preferred to spend most of his days on his front porch, where he could see the comings and goings of his neighbors and use the sixth sense he had developed during his years on the force to keep his small world safe. He had called in half a dozen complaints to the department since his retirement and not once had he been wrong about someone lingering too long on the block, claiming to be a delivery man, or sitting in a car outside the elementary school watching the children play. He was still good at what he did.

Maggie greeted him by tucking his blanket around him and

scolding him for not being more careful of his health. Colin endured her babying because he loved her beyond all reason and knew that mothering him made Maggie happy.

At first, I watched them from a distance, cautious about approaching Colin. He could sense my presence with the same remarkable intuition that enabled him to spot a con man. But I finally joined them on the porch, too curious to stay away. I had just settled in when the old man snapped his head toward me, but said nothing. I smiled, knowing that claiming to sense a ghost would do nothing for his reputation for still being sharp as a tack.

It was as if he could read my mind. He gave me the same Colin Gunn glare that had once stopped juvenile offenders in their tracks, but turned back to his guests without comment.

'I saw your name as one of the investigating officers,' Maggie said to her father. 'I thought maybe you remembered what was left out of the jacket?'

'Oh, I remember plenty,' her father said. 'I remember that the kid was the one who found her when he got home from school. He tried to resuscitate her, never mind that half her face was gone. A neighbor saw him screaming in the middle of the sidewalk, covered with blood, and called 911. The father was a plumber and out on an emergency call when it happened.'

'Jesus,' Calvano said. 'That'll warp a kid for good.'

Colin Gunn was no fool. 'What's this all about? Is this about the murders?'

'It might be,' Maggie admitted. 'Adam Mullins used to date Darcy Swan, the girl who was killed last week. We're looking into his background. He seems unnaturally poised for his age. My guess is he's keeping an awful lot inside.'

'He was like that when it happened,' Colin remembered. 'Don't get me wrong – it was horrific. It was one of the last calls I ever took before retirement and it was also probably the worst call I ever took. His mother must have wanted to check out an awful lot, because that was one serious shotgun wound. But I never could understand her doing it when she had to know her kid might find her. That's just unforgivable.'

'Yes, it is,' Maggie agreed. 'I can't think of a woman who would let that happen.'

Colin glanced at her. 'You don't think it was a suicide?'

'I have no idea. I'm asking if you think there's a chance it was something else.'

'We looked into the possibility,' Colin admitted. 'The cops had been called out to the house a couple of times for domestic disputes. Her husband liked to use his fists. But that's not uncommon for that part of town. There were never any allegations about child abuse, and the kid was doing really well in school, as I recall. That probably didn't continue after her suicide, of course.'

'He dropped out of school for a year,' Maggie said.

Colin nodded. 'That makes sense. If I recall, Social Services stepped in to make sure the kid got the counseling he needed. You can't live through something like that at that age and get through it without help. Like I say, he was the one who found her.'

'Could something like that turn a kid bad?' Calvano asked.

Colin gave Calvano the look he used on people he wasn't quite sure he liked. 'I'm not a shrink,' he said. 'But I doubt it. Not unless there were a lot of other factors at play. Besides, I think the kid was in pretty heavy-duty therapy for months after it happened. The system did everything right. There was even some question about him going back to live in the same house. But he wanted to go back there, and the grandmother stepped forward to move in with them, so Social Services OK'd the deal.'

'The grandmother got sick a couple of years later,' Maggie told him. 'Adam Mullins ended up having to take care of her.'

Colin Gunn shook his head. 'This world can be a tough place.'

'Could the husband have done it?' Maggie asked.

'I suppose,' Colin admitted. 'But no one really thought so. He seemed pretty broken up and she had been suffering from depression, and the whole thing was so awful that we all just wanted to close the file on it. I remember that I didn't like the husband. He was a bully and he didn't ask about his son once, at least not in front of me, and I think he was hitting the sauce pretty hard. But if I suspected every person in this town who was a drunken bully, there wouldn't be enough room down at the station to hold them all.'

'Could the kid have done it?' Calvano asked.

Colin looked startled. 'Son, if you had seen what finding his mother did to that kid, you would not be asking me that question. No, he could not have done it.'

'How old was Adam Mullins at the time his mother died?' Maggie asked.

'He was still in elementary school, as I recall. I believe in fifth grade. The principal pulled me aside to say that he wanted to make sure Adam got some help to deal with it, that he was not convinced the father could look after the kid. In fact, the principal is why we called in Social Services.'

'Did you have anything to do with the Otis Parker case?' Calvano asked him. 'You remember the one?'

'Of course I remember it,' Colin said. 'Fahey and Bonaventura caught it, but the Chief asked me to keep an eye on what they were doing to make sure they didn't screw it up.' *Ouch. No one had ever told me that.* 'In the end, the Feds took over anyway once we figured out some of the murders took place over the line in New Jersey. But I still made sure Fahey and Bonaventura got some of the credit. They needed it at that point.'

Another self-delusion bites the dust.

'But it was a solid case, right?' Calvano asked.

'Oh, yeah,' Colin said emphatically. 'As solid as they get. It was right before we started routinely testing DNA, it still cost a boatload back then and the Chief wouldn't spring for it. We didn't really need it anyway. There was plenty of trace evidence and some credible eyewitnesses. Parker did it, all right. Of course, it didn't matter in the end since he pulled his bat-shit act and the jury believed him.'

Maggie and Calvano were silent, absorbing this information.

'Why are you asking me about Otis Parker?' Colin asked them.

'It's nothing,' Calvano mumbled. 'It's just a stupid idea we had.'

'Let me guess,' Colin said. 'Darcy Swan was murdered in a way very similar to how Otis Parker killed his victims?'

Maggie looked surprised. 'How did you know?'

'Don't ever underestimate Otis Parker,' Colin warned them. 'You have to meet him to understand how truly dangerous he is. People who have never met him have no idea. You have to feel him to get it.'

'We have,' Maggie and Calvano answered, almost simultaneously.

'Then you know that he'll act like he's some dumb-ass country cracker, or the victim of a lousy childhood, or he can be as crazy as a loon if it suits his purpose,' Colin said. 'But underneath all that, he is one devious son of a bitch. He is smart. If that girl's death seems connected to him, it is. I'd bet all the money I have in the bank on it.'

'That's what we think,' Maggie said. 'But we're not getting a lot of support on it.'

'Gonzales thinks we're wasting time,' Calvano explained. 'He acknowledges the murders might be connected, but he thinks it all connects back to Holloway and some kind of a drug ring. He thinks the Otis Parker similarity is just a coincidence. He's pissed off the press keeps reporting Parker is involved.'

'That's because Gonzales doesn't want to deal with the possibility,' Colin said. 'It's bad press and, believe me, press coverage is the defining factor in most of his decisions since he rose up in the command. Sometimes he lets it get in the way of the facts.'

'The trouble is that I don't have that good of a theory as to why Otis Parker would want to orchestrate Darcy Swan's murder,' Maggie admitted. 'Other than to screw with us. Maybe he likes us knowing he had something to do with it, and he likes to taunt us with that because we can't do anything about it. It pisses me off.'

'Fight that impulse to get angry,' her father advised. 'That's his way of throwing you off balance. He knows he'll make mistakes if you make it personal. You think he's got something to do with all the murders?'

'We do,' Maggie said. 'We can't find any other connection to Darcy Swan beyond the way she was killed, but her torture matches his signature right down the line. The connections with the other victims are more clear. He had a beef with Vincent D'Amato, the orderly who was killed. The guy was always hassling him, and for Parker that would be enough to have him killed. The psychiatrist who was murdered was Parker's shrink. According to his notes, he was going to testify against Parker's release at a competency hearing and now he's dead, too. Parker can't have done any of these things himself. Someone is doing them for him. We just can't figure out who it is or how Parker is pulling the strings.'

'Plus we've got no proof,' Calvano added. 'And we're the only ones on the squad who think Parker is involved.'

'Well, I don't know about you, son,' Colin told Calvano, 'but my daughter's instincts are good. If you both think he's behind it, he probably is. From what I know of Parker, if it's benefiting him in any way, he's behind it. He is a natural born and bred killer and he thinks of no one but himself. You couldn't have raised a more perfect predator if you had done it in a laboratory. Parker's mother took off as soon as she could and his father made it worse by beating the hell out of him every chance he got. You know that brand Parker burned into the skin of his victims? He learned that trick from his father, who used to whip him with a coat hanger he'd heated up in the fireplace. Parker grew up on violence and, when he got big enough, he turned that violence against anyone he could.'

'They sound alike,' Calvano pointed out. 'Otis Parker and Adam Mullins. Both lost their mothers. Both had drunken fathers.'

'I don't know,' Colin said doubtfully. 'Otis Parker is a special breed of killer. It takes a long time to make a man as bad as that one.' He looked worried. I was surprised. He usually hid that from Maggie.

'What is it?' Maggie asked. 'Why are you looking at me that way? I'm not afraid. I can take care of myself.'

'It's not you I'm worried about, Maggie May,' Colin said. 'It's what could happen to this town if they actually let Otis Parker out. He'll have a long list of people he wants to get revenge against. That's how he works. You'd be on it, but at the bottom of the list. He'll go after everyone who put him away for what he did to those other girls first, and if they're gone – you better believe he'll go after their families.'

Was it my imagination or did he glance my way?

Maggie looked alarmed. 'That's a long shot, though, isn't it? His first competency hearing has already been postponed.'

Colin shook his head. 'When it comes to Otis Parker, nothing is a long shot. He's not going to stop with a competency hearing. My guess is that it's just his first step. If the competency hearing fails, and he's got a decent lawyer, I'd bet my badge that he is going to file to have the verdict against him vacated on the grounds that he was not competent enough at the time of the first trial to assist with his defense. He'll ask for a whole new trial on those murders. He could win that motion, too. It's happened before. In the meantime, he'll be released from Holloway. And when he brings up new evidence at his second trial, he could very well walk out of that courtroom a free man forever.'

'What new evidence?' A hint of fear crept into Maggie's voice.

'He'll argue that whoever killed Darcy Swan killed the other girls,' Colin explained. 'That her death is proof he didn't do the earlier killings. Think about it – no matter what the press says, Parker has the perfect alibi. He was locked up at Holloway when the Swan girl was killed. And the death of the others just proves there's another crazy killer on the loose.'

'You really think that's a possibility?'

'I know it is. It's probably the motive behind that poor girl's death. Parker didn't know the Swan girl. He just needed a convenient victim. But whoever killed her for him certainly knew her. Parker is orchestrating all of this just to get himself out of Holloway and safe from the possibility of prison once he's out. Like I said, Parker is smart. He's had a long time to think about this strategy. You have to be smarter.'

'How?'

'You have good instincts. Just follow them. I know you can take care of yourself. Besides, I've got a feeling that you have a guardian angel watching over you.'

This time, I knew he was looking my way.

THIRTY

I knew Colin Gunn was right about Otis Parker. I just didn't know who he was getting to do his dirty work for him. I thought back to everything I had ever overheard about Parker, even from the patients at Holloway. The teenagers had claimed to my son that killers were loose at Holloway and attacked you at night – the usual teenage nonsense if you added in a bloody claw hanging from a car door. But Olivia had said that Lily was going around telling other patients that dark angels crawled out of the ground at night to take people away. I had been in the dark forest of Lily's mind and I'd never seen creatures like that. Maybe she really had seen something?

That night, I decided to keep watch out the windows of the long-term unit just as Lily liked to do, looking for dark angels. Lily was already in her room, sleeping the near catatonic sleep of the over-medicated. She looked tiny and abandoned curled up in her bed, her ghastly teddy bear peeking out from beneath the covers with its mutilated, red-rimmed eyes.

I stood vigil in the common room, choosing a window toward the back where I'd most often seen Lily standing watch. I was kept company by Harold Babbitt and a handful of other patients waiting out the last of the evening hours in the common room together. Harold was definitely tuning up for one of his episodes. He wore his soft helmet and looked like an old-fashioned football player psyching himself up for the second half as he marched back and forth across the room behind me. I stood at the window, wondering how long it would take before anyone appeared – or if they would appear at all. Sometimes a delusion was just a delusion.

One by one, Harold and the other patients were led to bed. I was left alone beside the window. I found myself wondering about my son. Was Michael safely asleep at home in his bed, content that his mother was near, happy to be freed from

Holloway? Had his stay here been enough to encourage him to turn from the darkness? Would it keep him from following in my sorry footsteps?

Just past midnight, I saw Lily's dark angels. One shadow emerged from the ground, near one of the sheds close to Holloway's back fence. The second shadow appeared on the other side of the fence, balanced on a narrow strip of grass that marked the edge of a cliff. It was too dark to tell who they were, but judging from its size, I knew that the shadow on this side of the fence was probably Otis Parker.

He had found a way to escape his unit. He was not yet free upon the world – but he was surely free within Holloway. It would not be long before he found a way out of Holloway.

But why had he not left yet? I thought about it. He had needed to be inside Holloway when his psychiatrist was murdered to establish his alibi. And now that he had decided to escape, the entrances were too well guarded. But he would find a way. When the time came, it would be his accomplice's job to break Parker out of Holloway.

The two shadows had a brief conversation at the fence before the second one disappeared down the incline and the other entered one of the sheds.

I decided to follow, though I worried about the effect that being near Otis Parker had on me. My feeling of unease had never been stronger than when I approached the shed behind the long-term unit, hoping to pinpoint what Parker's plan might be. My courage has seldom been tested in the afterlife. I am in no physical danger, since I am no longer a physical being, and the only real thing I fear is the unknown. But approaching the shed filled me with uncommon dread and I realized that what I was feeling was more than unease. It was more like the prickly feeling I'd had when I was still on the job and had to round a corner, gun drawn, unsure of what I was about to face but forced to take action because others on the squad were watching me.

In short, I felt afraid for my survival.

It was a feeling I had not experienced since my death. As the feeling of danger grew, I began to wonder if I was strong enough to withstand what might lie ahead.

I reached the spot where one of the shadows had been standing and discovered a manhole just outside the shed's entrance. It had a heavy metal top with handles on it, making it easy to lift up if you were above ground. But it would also be equally easy for someone inside the pipe to lift up the manhole and escape from the drainage system below or, conversely, replace the manhole cover above him after he had disappeared back into the system. No one would be the wiser. If the larger shadow had been Parker, it meant he had some way inside the maximum security unit to enter the drainage system. But his room and, indeed, the entire unit had been thoroughly searched since Darcy Swan's murder.

How could I find out where he was getting in and, even more important, bring someone else's attention to it?

The manhole had been left open. I peered into the darkness and saw a metal ladder that led down to a massive pipe extending back toward Parker's building at a slight upwards slope. But a wrought-iron grid blocked the mouth of the pipe in the other direction, probably to capture debris for easier cleaning. I suspected that it was this underground gate that had forced Parker to exit the drainage system behind the long-term unit and had motivated Parker to enter the shed. Curious, I stepped inside it.

The shed was barely ten feet square. An assortment of breaker boxes and tools had been mounted along three of its walls, along with some sort of suction device that looked like a giant vacuum cleaner hose. The center of the room was dominated by a second manhole with a cover that could be swung to the side to open it, eliminating the need to lift the heavy top at all. The cover had a metal sliding bar six inches wide embedded into its design, making it easy to lock the manhole shut by sliding the bar over the cover and securing it in a steel slot on the other side. At the moment, the cover was swung open, revealing a black hole that led into absolute darkness. A metal ladder was permanently affixed to one side of the opening so that workmen could access the pipe to perform maintenance. It was the same drainage pipe that led to Parker's unit, but this opening allowed you to access it on the other side of the metal grid that trapped debris for removal.

I ventured down the ladder and into the pipe, wondering if I had somehow stumbled upon the entrance to Hell itself. Certainly, when you are dead and still wandering the earth, the idea of Hell is much more than an abstraction.

The pipe was made of heavy iron. Mineral deposits clung to its sides, and the floor held several inches of run-off. Scurrying and skittering sounds, followed by splashing, told me that the rats living in Holloway's drainage system could sense my presence. As I wandered through the pipe, I discovered smaller pipes feeding into it at various intervals. Clearly, I was in the main pipe of a master drainage system. I followed the tunnel toward the outer fence of Holloway, knowing that before long I would reach the end of the pipe where it protruded out over the cliff's drop-off. A few days before, when I was standing near Darcy Swan's body and looking back up at Holloway, the mouth of the pipe had gaped open like a huge black eye in the center of the cliff behind Holloway. But I also recalled that the opening had been blocked by another iron grid. I wondered how Parker intended to break through it. If he had gotten this far, all he really needed to do was cut through the iron bars. A short jump and a roll down the incline later, he would be free and running.

I needed to know what Parker was doing in the pipe. I was sure I was close to the edge of the cliff, but as I rounded a curve in the passageway, I was hit with a feeling of dread so profound I could go no further. It was as if the pipe had filled with a malevolent force so powerful it had sucked all oxygen out of the air, replacing it with a heavy darkness that pressed in on me and filled me with the fear that I might somehow disappear into that darkness.

It was the same feeling I had experienced near the pedestrian overpass the night someone had stalked Connie. I knew then that it had been Otis Parker following her, and that Parker had probably killed Vincent D'Amato, too. He had been loose within Holloway for days, including when my own son had been there within his reach. The possibilities of what might have happened ran through my mind with unspeakable clarity, like a horror movie playing the same scene over and over. I was filled with pure unadulterated terror.

I heard Parker up ahead whispering to someone on the other side of the bars that marked the end of the pipe, but I could not bear to go any closer. Tendrils of despair had insinuated their way into my core, reminding me of every failure and sorrow I'd had in my life. The cumulative weight of these memories was paralysing. I felt myself falling into blackness and thought it. I feared what might happen if the feeling reached the center of my being.

I turned around and left.

I reached the shed again and emerged into the night air. I sat down against one wall of the shed and waited, unsure of what I was waiting for or what I could do. If Otis Parker did not escape tonight, he would simply return to try again.

Several hours before dawn, before bed checks were conducted, when the sky had barely turned to a deep gray, Parker poked his head out of the manhole opening and crept up the ladder, hopping on to the dirt floor and darting outside so quickly that he was already climbing down into the pipe on the other side of the dividing grate by the time I could react. I thought about going into the pipe after him, but the crushing despair I had felt earlier stopped me. I didn't have the courage.

Instead, I made my way to the maximum security unit, where the rest of the patients were still asleep. The staff had that sleepy, slightly bewildered look that came with surviving another night shift. I paced the empty hallways and thought of where the pipe might feed into the unit. I knew it wasn't in Parker's room, but it had to be someplace where he could gain access without being noticed.

I went back over Parker's actions in the past week, looking for a clue. There was little he had done that was out of character, at least not for a psychopath like him. But he had made his lawyer fight to get him out of solitary confinement – and Otis Parker was not a man who enjoyed the company of others. My guess was that the pipe fed into a common area. The most likely places were the dining area, recreational yard or the shower room, which could accommodate six people at a time to make it easier for the orderlies to supervise more than one man at once. Not that they ever took that chance.

My bet was on the bathroom. Parker had access to it nearly twenty-four hours a day and he was notorious for showering incessantly.

I reached the bathroom in time to see the lower half of a small tiled wall move straight toward me as if it was levitating in the air. It was then slowly lowered to the ground by an unseen person on the other side of it, leaving an opening in the wall about four feet square. Parker squeezed in through this opening, picked up the wall section and pressed it carefully back into place until he heard a click. The craftsmanship was meticulous. The edges of the hatch matched the rest of the wall perfectly. Once pressed back into place, the entrance to the drainage system pipe was invisible. You'd have to know exactly the tile to press to unlatch the lock in order to access it from this side. It was impossible to detect.

Before Parker had been able to maneuver it back in place, I had caught enough of a glimpse to know that someone – Parker, his accomplice? – had cut an opening in the side of the pipe on the other side of the wall as a doorway for Parker to enter and exit the drainage system at will. It would have been a noisy, messy task. It would have required skill and it would have taken time. I did not see how anyone less than an employee working for hours at a stretch could have accomplished it. Parker definitely had help on the inside.

I shrank from Parker's presence as he stripped naked and turned on a shower, whistling as he adjusted the water temperature. As the unit slowly woke up around him, Parker scrubbed the sludge and grime from his body, removing all traces of his adventure. He rinsed the clothes he had been wearing and wrung them out, then tucked them under his arm and slipped back down the hallway to his room. Had anyone seen him, they would've thought he was simply indulging his incessant need to wash.

Parker climbed into his bed and his breathing quickly slowed. He fell asleep in moments, unfettered by conscience or concern for others. Innocence did not slumber as deeply.

The terror that had overcome me when I was inside the pipe subsided as he drifted off. Perhaps it, too, was sleeping.

THIRTY-ONE

I had to find a way to let someone know that Otis Parker was, for all intents and purposes, no longer confined. I could not depend on my Holloway friends for help. Olivia could see me, but I feared how she might be judged if I tried to get word through her. I wanted her to leave Holloway and resume her life. If she started talking about conversations with people who weren't there, they'd keep her on The Hill for sure.

I traveled down to town early the next morning, unsure of what I could do. Even filled with distress, I enjoyed the morning sun and the feeling of being a solitary traveler wandering through sleepy fields and equally sleepy suburbs rising to greet the dawn. But as soon as I entered town, I could feel a change in the air. The atmosphere was tangy with suppressed energy. The feeling grew stronger as I approached the station house where the parking lot was nearly full and more cars were pulling up by the minute. It looked as if everyone on the force had been called into duty. There were faces I did not recognize, many of them dressed in body armor. A SWAT team had arrived, I realized, most likely called in by Gonzales from a larger jurisdiction.

Had they finally identified Parker's accomplice? Perhaps they had discovered him in time and I had no need to fear Parker's escape from Holloway.

I passed Gonzalez on my way up to the conference room on the fourth floor, where I knew Maggie and Calvano would be gathered with the other detectives assigned to the task force. I hurried, wanting to gauge the mood in the room before Gonzales arrived.

Whatever was going down was big. Most of the guys were juiced up on adrenaline. They were checking their guns, adjusting holsters and making way too many jokes for just another day. Tellingly, Maggie and Calvano stood apart from the others and were looking at a schematic of a large building, marking entrances and exits with a pen. Calvano was leaning over the blueprint, obscuring the drawing's title. I did not know if it was Parker's ward or some other building they were planning to storm.

As the clock on the wall ticked toward eight o'clock, the excitement in the room rose on an incoming tide of testosterone. Gonzales's arrival only added to it.

'Sir, a word,' Maggie asked him the moment he entered the room.

He guided her out into the hallway. 'Make it quick.'

'I think this is a mistake,' she told him. 'It's too easy. Something is off, it doesn't make sense to me.'

'Gunn, I've indulged your theories until now but, as of this moment, I am taking command. We set up a hotline and we set it up for a reason. We've had not one, but two, tips about this. We have a moral obligation to pursue action. Do you want off the task force? Are your personal feelings interfering with your ability to do the job?'

'What do you mean?' Maggie asked.

'I'm not sure you're objective enough to be in on this. It might be better if you stay here.'

'No,' she said at once. 'I want to be there. We've agreed that you are only taking in one of them. You said you would let me handle the other one. You promised me. It's the only time I've ever asked you directly for something, sir. And you owe me.'

'Don't ever play that card with me again,' Gonzales warned her. 'And don't interfere with the rest of the operation.'

'I won't, sir,' she promised. 'But I am telling you, this is a mis—'

'Save it,' Gonzales ordered her. 'We can't afford to wait. Both callers were very clear. The danger is imminent. Now go inside that conference room and pull the trigger.'

He walked away, leaving Maggie standing in the hallway, looking grim. As she re-entered the room, she nodded at the SWAT commander. He gave his men the order to move out and, just like that, the crowd seemed to evaporate. Their energy was irresistible. I followed them out into the hall and on to the elevator, just to feel like I was one of them. They piled into vans and sped out of the parking lot in a convoy headed toward the north of town. I chose a spot on a SWAT van and snagged an empty window seat toward the back. Having missed the chance to participate in their front page raids while alive, I was not about to give up the opportunity now.

I enjoyed the feeling of being surrounded by men who crackled with energy and exuded confidence. They joked in that familiar way of cops: relentless and offensive ridicule of each other. God, but I had missed it. I had been a lousy member of the team, but I had enjoyed belonging to the brotherhood.

The wind whistled in through the windows of the van and someone in the front row burst out in laughter, shedding nervousness. I had been reduced to being an ineffectual hitch-hiker in life – but at least I could experience it all through better men.

Maggie's car was in the lead. She drove quickly once she reached the highway then veered off at the exit that led to one place and one place only: the high school that had been built a few years before to accommodate the never-ending growth of suburbs on this end of town. It had opened up just in time for Michael to enter its magnet program. We were heading to the high school.

What if Adam Mullins was involved after all?

What if he took Michael down with him?

School had started nearly an hour before. The parking lot was deserted when the convoy pulled up. Men and women leapt from the official cars and Maggie was met at the back entrance by the school's somber-looking principal. He clearly had been alerted beforehand. He opened the entrance doors wide, allowing a dozen officers to flood into the school and take up points along the hallway. A bomb specialist leading a German shepherd on a chain hopped from a pickup truck and hurried inside. The principal led him down the hall with Maggie and Calvano following close behind. The dog slowed on instructions from its owner, but barked when it reached the lockers near the end of the hall and refused to go further. The principal looked frightened. After a nod from Maggie, he went into the classrooms closest to the locker and spoke to each of the teachers in a rapid whisper. Maggie and the other officers tried to melt into the sides of the hallway, to no avail, as frantic-looking teachers ushered kids from their classrooms and hurried them down the hall and through a pair of double doors that lead outside to the athletic fields.

Bolt cutters were produced and the combination lock securing the locker clipped. By now, the German shepherd was quivering with anticipation. It had assumed a rigid position, its gaze never leaving the locker. Maggie started to stop the dog's owner from opening the locker, but he reassured her and reached up and opened its doors. Inside, leaning up against the back of its wall, I saw two assault rifles, with handguns arranged on the locker floor below. Maggie exchanged a glance with Calvano, who waved over four men. They followed him to the other wing of the school, which had remained oblivious to what was happening nearby. Accompanied by the principal, Calvano entered a classroom filled with restless students sleeping and doodling and napping in various stages of boredom as a teacher dressed in khakis and a polo shirt spoke earnestly at the front of the classroom, a copy of George Orwell's *1984* held in his hand. He looked up, startled, as cops swarmed the room. His lecture had become very real.

The teacher opened his mouth to speak and then abruptly shut it. He looked frightened and took a step back. The kids were silent, wondering if this was some sort of stunt to illustrate what a police state was like. But when Calvano marched over to Adam Mullins and dragged him out of his chair and threw him on the ground, then two uniformed cops leapt forward to help him, pandemonium broke out. Students began shouting, books were thrown, even the teacher lost his composure and rushed over to Adam before being jerked roughly away by a pair of plain-clothes men. I looked for Michael in the chaos and found him at the back of the room, standing on a chair, trying to see what was going on. He looked stricken. Some of the other kids cast him sidelong glances. They knew that he and Adam were friends. They wondered if Michael was a part of this or knew what was going on.

Maggie was staring at Michael, too. A feeling of dread

flooded through me and I ached for my son. I could feel his heart hammering in my chest, as if it were my own, when he realized that Maggie was looking at him. A uniformed officer moved toward Michael, but Maggie stopped him. She shook her head slightly and beckoned for Michael. My son stepped forward numbly, pale with shock, automatically obeying her command. She whispered something in his ear and he nodded.

She was taking Michael with her back to the station.

I was gripped with a sudden, terrifying doubt. *Did I really know my own son at all?* I had never paid attention to him when I was alive, I had left him without a father's influence to grow up on his own, finding male guidance wherever he could. What if he was involved? What if he had made one silly, stupid adolescent mistake and ruined his life forever? I thought of the prisons I had visited and the animals who lived inside them – and I felt sick in every fiber of my being. Not my son, not my Michael. *He would not last a day.*

Michael stared down at Adam, held face down on the floor by four different officers as they handcuffed his hands tightly behind his back. Adam twisted his head and looked up at Michael. Their eyes met, but I could not read the look that passed between them.

'I'm going with you, man,' Michael told his friend. 'You won't have to go through this alone.'

Adam Mullins was hauled to his feet and did not resist. He looked confused and frightened as the officers pulled him toward the door and still more members of the SWAT team surrounded him, creating a wall of authority. As Adam was marched down the hall, Maggie escorting Michael right behind him, students exchanged looks of shock and some of the girls began to cry. No one looked titillated, no one looked entertained. No one even pulled out a cell phone to begin recording. These kids were devastated.

Of all of the things that had happened so far that day, I thought this reaction by his classmates the most telling. Whatever was going on, there wasn't a kid in the school who thought it was possible that Adam Mullins would be involved.

I wondered if their confidence extended to Michael.

Maggie kept my son close by her side, twice signaling other

officers to back off as she led Michael to her car. She wanted to put him at ease and waved him into the back seat as if it were entirely his decision to come along for a ride.

For the first time since I had known her, I felt myself on the other side of one of Maggie's battles. I did not know if she was trying to protect my son or was simply being a good detective. Michael would be no match for her.

Calvano did not look happy at the approach she was taking. He climbed into the front seat looking like he had just swallowed a fish hook. I wondered if I had misread the mild animosity between us when I was alive. Had he resented me more than I realized? Was he now going to take it out on Michael?

I was not about to let my son ride in the back seat of a police car for the first time alone. Although I would get no credit for it from him, I climbed in next to Michael, determined to give him what strength I could. He was close to tears and I could feel the panic welling in him. I prayed word would get to Connie soon, and that Michael would have the good sense to shut up until she arrived.

My prayers were answered. Michael knocked on the bullet-proof partition that separated him from the detectives. 'Am I going to get to call my mother and tell her where I am?' he asked. 'She'll get worried if she hears about this from someone else.'

'Call her now,' Maggie suggested. She handed Michael her cell phone. Michael looked confused at this show of trust, but took it and dialed Connie, reaching her on the department store sales floor where she worked each day.

I could hear her horrified squawking from where I sat. This was going to get interesting.

Up front, Calvano was arguing with Maggie. 'What the hell?' he said, not bothering to whisper. 'You ever hear of a kid going on a rampage alone? Isn't the whole point of it to be a badass with your buddies? Why the hell is one of them in handcuffs and the other sitting in our back seat, acting like we're on the way to Dairy Queen for a friggin' ice cream cone?'

Maggie looked surprised at Calvano's reaction. 'Look,

Adrian, he's the son of a fellow officer. He hasn't been directly implicated. On top of that, you met his mother. You really think we'll get anything from him if we go the formal "talk to my lawyer" route?'

Calvano sat back, accepting her judgment but unwilling to acknowledge it out loud.

Michael had overheard the last of their conversation. He passed the cell phone through the partition opening. Calvano grabbed it out of his hands like a petulant child.

'My mother's going to meet us at the station,' Michael said timidly. 'She wants to know what this is all about.'

It was his way of asking what was going on and Maggie understood this.

'You know Adam better than anyone,' she explained to him. 'We just want to ask you some questions about his other friends, what his habits are. That sort of thing.' She glanced at Michael in the rear-view mirror. I knew she saw the same thing that I saw: a frightened kid, torn between loyalty and honesty, sitting back against the seat, arms crossed, his mouth clamped shut as a sign of his determination to stand by his friend.

'He's not going to talk,' Calvano predicted.

'I'm definitely not talking to *you*,' Michael told Calvano angrily. 'My mom's right. You're a complete asshole.'

'See?' Calvano said to Maggie. 'The kid's just like his mother.'

Maybe. But when it comes to you, he's just like his father.

THIRTY-TWO

I knew Adam Mullins was on his way to processing and would be facing arraignment within hours. But for once in her life, Maggie drove slowly enough that, by the time she reached headquarters, most of the unfamiliar vehicles were pulling out of the parking lot as the borrowed manpower headed out to a less exciting part of their day. I liked to think she did that for Michael, to spare him the side of his friend being dragged inside like a dangerous animal, surrounded by dozens of armored men holding rifles on him. I had seen the drill before, and no matter how guilty the prisoner might be, the spectacle always left me feeling diminished. It would have scared Michael out of his wits.

Maggie led Michael inside past the desk sergeant, who recognized him as my son and looked a little startled. His eyes darted from Michael to Maggie as he gauged how much he should say. 'Your mother on her way?' he asked, trying to sound unconcerned.

'I already let him call her,' Maggie assured him, understanding the code of loyalty. 'When she gets here, send her up. We'll be in Conference Room B on the second floor.'

The desk sergeant looked relieved and I suddenly wished that I had been nicer – much nicer – to him when I was alive. I felt an overwhelming wave of gratitude toward him for looking after my son.

But Maggie did not wait for Connie to arrive to start the interrogation. The moment she seated him in the conference room, she sent Calvano to get Michael a soda and turned to my son. 'Tell me what you know about your friend,' she asked.

Bitch. That boy is my son.

'I don't know what you think he's done,' Michael said. 'But Adam would never hurt anyone else. He takes care of people. He takes care of his grandmother and he's always looking after me. He knows what it's like to . . .' Michael stopped, not wanting to betray any confidences.

'Sometimes people are much different than how they seem around you,' Maggie said.

Michael was having none of it. 'Not Adam,' Michael answered firmly. 'Adam hates all that stuff. He hates guns, he hates violence. He won't even play video games with shooting in them. His mother shot herself. That's why he hates guns so much.'

'But we have his computer,' Maggie explained, her voice filled with what I could only hope was genuine sympathy. Calvano started to barge in the door and Maggie waved him out again. 'There are some pretty hardcore sites listed on its browsing history. We're talking snuff films, soldiers of fortune type stuff. You must have known he was into all that stuff.'

'You're wrong,' Michael said stubbornly. 'Adam is not like that. He wants to be a writer one day. Just ask our teacher, Mr Phillips. He says Adam has a voice and the talent to share it. All Adam cares about is reading books and writing in his journal and getting out of that house one day. He's applied for a scholarship to a prep school and Mr Phillips thinks he can get in.' Michael's voice broke as he fought back tears.

'Sometimes we don't know our friends as well as we think,' Maggie said gently.

'I know Adam,' Michael insisted defiantly. 'Adam would never do this.'

'Why would his father lie?' Maggie asked. 'He says Adam stays up all night playing violent games on the computer, that he's always writing in his notebook about his plans to blow up the school. And you saw what we found in his locker.'

'I don't know why he'd lie,' Michael said, then added a flash of insight. 'But he hates Adam because he knows he's not going to end up being a big loser like he is.'

'Two people called in tips to our hotline,' Maggie explained. 'They both said that Adam killed Darcy and was going to start shooting at school today because he didn't care what happened to him any more.'

'That's crazy,' Michael said. 'That doesn't make any sense at all. It's just not possible. Those people who called were lying. It's probably the people who really did kill Darcy.'

I thought my kid had made a good point. Maggie didn't act like she agreed.

'One caller was a man and the other was a woman,' Maggie said. 'Do you know who it might have been?'

Michael shook his head helplessly.

'Some people think Adam was dealing drugs,' Maggie said. 'That he was getting them from the orderly at Holloway who got killed, and that maybe the psychiatrist who was killed found out about it. You can see how it all connects, can't you?'

'Adam does not do drugs,' Michael said fiercely. 'He doesn't do drugs and he doesn't sell them. If you could hear what he says about the kids who do, you would know I was telling the truth.'

'How do you explain the guns in Adam's locker?' Maggie asked.

'I don't know. Maybe someone put them there.' Michael looked around the room frantically, as if the answer was waiting for him in a corner. A thought occurred to him. 'Adam never goes to his locker until lunchtime. Everyone knows that. Anyone who knows his schedule could've put the guns in his locker during the night.'

'What about your locker?' Maggie asked. 'What are we going to find if we open up your locker? Because if you're involved in any way, now's the time to tell me, Michael. I can't help you unless you tell me the truth.'

'What's going on in here?'

Connie's voice cut through their rapport like a buzz saw. She stood in the doorway and stared at Maggie with fire in her eyes. Even Maggie – my bulletproof, Teflon-coated, unbelievably confident and infinitely capable Maggie – shrank from that look.

What a warrior Connie was. She was magnificent.

Maggie took a moment to regain her composure. 'Sit down, Connie,' she said, gesturing to the chair next to Michael.

'Oh, you can call me *Mrs Fahey*,' Connie said. She sat next to Michael, drawing him close, needing to physically protect him.

Calvano had followed Connie sheepishly into the room, holding a can of soda. Maggie sent her own fiery glance his way. It had been his job to warn her Connie was near.

'OK, then,' Maggie agreed. 'Michael was just telling me what a good person Adam is.' She leaned toward Michael. 'What if I were to tell you that I believe you about Adam?'

Connie looked suspicious and Calvano was visibly startled.

'If I were to convince you that I believe you, that your friend Adam is innocent, would you talk to us a little bit more about his life? About back when Darcy Swan was his girl-friend?' Maggie asked.

Connie looked even more suspicious at this turn in the

questioning, but before she could say anything, Michael spoke up. 'Why does that matter now?' he asked. 'It was like, I don't know, a whole year ago or something.'

'I want to know why Darcy Swan broke up with Adam,' Maggie said, then immediately corrected herself. 'I want to know why *you* think they broke up.'

Michael shifted uncomfortably, but Connie, who had never been a fool – with the sole exception of the day she married me – understood what Maggie was getting to. 'Answer her,' she ordered our son.

Michael looked up at his mother, unwilling to speak.

'Christopher Michael Fahey,' she warned him. 'Tell the detective what you think happened. Because, at this point, I want to know myself.'

Michael looked miserable and ashamed, though none of this was his fault. 'I think she was creeped out by Adam's father,' he mumbled. 'Darcy tried to tell Adam that his dad made her uncomfortable, that he was always looking at her or making comments. But Adam doesn't think that way, you know? He didn't even know what she was talking about. He respected Darcy. I don't think he realized how other guys saw her. She was pretty hot, but I don't mean that in a disrespectful way.' He looked at his mother nervously. It had not been that long since she had stopped slapping him up side of the head as a way to correct his adolescent boy attitude.

'It's OK,' Connie assured him. She exchanged a glance with Maggie. 'Did she talk about anything specific happening?'

Michael shifted uncomfortably.

'Tell her,' Connie ordered him.

'There was this one time when she said something about Adam's dad grabbing her when she got there before Adam was home from school. She left and Adam got mad at her for not showing up. She was just trying to explain that she had been there but had to leave and why.'

'Why didn't she tell her mother what was going on?' Maggie asked. 'Or did she?'

Michael sounded angry when he answered. 'Darcy's mother wouldn't have cared. She thought men making creepy comments was a good thing. I've even seen her flirt with

Adam's father, which shows you how desperate she was for a boyfriend.'

Connie looked disgusted at the thought of anyone flirting with Eugene Mullins. So did Calvano.

'Do you think her mother could have had anything to do with her death?' Maggie asked.

Michael looked confused. 'No,' he stammered. 'I mean, she was really selfish and she drank too much, but I don't think she'd ever have hurt Darcy.' He looked up at his mother, not wanting to believe that such a thing was even possible. 'Besides, she depended on Darcy for money. She'd want that money to keep coming in, right?'

'You can't really think that,' Connie said to Maggie. 'Please tell me you're not serious.'

Calvano had said nothing so far, but he looked as if he agreed with Connie on this one.

'I don't know what to think,' Maggie admitted. 'I've been trying to get in touch with her for the past four days and she's not returning my phone calls.'

The room was silent, some wondering if something had happened to Belinda Swan and others telling themselves that she was holed up in a hotel room in New York City getting ready to be interviewed on some morning television show.

Michael shifted uncomfortably in his chair and I was not the only one who noticed. He opened his mouth, as if he were going to say something, then abruptly shut it again. Connie saw it all.

'Christopher Michael Fahey,' she said in a deadly voice, 'you better tell the detectives right now what you were about to say.'

'*Mom*,' Michael said as he glared at his mother. 'I wasn't going to say anything.'

'Don't you dare lie to me,' Connie said. She moved her chair closer to Michael and I thought, for just an instant, that she might actually slap him. 'That girl is dead and if you know anything that can help them, anything at all, you tell the detectives what it is right now. Or so help me God . . .' Her voice trailed off and she left the threat hanging in the air.

No one in the family had ever been able to figure out what

she meant by 'so help me God . . .' but then no one had been able to risk finding out, either. Michael was no exception.

'I don't want you to think bad things about her,' Michael said quietly.

'About who?' Maggie asked. 'About Darcy?'

Michael nodded miserably.

Maggie's voice was kind. 'Michael, there is nothing that Darcy could have done that would make me think badly of her. Whatever she did, she didn't deserve what happened to her and I would never, ever think that.'

Connie was not in the mood to coddle Michael. 'Just spit it out, Christopher Michael Fahey,' she ordered him.

'Darcy really needed money,' Michael mumbled. 'She was having to give her mother money for rent all the time, so she wasn't saving enough to get out of town like she wanted to. The tips from the diner were pretty bad, so she was thinking about becoming a dancer.'

'What kind of dancer?' Connie asked, beating Maggie to the punch.

'An exotic dancer,' Michael whispered, ashamed. 'There was this new club that opened up out on the highway and Darcy heard that the girls were making something like six hundred a night in tips just for dancing. She wasn't going to strip or give lap dances or anything like that.'

Oh, the innocence of youth.

'Who knew about that?' Maggie asked. 'Did her mother know? Did Adam know?'

Michael looked both stricken and a little proud. 'I was the only one she told,' he said. 'I used to call her and we would talk on the phone. She said she needed someone to talk to and she didn't want to lead Adam on, so she couldn't call him. She said I was her friend.'

'What exactly did she tell you about her plans for dancing?' Maggie asked.

'She said she was going to go out and talk to the owner of the club, and if it all worked out that she would be able to leave here and start over someplace else by summer. That she would only need to do it for a little while and she'd have enough to leave.'

'Are you sure Adam didn't know about this?' Maggie asked him.

Michael nodded. 'Adam had this picture of Darcy as the perfect person. He put her on one of those things, you know—'

'A pedestal?' Calvano interrupted.

'Yeah, one of those,' Michael said. 'Darcy said it drove her crazy, that she felt like she always had to be perfect around Adam. He had built this imaginary world around himself where she was like a princess, and his father wasn't a mean old drunk and there were puppies and flowers and stuff like that everywhere. She said she couldn't bear to burst his bubble, so she didn't tell him about stuff like that.'

'But she told you?' Connie asked grimly. With a mother's instinct, she had figured the same two things I had: one, that Michael had loved Darcy Swan as much as a fourteen-year-old boy can love anyone; and two, Darcy had somehow known that Michael was the kind of person a damsel in distress could turn to. I wasn't sure that signified much for his future love life. Connie was living proof that being a rescuer took its toll.

'She trusted me,' Michael said. 'She knew I wouldn't tell anyone.'

'How did she find out about the dancing job?' Maggie asked. 'Did she tell you that?'

'I think she said someone who came into the diner told her.'

'But no name for this person?' Maggie asked.

Michael shook his head.

'What's this all about?' Connie asked Maggie. 'You can't really think that Adam had anything to do with Darcy's death?'

'He is still one of the few people to link Darcy to Holloway,' Maggie explained. 'It's hard to get beyond that. I'm convinced Darcy's murder is linked to what is happening at Holloway and Adam is her only link.'

'That's not true,' Connie said. 'What about Adam's father?'

'What about Adam's father?' Maggie and Calvano asked her simultaneously.

'He works at Holloway,' Connie said. 'Trust me, I know. I made a point of avoiding him every time I went there to see Michael.'

Maggie stared at Calvano pointedly.

'He wasn't on the list of employees,' Calvano said. 'I would have noticed his name.'

'He's not an employee,' Connie explained. 'He owns his own plumbing business. He's been working there for about six months now, I think.'

'It's true,' Michael said, backing up his mother. 'That's how Adam was able to get a ride home at night after seeing me. His father was getting off work.'

Maggie was staring at Calvano again.

'There are a lot of people on the list of contractors,' Calvano said, defending himself. 'And Gonzalez pulled all of my help on it because he thinks we have our suspect. I was trying to get through the list as fast as I could.'

'Oh, God,' Maggie said, as if to herself. 'This changes everything.'

'So? Go arrest him,' Connie said, always the practical one. 'Trust me, no one will be surprised to see that man behind bars.'

'It's not that easy,' Maggie said.

'Why not?' Connie asked. 'You heard what Michael said. Adam's father was hitting on Darcy all the time and she thought he was a creep. You know what that means. You know what his father's temper is like.'

'Adam has already been arrested for her murder,' Maggie explained.

'That and a whole lot of other things,' Calvano added.

Connie looked as if someone had ripped her heart out and thrown it on the floor. 'You've already arrested Adam Mullins?' she asked them in a near whisper. 'Don't tell me you arrested him based on anything his father had to say.'

Maggie and Calvano were silent.

Connie was fighting back tears. 'Are you telling me that you arrested a fifteen-year-old boy who has no one to stand up for him? Are you telling me that Adam is having to go through this all alone, that he is sitting in a cell somewhere all by himself, knowing he is accused of killing the girl he loved and that there is no one in his life left willing to come to his rescue?' Connie ran out of words. The silence in the room built.

'When is he being arraigned?' Connie asked.

Maggie looked at her watch. 'My guess is right now,' she said to Connie.

Connie stood. 'Let's go, Michael,' she said. 'Adam needs us.'

THIRTY-THREE

A dam Mullins was as alone as he had ever been in his young life. He sat on the edge of the metal bench in a holding cell, the only occupant in a room designed for high-risk prisoners. He wore an electric security belt designed to allow the guards to shock him at any point during the transportation and courtroom process, a precaution reserved for those criminals who were considered as close to human monsters as you can get. The kid was dwarfed by the apparatus.

A few yards down the hallway from his cell, Gonzales stood arguing with a trio of other suited men about who would be taking Adam Mullins to his arraignment. I knew then that the Federals were going to take over, whether Gonzales liked it or not, that Adam Mullins had fallen into the no man's land of being considered a home-grown terrorist and would be placed under federal jurisdiction. All bets were now off. It was conceivable Adam could disappear within the hour and never be seen or heard from again. It had happened before.

If Adam realized this, he did not show it. He was lost in his own private despair. For fifteen years, Adam had struggled through a life that surely had not lived up to his expectations and had suffered one disappointment after the other. He had endured the blows of an abusive father, the horror of losing his mother and the need to take care of a grandmother dying before his eyes. Through it all, he had retained a poise remarkable for anyone, much less someone his age. But this final indignity, this being locked in a cage with some space-age torture device cinched around his middle, had proved too much for the kid. He was crying without making a sound, the tears flowing down his cheeks to stain his hands. Five years of being kicked in the teeth, without even a mother to console him, had finally claimed its toll. The kid could take it no longer.

I could not leave him there alone. I sat back against the concrete wall in a corner across from him and I asked myself why this kid should be asked to pay such a heavy price in life when people like Otis Parker were given every break.

The jail was noisy and overheated, and the catcalls and jeers of other prisoners rang from cell to cell. Adam heard none of it. Gonzales and the trio of well-suited Feds walked past the cell, looking in curiously at him, and Adam did not even notice.

They would be coming for him soon, I knew. They would not wait long with a case like this. They would move as fast as they could, so that no one had to linger too long to consider what it was they were actually doing. A guard came by in the middle of it, glanced in on him and walked on. No one wanted to witness his despair.

The kid cried in silence until he could cry no more. I wasn't sure what I could do. I did not think there was anything I could do.

Most remarkable to me was the utter lack of hatred in Adam Mullins. As badly as he had been treated by those he loved, he had not yet turned mean. I could feel no trace of hostility, no need for revenge, no desire to blame others for his troubles. I just felt a weariness from him, an overwhelming, bone-deep weariness and a desire for it all to be over.

I hoped he was on suicide watch.

Adam's breath began to slow and I felt him slip under into a quieter state of mind. I realized that he was meditating, that he was consciously trying to find peace in a deeper state. I wondered if he had learned that technique while in therapy after the death of his mother. Maybe this was how he had been able to maintain his remarkable calm as a young man.

Whatever it was, it worked. I felt a tranquility settle over me as the same feeling filled the cell. I felt the kid's sorrow start to lift. I felt a flicker of his spirit come alive.

That was when I realized that I was not alone in the cell with Adam.

There, standing in a corner across the room from me, was

the figure of a tall woman with high cheekbones and a weary face. Her bony red hands and plain house dress were evidence that life had been hard on her. Her hair was pulled back in an indifferent bun and she wore neither jewelry nor any make-up. She was staring intently at Adam. I examined her face and saw traces of him in her features. He had her eyes, and those cheekbones had been passed on to him, too. I knew who she must be.

Adam's mother had come to him in his darkest hour, traversing who knows how many worlds to get there, and while I did not understand the form she took – she looked there, yet somehow not there, her body seemingly carved out of the air – I could feel her presence undeniably. She stood a few feet away from her son, radiating a warmth that I can only describe as golden and comforting in its power. I experienced every moment of it with Adam. It washed over him as he meditated and calmed his mind. It filled his being and healed his heart. It settled around him like a cloak. It gave him hope and the will to live.

'You ready, kid?' The guard was back and he held a bullet-proof vest in one hand. 'I'm going to have to put this on you, and it's going to be tricky because of the belt.'

Adam stood, staring at the vest. 'Do I really need to wear that?' he asked. His mother had faded away at the guard's arrival, but she had left him with new strength.

'I think so, yeah. I think maybe you better.'

'What happens after that?' Adam asked.

I don't think the guard liked what was being asked of him by Gonzales. I don't think he thought of Adam as a monster, the way Gonzales and the Feds seemed to. 'After that, you get arraigned in court, kid,' he answered. 'And I hope to God you have a good lawyer.'

I rode with Adam to court, squeezed in beside three guards who sat motionless and silent on the bench across from a shackled Adam. He was dressed in a bright orange jumpsuit that covered the security belt and bulletproof vest, but made him look like a kid in a Halloween costume instead of a dangerous prisoner.

Adam was someplace far away. His body was there in the

van, shackled to rings in the wall, but he wasn't there. I hoped he was someplace beautiful, and I hoped that wherever he was, his mother was there with him.

Word had leaked to the press, probably deliberately, that a Columbine-style shooting at a local high school had been thwarted and that there might be a connection to the recent murders in town. By the time Adam Mullins was pulled from the transport van, he had already been dehumanized and reduced to everyone's worst fear – a diabolical young villain, devoid of all morals and empathy, caught just in time, intent on random destruction of those more innocent than he. He was the perfect poster boy for those who feared the world changing around them as much as they feared getting old.

Me? I had not bought it as a cop and I sure didn't buy it now. I knew that the real villains were never as obvious as Adam Mullins, that they did not display their weapons neatly in lockers or leave blueprints to destruction on their computers for everyone to see. The real people to fear were the ones who spent a lifetime hiding behind others, reaping the benefits of their well-directed destruction. Beyond that, I could feel the terror in Adam Mullins – and no one could be that afraid without having some innocence left in them.

As the angry shouts of a gathered crowd reached him, I could feel Adam clinging to fading memories of time spent with his mother, frantically attempting to return in his mind to afternoons by the creek, building forts and playing war, of times before his world shrank to four walls that trapped him and held little more than a sick grandmother and violent father.

My heart ached as I experienced these memories with him, knowing they did not have the power to obliterate the threats of the crowd gathered to watch him being hustled inside, their shouts and fear fueled by the presence of television cameras.

Overhead, the sky had turned a deep gray, as if the heavens themselves were angry at what was playing out beneath. I looked up, smelling rain in the air. A storm was on its way.

I passed Maggie and Gonzales in the hallway outside the main courtroom, arguing in furious whispers. I stopped to eavesdrop. I had never seen the Commander more angry at Maggie. His face was flushed and his mouth set in a dangerously thin line. He was world-class pissed off.

'Your actions could cost us this entire case,' he said to her. 'How many times have I made my feelings very clear on that point? No interviewing minors without a parent present.'

'He had an adult there representing him,' Maggie protested.

'I'm not talking about that interview, Gunn,' Calvano said angrily. 'Don't play games with me. You went out to his house, and you talked to him alone, and if he has a halfway decent lawyer, that could well cost us this case.'

'What case?' Maggie asked. 'Look at what's happening around here. You brought in the Feds and you know what can happen. They've labeled the kid a terrorist. They don't need any evidence now. He could well end up a thousand miles away from here and we'll never be able to find out what happened. He may well have done nothing. His father is far more likely to be guilty. Just stop to think about it. Every scrap of evidence you have against the kid is either from his father or could apply equally to his father. And the old man worked in the very unit where Otis Parker lives.'

'From the very beginning, you have let your theory about Otis Parker color every piece of evidence we've found,' Gonzales told Maggie. 'You have ignored the facts. The evidence against this kid is overwhelming and I'm not going to discuss it any further.'

'Sir, you are making a mistake.'

'The only mistake I made was moving you up too far, too fast,' Gonzales said. 'I plan to correct that mistake once this afternoon is over.'

With that, he left Maggie standing, stunned, in the middle of the hallway. Typically, Calvano waited until Gonzales had disappeared into the courtroom to step out from around the corner and approach his partner. Christ, the guy was better at skulking around than I was.

'That sounded pretty bad,' Calvano ventured. He looked genuinely shocked when he realized that Maggie was wiping away tears.

'I don't give a shit about my career,' Maggie said. 'We've

all made a horrible mistake and that kid is going to be the
one to pay for it once he steps into that courtroom.'

Calvano put an arm around her and pulled her tight. 'Pull
yourself together, Gunn. Let's just go in and see what we're
up against.'

I followed them in to the courtroom and saw that Connie
and Michael were both already there. They were sitting directly
behind the defense table and looked as if they both wanted to
throw up. Then I saw the reason for their distress: Adam had
been assigned a public defender who looked nearly as young
as he did. His suit hung off his gawky frame and he looked
panicked at the growing crowd trickling in, as if he wasn't
sure he could handle the task ahead.

The judge was cause for even more concern. I knew her
well, she'd chewed me out often enough, and she looked like
she was in no mood for mercy today. She was a prosecutor's
judge, and the DA's office did everything they could to rig the
system and draw her name when a big case like this one was
on the docket. Adam Mullins would not get a break from
Judge Hobart. She was a large woman with a perpetually
unhappy face and an attitude that made you believe she felt
the world had been unfair to her and therefore she was entitled
to impose a rigid justice system of her own when it came to
her courtroom.

The prosecutor hadn't liked me much either and had once
famously referred to me as 'a waste of space who is not worth
the tarnish on his shield,' right here in this very courtroom.
She'd been speaking privately to a peer and was unaware that
the microphones at her table were on. From the look on the
judge's face at the time – and his failure to instruct the jury
to disregard the remark – I had the uncomfortable feeling that
he agreed with her about my credentials all too readily. In the
end, I had not been called to testify in the case and, had I
been sober at the time, would have slunk shamefacedly from
the courtroom. As it was, I remembered with even more shame
that my partner had tapped me on the shoulder to let me know
that the session had been adjourned and I could go home and
sleep it off. I'll never forget the way the jury was looking at
me as I trudged from the courtroom.

That had been the last time I ever appeared in court until now.

Adam Mullins was led to the defense table in chains. He stared down at his defense attorney, not knowing who he was. He saw Michael and Connie sitting a few feet away and looked so grateful, I thought he might start crying again. His eyes swept over the courtroom and I felt absurdly grateful to see another friend of Adam's among the crowd – his English teacher, Mr Phillips. He had seen his favorite pupil dragged from his classroom and now sat a few rows behind Connie and Michael, clearly furious at what Adam was going through.

And, then, just as I thought that Adam had been abandoned to the kindness of strangers, I noticed his father sitting in the back row. Eugene Mullins made no attempt to speak to his son and Adam did not make eye contact with him.

Eugene Mullins was dressed far nicer than I had ever seen him dressed before. He wore a pair of clean khakis and a pressed white shirt and his hair had been combed straight back from his cleanly shaven face. He looked like the epitome of an honest, hard-working citizen – right down to the pained expression on his face, as if he was disgusted with his son and wanted the world to know that he had regrettably washed his hands of him.

I wanted to get closer, to probe his memories and see what I could find out but Adam was suddenly instructed to sit down next to his counsel with a clanking of chains and Judge Hobart gaveled the courtroom into order.

It was a packed room, with reporters jostling for seats among the spectators. It took a moment for the crowd to settle down, and even then there was barely a second of silence before the doors at the back of the courtroom opened and a handful of nervous-looking teenagers entered, dressed in their church clothes. Adam turned around and spotted the three girls and a solemn-looking boy as they inched their way to a spot standing against a wall. He bit his lip and tried not to cry.

Judge Hobart had noticed their entrance, too. I was certain she at least knew who the kids were, and that they came from good families – our town was small enough that she could still keep the troublemakers catalogued separately from the good kids. I hoped that her opinion of Adam had been dislodged just enough to make mercy a possibility. The kid deserved some hope.

The crowd had been expecting a good show, but even the spectators gasped as the charges against Adam were read. He was being charged with more than the attempted murder of his classmates: the prosecutor announced in a clear voice that they had evidence that he was involved in the murders of Darcy Swan, Vincent D'Amato and even Otis Parker's shrink.

When Maggie heard the charges, she could not hide the surprise on her face. But her expression changed instantly to one of anger as she searched the crowd, finding Gonzales in the opposite corner of the courtroom, studiously avoiding her gaze.

The prosecutor was the best one the department had, but she was also deeply self-righteous and loved the attention that came with being the one who led the battle cry for justice. She could never resist trying her case in the press and at other inappropriate times, such as during an arraignment. Sure enough, she gave in to her need for glory and tried to introduce her opening argument. 'The state intends to prove that Mr Mullins is responsible for multiple murders, and planned to commit dozens more by taking revenge on his classmates for shunning him,' she announced. Her voice was as trained as a news announcer's and rumor was she'd taken lessons for years. 'The state intends to present overwhelming evidence against Mr Mullins, including the testimony of his own father.'

'Save it for the opening argument,' Judge Hobart intoned automatically and waved for the prosecutor to go on.

There was at least one person in the courtroom who clearly could not go on. His lawyer had instructed him to stand for the next part of the proceedings, but Adam swayed and turned white as he realized the magnitude of the charges against him – and the fact that his father was going to testify against him.

Worse, his lawyer clearly shared in Adam's disbelief. He was staring down blankly at his notepad and his hands were shaking.

I knew then that the kid was in real trouble.

'How does the defendant plead?' Judge Hobart prompted Adam's lawyer.

The lawyer looked too confounded to speak.

My god, could this really be his first trial? Would they do that to him?

I was not the only one to wonder if what was happening truly served the cause of justice. Connie looked like she was contemplating leaping over the railing so she could represent Adam herself. His teacher, Mr Phillips, was scanning the crowd as if seeking someone, anyone, who might agree with his belief that something had to be done. Even Judge Hobart looked doubtful as Adam's defense attorney remained silent, paralysed with stage fright.

A painful silence followed as the courtroom waited for a response. But the young lawyer just stood there, looking frightened. He was in over his head and he knew it. The seconds stretched out and the tension grew. Spectators began to glance at one another. Whispers broke out. Judge Hobart frowned, not sure what to do.

'Do something,' a voice cried out, and there she was – Connie, standing up alone when no one else was willing, determined to protect someone else's son out of love for her own.

Connie's courage tipped the balance of another's.

'Your honor,' a deep voice said as a well-dressed man rose from his seat in the center of the courtroom. 'The charges against Mr Mullins are both complicated and as serious as charges against a defendant can get. I am an experienced criminal defense attorney and I would like to offer my pro bono services in assisting his counsel at this time. I realize this is unorthodox, but I believe it is in the best interests of the court that the proceedings continue at this time and I believe that my counsel would enable that to happen.'

As I realized who this unremarkable-looking man was, I experienced a sudden and irrefutable flash of understanding, as if a door had been opened and I had been allowed to see the truth on the other side. I realized then that true miracles don't occur when prayers are asked and answered. True miracles occur before we even reach the point of prayer, when fate, or God, or some other force I cannot begin to explain, intercedes and sends events barreling in a new direction just before we are about to believe that there is no hope. People can call these strange turns 'twists of fate' or coincidence, but in that instant I knew better: I knew a greater force was at work.

Judge Hobart looked too astonished to comment, but the prosecutor was outraged. She jumped to her feet and shouted, 'Your honor, he can't do that,' just as the judge recovered and asked the lawyer, 'Why would you want to do that?'

A profound silence settled over the courtroom again as the crowd waited to see what might happen next. I stared at the man who had offered to rescue Adam Mullins and now stood, confident and poised, as only a man at peace with his conscience can be: it was Otis Parker's lawyer, the man I had discovered sitting on a bench a few days before, unable to bring himself to attend Parker's competency hearing, knowing in his heart that his client had arranged to have the psychiatrist killed, acknowledging that he had helped to kill another man.

'He can't do that,' the prosecutor repeated. Her voice rose with indignation and she glared at Parker's lawyer. 'He is representing Otis Redman Parker and we fully expect that Mr Parker will be called to testify as part of this case.'

The prosecutor had not wanted to disclose this information in public – but it was too late. The courtroom exploded with speculation as onlookers stared at Adam Mullins, wondering how such a timid young man could be connected to a known monster like Otis Parker.

The judge banged her gavel and silenced the courtroom yet again. The lawyer at the center of this controversy waited until all was quiet before he explained. 'Your Honor, I am no longer representing Otis Redman Parker. I resigned as his counsel yesterday. I have absolutely no connection to this case and I reiterate my offer to help.'

Not a person in that courtroom moved at that moment – except for one. While everyone else waited to see what this new development might bring, one man hurried from the courtroom without looking back: Adam's father. And wherever Eugene Mullins was headed, he was in a hurry.

Maggie saw him go. She rose abruptly and gave Calvano

a look that contained the sort of unspoken signal that only partners can understand.

Calvano was not a complicated man. He believed that when people talked, they lied more often than not, but that when they acted, they were telling the truth. The fact that Eugene Mullins had run from the courtroom told Calvano that he had a reason to run. He nodded back at Maggie and, as the lawyers clustered in front of the bench, arguing over Adam's representation, he and Maggie took advantage of the confusion to slip from the courtroom.

THIRTY-FOUR

I hightailed it out of the courtroom after them, knowing that once Maggie made up her mind, you needed to get on board while you could. When Maggie brought their car around to the front of the courthouse, I was in the back seat, ready to roll, before Calvano even reached the car door. She took off like a bat out of hell.

'Game plan?' Calvano asked, bracing himself against the dashboard as she took a corner too fast.

'Get evidence on Mullins so solid not even Gonzales can ignore it. We can't find him alone. We're going to need help or he's going to get away for good.'

'Meaning what?'

'Photo, diner, club, in that order.'

Calvano pulled out his cell phone and started making calls.

The two of them would have made excellent bank robbers. When Maggie pulled up into the parking lot at the station and made her own phone calls, Calvano ran inside the station and returned ten minutes later with a thick envelope. It had started to pour in that heavy, depressing way of spring and Calvano was soaked by the time he got back to the car.

'Gonzales?' Maggie asked him.

'On the way back to the station,' Calvano said. 'He saw us leave the courtroom.'

Maggie's response to that was to burn rubber out of the parking lot and speed toward the outskirts of town. I knew where we were going: to the diner where Darcy Swan had worked.

'Any luck at his house?' Calvano asked. His legs were stretched out straight as he attempted to brace himself for the inevitable rear-end collision. Maggie was in the zone.

'No,' Maggie said. 'And he's not going there, not with all the cops there searching through Adam's things. Just in case, a car is going to swing by his house every half-hour. If they see his truck, they're going to call me directly.'

Calvano looked relieved at that, but not as relieved as he did when they reached the diner safely.

It was warm and dry inside the diner and the air was thick with the smells of coffee, grease and frying potatoes. It was heavenly. A few hardy souls were lingering over their meals, staring out at the rain that pounded the world in fat, angry drops. No one was in a hurry to leave.

Maggie and Calvano's entrance shattered the dreamy atmosphere. Maggie commandeered a booth and, while Calvano ordered them coffee and tea, spread an array of photos out on the tabletop and gestured for the waitresses one by one. They recognized her and exchanged glances with one another. This was about Darcy, they knew.

The photos were taken from the state driver database, meaning that everyone looked like a serial killer. Most of the men were on the force, nearly all of them tired-looking, middle-aged men with droopy eyes and unshaven faces. I had been a popular volunteer for photo line-ups when I was alive. Apparently, all those years of drinking in bars and other bad habits had transformed my physical appearance into one that resembled an unhealthy percentage of criminals. It was not an honor I had been particularly proud of.

I sat next to Maggie, feeding off the excitement in the air. With a stab of vivid memory, I suddenly missed my old life. I missed all the chances I'd had to make the leap from theory to reality, to feel the triumphant flush that comes when you realize you've finally cracked a case. It felt good to be closing in.

Most of the waitresses went straight for the photo of Eugene Mullins, explaining that he was a regular at the diner. One said, without hesitation, 'Ham and cheese toasted, extra mayonnaise, fries and a regular Coke.'

Another told Maggie, 'He's a lousy tipper and plays grab-ass.'

One of the older women confided, 'Darcy always asked me to take his table. She hated waiting on the guy. He didn't bother me none, though.'

Still another offered the information that Eugene Mullins had last been in about a week *after* Darcy's body was found. 'He was with a heavyset woman,' the waitress said. 'She had a bad dye job and a worse attitude. Trash for sure. Which made her perfect for him. Only they were arguing, so I guess they didn't think so.'

'You sure it was after Darcy died?' Maggie asked the waitress.

The woman nodded. 'I remember thinking that the woman looked just like what Darcy would have looked like if she had lived. After about twenty years of cigarettes and bad food, of course.' The woman smiled philosophically. She was describing her own appearance and she knew it.

But it was the busboy with a crush on Darcy who knew the most about Eugene Mullins. 'Darcy hated that guy,' he offered. 'He always said crude stuff to Darcy, but she said she knew him and could handle him. She said she had shot him down in the past and he was going out of his way to come here and hassle her because of it.'

'Was he here the day Darcy died?' Maggie asked.

The boy's eyes widened; he knew what she was getting at. 'Yeah,' he said. 'He was here. I remember because Darcy had an argument with Ellen over who had to wait on him.'

'Who did wait on him?' Maggie asked.

The boy shrugged. 'Sorry, it was dinner rush and I don't remember. I was too busy cleaning tables. But Ellen would know. Ask her.'

Ellen turned out to be an overweight woman with over-plucked eyebrows and a bad attitude. Maggie's conversation with her was brief and to the point. Yes, Darcy had left early the night she died. For a job interview, she'd told Ellen, at a place where she'd get ten times the tips she was getting at the diner. Ellen had known what that probably meant and had not asked questions. 'Some of us got standards, you know,' she added.

The comment pissed Calvano off. 'Did it ever occur to you that the cops might need to know that?' he asked her. 'Did it ever occur to you to call us?'

She'd been meaning to tell the cops about it, she told him, but three kids, two jobs and life got in the way. 'It wasn't none of my business,' she said. 'But if you want to shake your ass for men, you better be ready to pay the price.'

Calvano looked like he was ready to *kick* her ass, but Maggie pulled him out of the diner before he lost his temper. Calvano slid into the front seat, muttering under his breath and wiping rain from his hair.

'Are you praying?' Maggie asked incredulously.

'To St Anthony,' Calvano explained. 'He's the patron saint of lost causes.'

Maggie stared at Calvano.

'What?' he asked defensively.

'Tell me you know where that new topless bar is?' Maggie said. 'The one the Fahey kid talked about that's out by the highway.'

'I know,' Calvano admitted. 'But not for the reasons you think.'

'Which way?' Maggie asked.

'North, about three miles.'

We made it to the club in under five minutes. Maggie left a spray of gravel in her wake as she pulled into the parking lot.

'Sure is aerobic riding around with you,' Calvano said drily.

Maggie ignored him. They stared at the Quonset hut and the blinking pink lights of The Pussycat Lounge. I recognized it from the night that Eugene Mullins had made his son wait in the truck, doing homework, while he drank and did god knows what else inside.

'How do you want to play it?' Maggie asked.

'You question the owner. I know him from high school. It'll be better if I just stand there and look menacing.' Calvano

smiled, and I realized that he loved this part of the job as
much as I did. He liked the hunt.

The club owner was a greasy little man with a pencil-thin
mustache and enough gold chains around his neck to keep
him at the bottom of the Delaware forever. He may have gone
to high school with Calvano, but his business had aged him
a solid decade beyond his years. He recognized Calvano the
moment he and Maggie entered the bar and waved the waitress
away from his table. When he gestured for them to join him,
his huge pinky ring glittered in the passing glare of a spotlight
sweeping toward the stage.

'Yo, Adrian,' the club owner said.

Calvano smiled painfully. He'd probably been hearing that
joke for thirty years.

Maggie got right to the point. 'It's about the girl who was
killed last week,' she said. 'We heard she was over here,
looking for a job.'

The club owner was silent as he gave Maggie the once-over,
evaluating her body first before moving on to her face.

'Hey, Richie,' Calvano said, snapping his fingers in the club
owner's face. 'She's a detective. She's not here looking for a
job. Answer the lady.'

Richie smiled at Maggie and it made me wonder why anyone
on this planet wore a mustache like his. It looked like two
caterpillars had died across his upper lip. 'We've been kind
of busy at the club,' he explained. 'Business is booming. I
haven't exactly been following the news lately. So I can't help
you unless you tell me more about the girl who was killed
last week.'

'We are talking about *this* girl,' Calvano said. He slapped
a photo of Darcy Swan on the table. It had been taken for her
high school yearbook a couple years before. She looked young
and hopeful that life held good things for her. I was sorry she
had not been given the chance to hold on to her illusions for
at least a few years longer.

'Oh, *that* girl,' the club owner said. He looked up at Maggie
and Calvano. 'She's dead?'

'She's dead,' Maggie confirmed.

In the silence that followed, the lounge seemed to take on

a presence of its own. I became acutely aware of the heavy metal music blaring from the speakers and the dim lights with their reddish glow. Everywhere you looked, sweaty men in suits were staring at bored women wearing little more than thongs gyrating on a narrow runway stage or wrapping themselves around poles. Jesus, it was depressing. The men all had that glassy-eyed look of afternoon drunks and they had not yet realized that Maggie and Calvano were cops. The girls knew, though. Most of them just kept dancing. But a couple of the girls, the ones on floor duty hoping to earn extra money giving lap dances, understood what the photo slapped on the tabletop meant. And they knew it could just as easily have been a photo of one of them. They inched closer to the table, circling like sharks. The club owner felt their presence and knew he needed to speak.

'She was in here about ten days ago,' he explained. 'I remember her because she was a nice girl. Smart, too. Too smart to be dancing in this rathole.' He glanced up at Calvano, as if seeking his approval. 'She was young and she looked good, no signs of drug use. At least not yet.'

'Did you give her a job?' Maggie asked.

The club owner shook his head. 'I knew right away she was under-age. She had a fake ID, but I didn't buy it. I told her to come back in a couple of years. I thought she looked kind of relieved, to tell you the truth. I'm not sure she had ever been in a place like this before.' He glanced out over the floor of his club. 'In my next life, I'm going to open up a daycare center. Better for your karma.'

'How did she react when you told her no?' Maggie asked.

'Like I say, she took it pretty well. But the piece of shit she was with threw a fit. This did not surprise me. I'd already thrown the guy out of here a half-dozen times and we've only been open a month. My guess is that he showed up with that girl, hoping to get in good with me so I'd let him have the run of the club. Trust me, he could've brought me Angelina Jolie and that wasn't going to happen. I got standards and this guy doesn't make the cut.'

Maggie exchanged a glance with Calvano. 'What did this guy look like?'

Calvano leaned over the table and shook the file folder he was holding, spilling photos in a line across the glass. He must've practiced the move. It was perfect. 'Any of these refresh your memory?' he asked.

'He looked like that guy,' the club owner said, tapping the photo of Eugene Mullins. 'Which is understandable, since he *was* that guy.' He looked up at Maggie and Calvano. 'Is he the guy who killed her?'

'We don't know,' Maggie told him. 'That's what we're trying to find out.'

'Well, you can stop wondering, because that is definitely your guy.'

'What do you mean?' Maggie asked.

'For starters, I've had to throw him out of here a couple of times for being grabsy with the girls. And while I run a completely legit establishment, and cannot vouch for this myself, I have been told by some of the girls, who operate their own businesses – totally without my consent or participation, you understand – that he likes to hurt them if he can.'

Maggie stared at him, evaluating his likely level of cooperation. 'Would you be willing to testify about that in court?'

'I would be willing to introduce you to girls who could testify about it in court.'

Maggie nodded. 'And you were sure that he was with Darcy Swan – that's the dead girl – the night she came in here?'

The club owner nodded. 'Not only was he with her, they started arguing on their way out the door.'

'Arguing about what?' Calvano asked.

'Toby will know,' the club owner predicted. He waved over a huge man with a rectangular head and missing front tooth who had been standing near the front door. The guy had hands like hams and I was pretty sure he'd used them to toss Eugene Mullins out of the club on more than a few occasions.

'You remember this scumbag?' the club owner asked his bouncer, tapping on the photo of Eugene Mullins.

The bouncer's eyes narrowed; he remembered him all right.

'You remember the night he came in with this girl?' The owner slid Darcy's photo toward the bouncer.

The bouncer picked up the photo and as he looked at it, I

could've sworn his shark-like eyes turned sad. He looked up
at his boss, his jaw tightening. He didn't have to be told what
had happened to Darcy.

'I remember,' he said in a thick Slavic accent.

'What were they arguing about as they were leaving?' the
club owner asked him, casting a glance at Maggie. She let
him do the questioning.

'She wanted to go home,' the bouncer said without hesitation. 'He said he knew a few more clubs where she could get
a job and he would be glad to drive her to them. She told him
to forget it, that she just wanted a ride home.' The bouncer
looked at Maggie and then at Calvano before addressing them
both directly. 'I told her that if she wanted, she could wait a
few more hours and I would be glad to give her a ride home.
But she said she was fine, that she could handle the guy.'

He didn't ask if she had turned out to be fine. There was
no point to that, he knew.

'Anything else we can help you with?' the owner asked,
casting an anxious glance at his customers. They were starting
to notice Maggie and Calvano and looked uniformly guilty at
their presence. They fidgeted with their drinks and unconsciously reached for the pants pockets that held their wallets.

Hey, I could've told them, *it could be a lot worse. It could
be your wives standing there instead of the cops.*

'I don't suppose you know where the guy who was with
Darcy Swan might be holing up?' Maggie asked the club
owner. 'We think he's good for more than just her murder.'

The club owner shook his head. He looked genuinely sorry.
'I got no idea,' he said. 'But I wish you luck, most sincerely.'

The bouncer held the door open for them as they left, and
watched Maggie and Calvano carefully as they walked to their
car. I knew he blamed himself a little for what had happened
to Darcy. Sometimes having a conscience sucked.

'What do we do now?' Calvano asked when they were back
in the privacy of their car.

She was silent for a moment, thinking. 'We go to Gonzales
and tell him what we've learned. Even he can't ignore that
Mullins was the last person seen with Darcy. He'll have to
give us some help searching for him.'

'What good is that going to do?' Calvano asked her. 'The guy could be anywhere.'

'We have to try,' Maggie said. 'He has to be somewhere.'

Maybe they didn't know where Eugene Mullins would run, but I thought I did. He was linked to Otis Parker by a bond that had a power of its own. Eugene Mullins intended to free Otis Parker before he left town. I knew it with a certainty. And it would be up to me to find a way to stop him.

THIRTY-FIVE

When you are dead, rain is like a gift from the heavens. It washes through you, leaving tiny jet trails of energy zinging around what passes for your body. But that afternoon, the heavens were going through mood swings like I had never seen before. As I left Maggie and Calvano at the station, preparing to tell Gonzales what they had learned, the rain stopped abruptly just as I reached the gates of Holloway. The clouds rolled back to reveal a sliver of late afternoon sun desperate to prove it had been there all along. A breeze wafted the clean scent of wet earth from the surrounding fields over the lawn. It was as if Holloway itself longed to be washed clean from its bout with death.

How I wished that it truly was over. But I knew that Otis Parker, at the center of it all, had not yet made his final move.

Parker was in the common room, watching the evening news with other inmates. There was no reporting on the arraignment's details, only footage of Adam being led into the courthouse in chains while the news anchor announced with relief that the killer who had terrorized the town had been apprehended. Satisfaction oozed from Parker as he watched the crowd shouting threats at Adam. I wanted to slap the smile right off his face. But at least I knew it would fade soon enough on its own. He may have known that his lawyer had resigned, but he clearly had no idea that Eugene

Mullins' involvement had been discovered and that the rest of his scheme was unraveling.

He was so smug that even the other patients could sense it and, apparently, not all of them liked it. A gawky patient with a prominent Adam's apple and bug-eyes kept glancing his way, annoyed at Parker's attitude. Parker noticed his stare and casually shot him the bird, mouthing something obscene as a kicker.

The inmate lost it. He leapt for Parker's throat, but Parker tossed him aside easily. He bounced off the wall and fell to the floor. While the other inmates laughed uproariously at this entertainment, the orderly with the braided beard rushed in from the hallway. He was in Parker's face within seconds. He pinned Parker to the back of his chair and calmly warned him, 'You touch another patient again, and I will see that you go into solitary for a week, and I don't care what your lawyer says about it.'

Parker immediately hunched down in his chair, trying to appear smaller, as if he were submitting to the orderly.

That's when I knew Parker was making a run for it that night. There was no other explanation for why Parker would deprive himself of the violence he loved so much. He had to have access to the shower room and could not risk being confined.

The orderly stared down at Parker suspiciously. He knew Parker was up to something. But there was nothing more he could do, so he turned his attention to the gawky inmate sitting dazed on the floor and helped him to his feet, telling him to sit across the room and stay the hell away from Parker. The other patient looked frightened but obeyed.

I was the only one to notice that somehow, in the confusion of the moment, Otis Parker had slipped the plastic cuff restraints from the orderly's back pocket. As everyone else watched the gawky patient shuffle across the room, Parker stuffed the cuffs into his pants and turned his attention back to the television set.

I did not want to know what he had in mind for those cuffs.

It would be hours before Parker made a move, so I left to check on my friends in the long-term unit, wondering if I could find a way to get a message about Otis Parker and his plans through to one of them. As I crossed the lawn, I saw cars traversing the roads in the valley below. There were far more cars on the highway than usual. Judging from the lack of extra guards in Otis Parker's unit, Maggie had still not been able to convince Gonzales that Parker was involved, but the extra cars told me that she had convinced him that Eugene Mullins was involved and been given help looking for him.

The news that Adam Mullins had been arrested for the murders had clearly reassured the long-term unit staff. They believed the killer was in custody and they were safe. Doors locked as a precaution were now back to their normal unlocked state and the signing in and out procedures had been lifted.

The patients on the unit were not so complacent. Restless from being cooped up inside on a rainy day, they worked out their pent-up energy by roaming the halls, squabbling in the common room or erupting in erratic behavior. Lily was the only beacon of calm among their chaos. Always alone from the others, she stood sentinel at the window in the common room, lost in her dark world as she looked out into the twilight, seeking monsters.

Harold Babbitt was in full form. Fresh red and neon green ointment had been applied to the scabs on top of his head, giving it an Easter egg-like appearance. His helmet was nowhere to be seen. He kept dashing down the stairs to the front door every few minutes, clamoring to be let out. Invariably, he would be retrieved before reaching freedom and led back up the stairs with a promise that tomorrow he would be able to resume his daily walks.

But Harold did not live in a world based on tomorrows. Harold lived in the right here and the right now. Two hours later, while the staff was distracted by a bodybuilding patient whose near-catatonic state had given way to mania, Harold slipped out the front door and escaped into the night. I followed him outside and passed Olivia sitting in the visitors' room, staring out a window at a world she was gathering her courage to rejoin. She noticed Harold leaving and followed him outside. I knew she wanted to sit by the waters of her beloved fountain.

Her step was strong. Olivia was getting better. She was

starting to shed the guilt she felt over her daughter's death and looking ahead to a life outside of Holloway.

I followed her to the courtyard and took a seat on the bench next to hers. She did not notice me. That was another good sign. She settled in to watch the water tumbling over the marble cherubs frolicking in the fountain. A few dozen yards away, obscured by the night, Harold was marching back and forth across the lawn chanting, 'Harold Babbitt walks a fine line across the lawn. Harold Babbitt walks a fine line across the lawn.'

And in life, my friend, and in life.

'Are you there?'

I was startled by Olivia's voice. It was clear and lovely, ringing out in the night air.

'Yes,' I said. 'I'm on the bench next to yours.'

'Are you an angel?' she asked. 'Sometimes I can see you and sometimes, like now, I can only feel you near.'

'I'm pretty sure I'm not an angel. That's definitely above my pay grade.'

'Then what are you?' She faltered. 'Are you real?'

'I'm real,' I assured her. 'I'm definitely real.'

'I'm going home,' she said. 'I told my therapist that I was ready to go home. I think I'm going to be OK.'

As she said it out loud, I realized that her recovery meant I would lose her. She was turning away from death and turning toward life. She would need to leave me behind.

She had been my only friend in this strange world of mine and I could not bear the thought of losing her. *Tell her about Otis Parker*, a seductive voice inside me whispered – *tell her of his plans to flee and the stolen handcuffs.* If they did not believe her, if the staff thought she was talking to invisible friends or taking wild rumors and turning them into fact, they would keep her here at Holloway, with me, a little longer. And if they did believe her, at least there would be more eyes on Otis Parker, maybe even enough to thwart his escape.

I could not do that to her. I could not risk the chance that her plans to start a new life might be blocked because of me, not after all the courage it had taken her to get to this point.

I had to find another way to stop Otis Parker. And I had to let Olivia go.

All I could do was let her know how much her friendship had meant to me. But I could not find the words to express how I felt. She had been my light in a dark world and now she was going. I let the silence grow around us as I gathered the courage to tell her goodbye. The minutes ticked by and I felt myself fading from her world. I knew I needed to say something before it was too late.

'I want you to know,' I began – but then, just like that, it *was* too late. The link between our two worlds had been severed.

I was, once again, nothing but a watcher.

We sat, watching rain clouds roll back across the sky to obliterate the moon. More rain was on the way. It was a fitting backdrop for my mood.

Our peace was disturbed by Harold's abrupt arrival. He came marching up the brick walkway, heading toward his building, repeating the same thing over and over: 'Harold Babbitt did not see a rabbit. Harold Babbitt did not see a rabbit.'

At first, I chalked it up to Harold being Harold. But as he hurried toward the front door of his unit, faster than I had ever seen him move before, I began to wonder. He had not seen a rabbit, but he surely had seen something. But what, at this time of night? It was nearing ten o'clock. The staff would not change shifts for another hour. The grounds were deserted.

Could Otis Parker have started his journey out of Holloway early? Could he be hiding in the trees?

I thought of the way he had looked at Olivia. I thought of the way his hands twitched when he called out to her. And that was when I knew – Otis Parker intended to commit one final, horrific act of taking before he left Holloway behind forever. He wanted Olivia.

I was afraid. I sat on the bench, knowing I should move, knowing that I needed to find a way to alert someone to what might happen. But I had felt the power of Otis Parker over me and I feared what he could do.

Olivia had started to hum. It was a children's song, one that held happy memories for her. But I did not want it to be her final song.

A distant rumble and a quickening of the breeze told me that the rain would arrive again soon. Soon enough to drive Olivia inside?

No. She lifted her face up to the sky and breathed deeply, finding freedom in the fresh air.

I felt a tremor in the night. Fear wrapped itself around me. I felt the urge to flee and fought it. Olivia needed me.

It took all my will to rise from the bench and confront what I feared. I would not be a coward now. I had spent a lifetime running from danger, afraid of both emotional and physical pain. I knew I had to change, that this could well be a test after a lifetime of apathy, a time to choose whether I would finally take a stand for something I cared about.

Behind me, a night bird trilled and an owl answered. Crickets chirped and frogs joined in their song, happy for the moist night. All around, I could feel the new growth of spring waiting out the evening, suspended and ready for the warmth of the morning sun. The air smelled of fresh earth, green shoots and rain. The air smelled of new life. It was no time to die. I had to do something to save Olivia.

As I moved toward the grove of trees, the powerful darkness that hovered around Otis Parker grew stronger. It was a poison that wrapped itself around me, reaching down into my guts, grabbing all the joy I had collected in my wanderings and trying to squeeze it from me.

The breeze shifted directions and brought me the acrid odor of Otis Parker's sweat. He was crouched inside the perimeter of the grove, his body obscured by shadows as he leaned against a beech tree and stared across the lawn at Olivia. He was excited by her helplessness, by the lack of barriers between them. He was savoring the moment, already tasting his power over her as he anticipated her anguish. Something ugly bloomed in him and demanded to be fed. His body vibrated with needs so dark I could not look at them further.

He moved away from the grove toward Olivia, slipping through the shadows. He had the ability to spot a patch of darkness and disappear into it, wearing the night as he melted from spot to spot. He was a trick of the shadows, here now and then gone, a predator at ease with his world.

The night grew still as if the crickets and frogs knew that death was near.

Up ahead, Olivia stood up suddenly. Parker froze. She looked up at the night sky, reluctant to leave it behind. An owl called to her from the direction of the distant front gate. She took a few steps toward it, curious as to where it might live.

No, I thought to myself, no, no, no. Go back into the building. Do not walk down that walkway. Go to the light, Olivia. Go toward the light. And by that, I do not mean go toward *the* light. Go toward the lights of Holloway. *Run.*

She turned away from the light. She took a few steps toward the front entrance and stopped to listen once again to the night sounds. Otis Parker took a few steps closer. His breathing quickened as he fought to keep his bloodlust under control.

The owl called again. Olivia stepped toward it.

I was close enough to see Parker smile. He froze, taking in the sight of Olivia posed in the night, her face upturned like a doe that hears an unexpected sound, never realizing it is the rustle of her killer coming closer, never knowing that the end will be swift and violent and sure. It was that pocket of peace that Parker longed to destroy. He lived for that single, overwhelming attack on the innocent, the moment when he annihilated the defenseless before they could react. It reaffirmed his power over what he saw as a clueless world.

I had to do something. I stepped directly in front of him and closed my eyes, willing myself to manifest, not knowing if I could do it. I had seen the shadow of his terrible black wings cast against a wall behind him. Perhaps I had the same vestige of being in me and I could use it as a show of strength. I imagined a hot, silver light in the center of my being and I concentrated on that light. I saw it flaring in my mind, growing in strength, taking hold, feeding on my will to protect Olivia until it became a conflagration.

Heat flashed through me and a dark hole of gravity opened at my core, as if I might tumble inwards on myself and disappear down it forever. Anger flashed through me as I thought of all the young girls who had died by Otis Parker's hands, and of how he had left Vincent D'Amato sprawled obscenely by the fountain, and unleashed Eugene Mullins on Darcy Swan and on his psychiatrist. I thought of how men like Eugene Mullins would always follow men like Otis Parker, admiring their cruelty and coveting their power. But unless I took a stand, it would never end. The evil would live on and live on.

Otis Parker had no right to destroy my world and I would not let him go unchallenged. I stood up straight and felt as if I was being yanked in a thousand directions all at once, as if the center of my being was stretching and stretching outwards, as if I were a great searing light illuminating the world. I was incandescent.

Parker froze and stared at what he saw before him. He faltered and the air behind him trembled. I could not see him anymore. I was blinded by my light.

Parker emitted a sound, little more than a gasp and, yet, it was enough. Olivia heard it.

'Harold?' Olivia called out into the night. 'Harold, is that you?' Her voice grew louder as she looked about anxiously.

Run, I thought to myself. *Run, Olivia, run.*

She stood, frozen in the darkness, looking about uncertainly. The heat and light radiating from me faltered and I could not sustain the river of energy flowing out from my core any longer. I felt my essence shrinking until I could not move. Had it been enough?

Parker was looking around him, assessing his need to escape against his desire for Olivia.

And then I saw him, striding up the walkway from the main gate, tall and strong, his white hair gleaming in the night air, his holster and gun outlined against his hip – Morty, the beat cop, still in uniform, holding a bouquet of yellow roses for his lady. He was heading straight for Olivia.

'What have we here?' Morty called out when he saw Olivia by the fountain. 'Surely, this is not the place to be at this time of night?' He reached Olivia and smiled at her kindly. She recognized him and smiled back.

'I just needed to feel free,' she explained. 'I needed the night air. Besides, they caught the man to be afraid of. Everyone is talking about it.'

'There's always a man to be afraid of,' Morty said gently. He took her arm and started guiding her toward the long-term unit. 'I've been out all afternoon and night searching for one.' He glanced at the roses in his arms. 'After days like this, I need to see her. I need a reminder that something beautiful still exists in this world. Do you ever feel that way?'

Olivia stopped and stared up at him, her eyes full of tears. 'I do,' she whispered. 'I do.'

They reached the door of the long-term unit, and Morty pounded on it loudly. A harried aide opened it soon after, looking relieved when she spotted Olivia. 'Oh Lord,' the aide said. 'I just noticed you weren't in bed and it gave me a heart attack.' She looked up at Morty gratefully. 'You're here mighty late, aren't you?'

'Better late than never, I always say,' Morty said as he stepped into the hallway.

Truer words were never spoken, I thought to myself.

Behind me, Otis Parker stood frozen in the darkness of the lawn. He was looking right through me and I knew that however I had appeared a few moments before, I had been discarded as beneath his notice now. His confidence in his own power had returned. He stared after Olivia and Morty with such resentment and hatred in his heart that I suddenly feared for both should Parker's escape plans change. Otis Parker liked to get even.

Above, a crack of thunder split the air and the heavens exploded in an angry, pelting rain. When I turned back around, Parker was gone. He'd left as quickly as he had appeared. I followed Olivia into the long-term unit. Morty was placing the yellow roses in a vase on the bedside table next to his sleeping lady friend and Olivia had already returned to her room, where she would find the solitude she craved. But Harold Babbitt was still marching up and down the hall, wearing only a pair of pajama bottoms.

He was being scolded by a weary nurse. 'It is past time for bed now, Harold. I don't have time to look after you all night long,' she said sternly, holding up the other half of his pajamas.

'Harold Babbitt is a man of the night,' Harold announced as he pushed away her attempts to help him. He began to put the top on himself. He wore real pajamas, light-blue cotton with dark-blue and red stripes, and they triggered a memory of my father. He'd had pajamas like that and wore them every Sunday, pretty much all day, in fact, even when he'd become enraged at me and my brothers for making too much noise and chased us out into the yard, a beer in hand, his face beet red from alcohol and anger.

'Your father did the best he could,' Harold Babbitt said, staring right at me.

I froze.

'If you talk to her, to the little one, she will be able to help,' Harold said distinctly. He blinked and examined the buttons on his shirt as he concentrated on fastening them.

'What are you going on about now?' the nurse said kindly. She brushed imaginary lint off Harold's shoulders. 'You look very handsome, Harold.'

'Harold Babbitt is a man of the night,' Harold said matter-of-factly.

'Yes, you are,' the nurse agreed. 'You most certainly are.'

THIRTY-SIX

S tunned that Harold had somehow penetrated my world, I returned to the common room. A few remaining patients still sat aimlessly, lost in their own worlds, following jumbled thoughts to the same private conclusions that had brought them to Holloway in the first place.

Lily had changed into a nightgown and was standing at the window, staring out into the night as if she were waiting for Peter Pan to come by. It was impossible to believe that this was the same child who had burned her little brother with lit cigarettes and killed the family cat with a kitchen knife. She clutched her teddy bear by the neck and her other arm moved up and down as if she were trying to fly. No one paid much notice. The staff did their best to look after Lily, all the while disapproving that she'd been parked here at Holloway among people many times her age. But when she was quiet like this, distracted by her inner world, they often left her to her thoughts and took the opportunity to check on other patients.

I joined Lily at the window. A clap of thunder erupted outside, but she did not flinch. She was staring at a corner of the side yard where the shadows overlapped. She had seen something there. I waited with her, wondering when Parker might reveal himself, wondering if he was standing outside in the darkness, staring back up at us, gauging whether it was worth it to find a way in and finish what he had started with Olivia. I could sense his terrible hunger even from a distance. He had been excited by her frail melancholy and he was finding it hard to leave his chance at one last kill behind.

Lightning flashed and illuminated Parker in a series of silver strobes. He was standing motionless by the fence behind the long-term unit. But when another clap of thunder echoed across the valley and the skies opened up even more, Parker moved toward the shed that protected the opening to his route to freedom. The time had come for him to run.

Lily saw him, too. She clutched her teddy bear tightly as the dark forest in her mind flared to life. The monsters who lived in her imagination were keen to get to know the monster who lived in her world. I willed myself to enter her mind. It was not the same as when I shared in someone's memories, it was a brutal, disjointed sensation that left me feeling as if I were chasing something in the wind and could not quite grab its tail. I saw dark trees arrayed starkly against a permanent twilight and sensed dark shadows slipping from tree to tree. The grinning cartoon cat was there, confident in its ability to control what Lily did. But, suddenly, her mind focused outward and I followed.

Parker had reached the edge of the shed. Seeing that the manhole to the first drainage pipe was slightly askew from when he had exited from it earlier, he pushed it into place. If anyone chose to check the drains, they would not know it had ever been opened.

I thought of Otis Parker descending the ladder down into the second section of that pipe. I knew that Eugene Mullins would be at the other end, ready to free him. I indulged in a fantasy of trapping Parker by locking the second manhole cover shut once he was in the pipe system and then frightening Mullins away with a fiery manifestation.

I did not have the power to do either.

I felt a chill and when I looked around, I realized I was still standing in the dark forest of Lily's mind. I willed myself back to the room. All of the patients had given up on the day and headed to their beds. Only Lily remained – and she looked as if she did not intend to budge.

'You are a stalwart warrior,' I said to her as I left her to her solitary vigil.

It was time to follow Otis Parker.

The rain was coming down harder now, the deluge so profound it felt as if a waterfall was pouring from the sky, unearthing the smell of rich loam and new grass all around me. I could not bear the thought of leaving that smell behind and descending again into a claustrophobic pipe filled with Otis Parker's evil. I did not fully understand what I was up against and I feared his power. Instead, I made my way to the other side of the rear fence and down the steep incline that marked the back of Holloway. I spotted a shape huddled beneath an overhang in the slope, seeking refuge from the rain.

I had found Eugene Mullins.

He was wearing a dark windbreaker and crouched over the opening to the massive drainage pipe that wound underneath the grounds of Holloway. I knew Parker was making his way toward that very same opening from the other end of the pipe. Mullins was already at work, his toolbox spread open on a lip of concrete that protruded beneath the pipe to create a narrow work area protected by the overhang from the rain above. I could smell his sweat from yards away. He had been running from the police all day and his adrenaline was stuck on high. I wondered if he had also been drinking.

He held a strange-looking tool resembling a cross between a large pair of pliers and a bicycle chain. He looped the chain around one of the heavy metal bars blocking the pipe's exit, ratcheted it into place and pumped the handle. Once he had made a crude cut in the bar, he used a hacksaw to try to cut

through the iron more quickly. It was hard work but he had
no other alternative: the bars were firmly embedded in concrete
above and below the pipe.

I didn't know how long Mullins had been working on the
pipes, but he had already removed one of the bars, creating
an opening half the size of a file cabinet. It would not be
enough for Otis Parker to squeeze through. Mullins had at
least two more bars to go.

I watched Eugene Mullins work, wondering what motivated
him to help a monster like Otis Parker. Did it make him feel
more important? Had the rest of the world overlooked him so
thoroughly that Parker's attention had overwhelmed his morality?
Or had he simply discovered a kindred spirit in Parker, someone
who shared his dark interests and was quick to assure him that
what they were doing was nothing more than their due?

Mullins lay the strange cutting tool down and stretched out
both of his hands, interlocking his fingers to work out the
cramps in them. He was weary from exertion and, judging by
the way he kept turning and surveying the valley below, also
worried about being caught.

'What the hell are you doing just standing around?' Parker's
angry voice cut through the sound of the rain. He emerged
from the inky darkness of the tunnel and crouched on the other
side of the bars, his eyes narrowed as he stared at Mullins.

Mullins was tired and the remark made him angry. 'I've
been at it for almost two hours,' he snapped back.

'Hurry up,' Parker ordered.

I wondered how long Mullins would be willing to play the
submissive in their relationship. If the murder of Parker's
psychiatrist had been any indication, Mullins was determined
to surpass his master and intended to leave Parker's finesse
behind.

Parker's attitude irritated Mullins further. 'Look,' Mullins
said as he picked up a hacksaw to begin working at the marks
he'd made on the heavy pipe. 'I'm the one who's taking the
risk here. I'm the one who could end up behind bars a hell
of a lot more secure than these if I get caught. I told you it
was overkill to try and frame the kid. I told you some jackass
would step forward to help him.'

Parker reached a beefy arm through the bars and grabbed Mullins by his collar. He jerked him forward so hard his head bumped against the iron bars. 'Don't think I don't see the scratches on your face. You let that woman make a little bitch out of you, didn't you? I told you to leave the girl's mother alone.' Parker's tone was so deadly calm that I felt a tremor of fear pass through me. It was Parker's control I found most frightening. Mullins had trouble keeping his anger in check; Parker never did. It was as if the evil that lived in Parker was so evolved that nothing could make it veer from its chosen path.

'Yeah?' Mullins said. 'You're also the one who told me to kill the shrink.' He tried to sound as tough as Parker, but he failed and his voice faltered. 'Let go of me or I will walk away.'

'I told you to make it look like suicide,' Parker said calmly. He released his grip as if he found the touch of Mullins distasteful. 'I didn't tell you to beat the guy into hamburger. That's amateur hour, my friend.'

'I'm not your friend.' Mullins picked up the peculiar cutting tool and began to work on the pipe again. He had to crouch over to reach the bottom of the pipe in front of Parker. The posture made him look like a supplicant kneeling before his master. And perhaps he was.

The rain showed no signs of slowing and, if possible, was growing in intensity. Parker looked up at the sky, his brow furrowed with worry.

'Give me that thing,' Parker ordered him. 'I'm stronger than you and it won't take so much time.'

Mullins would not give up control. 'Ever used a snap cutter before?' he asked Parker, relishing at least one area where he knew more than Parker.

'So what?' Parker said. 'It's not rocket science.'

Mullins was enjoying his position of superiority. 'It's not brute force, either,' he said, holding the tool out of Parker's reach. 'The wrong angle can damage the tool. You have to know how to use it, when to slant it, or you're just wasting your time. I know how to use it.'

'Fine,' Parker said reluctantly. He looked behind him into the darkness of the tunnel. 'How long is this going to take?

They've got a couple of real slackers on night duty, but I can't push it much longer. Someone's going to notice I'm gone.'

Mullins shrugged. 'Another hour, maybe. If you weren't such a fat ass, you could squeeze out sooner but I've got at least two more bars to go.'

I wondered at their inability to get along for more than a few seconds at a time. This was not a partnership that was going to end well.

'You're going to give me my money right away, right?' Mullins asked Parker. 'Enough to afford a place to lay low in style? And if you're taking my truck, I want cash for that, too, plus a ride at least five hundred miles from this hellhole.'

Parker looked bored and kept looking behind him into the darkness of the pipe. 'Yeah, yeah, yeah. Women have been sending in cash like you wouldn't believe and they're willing to do anything I tell them to do. You'll get what I promised. I got one sketell in Atlanta who will put us up for a night. But she's mine before we leave, so don't get any ideas. After I take care of her, we go our separate ways.' Parker wanted to regain the upper hand and he could not resist adding, 'You're too sloppy. You butcher the moment. I can't work that way.'

Mullins froze. He stared at the bar he was cutting through for a few seconds before he answered Parker. His voice was hard. 'Do you really think you're any better than me?' he said. 'You think because you kill them more slowly, or mark them with some half-ass prison brand, or have some sick need to spread them out, that you're any better than me?' Mullins bent back over his work. 'You're no better than me. We both just kill them. There's not much more to it than that.'

Mullins knew what he had done to Darcy Swan and the psychiatrist was wrong. And judging from his tone of voice, I'm not sure he had enjoyed it, not in the way Parker enjoyed killing. Mullins sounded almost as if he was ashamed of himself and I wondered again about the hold Parker had over him. How had Mullins got himself into this mess?

Parker's mind was elsewhere. He looked up at the sky and then behind him. 'Another hour? You sure?'

'We'll still have plenty of time to get the hell out of here,'

Mullins pointed out. 'We've got at least four more hours of darkness and the truck's parked down the hill in some brush where no one will ever see it, at least not till daylight. We could be in and out of here and two states over by daybreak.'

Parker wasn't interested. He had already figured all that out. He had something else on his mind. 'I'm not sure I put the manhole lid back on completely,' he said to Mullins. I knew he was lying. 'I want it to look like I just disappeared, and I don't want any of them to figure out the connection between you and me.'

'A little late for that, don't you think?' Mullins asked.

'There's a difference between suspecting and knowing,' Parker said, but he was almost automatic in his arrogance. I felt the darkness rise in him. The hunger that had frightened me earlier on the front lawn grew and filled his being. 'I'm just going to go back and check it one more time,' Parker said. 'I'll only be a moment.'

Mullins glanced up at him briefly and risked sarcasm. 'Don't rush back on my account.'

Parker crouched down to fit inside the pipe and began loping back toward Holloway, his gait as smooth as a wolf's.

Why was Parker really heading back to Holloway?

And in one terrible moment, I realized what it was: the hunger had risen in him and that hunger was the one thing he could not control. He was going back to take Olivia. It would be his final act before he disappeared. He had seen her and wanted her and felt a right to take her. But he had been thwarted – and Otis Parker was not used to failure.

I hurried back up the slope. It would take Parker no time to reach Olivia. He was smart and he was willing to take the risk. He knew there were plenty of precautions taken to keep patients inside the long-term unit, but not many ways to keep people on the outside from getting in. He'd be in her building and up the stairs and in Olivia's room within minutes. It would take him no time to finish what he had set out to do.

I could not let that happen to her.

I did not know what I would do. I reached the grounds of Holloway and headed toward the long-term unit but stopped short as I noticed a shape ahead of me in the darkness. It moved and I saw it again. An animal, perhaps? Maybe a dog. No, it was too big – and it was walking upright.

It was Lily, the mutilated teddy bear tucked under her arm, tiptoeing toward the shed in the rain, intent on finding the monster she had seen from the window above. I could feel her heart beating from where I stood. She was afraid, and yet she kept moving through the darkness, compelled by something greater than her fear. I willed myself to feel what she was thinking. The grinning cat was fully awake in her mind and he was calling the shots, telling her to stop the monster forever.

Could she? I did not dare to hope.

I followed her as she slipped into the shed and spotted the manhole cover. Parker had swung it back into place from below as he descended into the pipe system, but he had not been able to lock it behind him. The locking bar protruded to one side and, as she stared at it, I could see the images flickering through Lily's mind. Yes, she understood how it worked. Somehow, she had learned it. Had it been from me?

Lily took a step toward the manhole cover and stopped. I knew Parker was moving up the pipe toward her. I wanted to scream at her to hurry, to gather her courage and move. She took another step toward the manhole cover and stopped again.

'Go,' I willed her. 'Just go now.'

I heard a clanging below. Parker had reached the bottom of the metal stairs that led to the manhole opening and was starting to climb up.

Lilly heard the clanging, too. She froze. My heart sank. But then I saw it, even as she saw it: the grinning cat, content in the shadows of her imagination, widening its hideous grin as it peered at her through her thoughts. 'Close it,' the cat ordered Lily calmly. 'Close it now.' It smiled again, looking pleased with itself.

Parker's heavy footsteps made the whole shed shake as he thundered up the metal ladder.

Lily reached the manhole cover. With all the weight of her little body, she pushed the metal bar. It did not budge. She did not have the strength to slide it shut. Beneath her, the clanging intensified. Parker was nearing the top. There was no one to stop him now.

'There you are, little one,' a deep voice called out from the doorway. The huge orderly with the braided beard was across the dirt floor in two huge strides. The tiny gold bells on the ends of his braids tinkled as he stared down at the manhole cover, listening to the sounds of metal on metal below it as Otis Parker climbed upward. He spotted the metal locking bar and pushed it into place. It slid across the manhole cover and lodged under the bracket on the other side, locking the cover so securely in place that not even a dozen Otis Parkers could have pushed it open from below.

Parker recognized the sound of the bar sliding into place and knew he was trapped. A roar echoed in the darkness beneath the shed and the manhole cover rattled with his rage.

Lily did not flinch. She stared down at the cover with satisfaction and looked up at the orderly. 'Tambours told me to stop the monster,' she explained to him. 'And I always do what Tambours says to do. So I followed the monster here.'

The orderly crouched down so that his face was even with Lily's. His voice was kinder than I had ever heard it before. 'So you did, little one,' he said. 'And I followed you. There I was, about to go home to some boring TV show when I saw you creeping around outside and I thought to myself, "Now what would a little one be doing that for on this sort of night? There must be a monster that needs stopping."'

Lily's face broke out into a huge grin. 'We got him,' she said. 'Tambours will be glad.'

'We got him,' the orderly agreed. 'He'll never bother anyone again.' He picked Lily up and cradled her in his arms, placing a palm flat against her forehead.

Parker roared in the pipe below them, spewing vile threats at them, not caring that he was giving away his presence. Neither took notice of him. Lily stared at the orderly and then ran a finger across the tiny braids of his beard, triggering a tinkling of bells. She smiled.

'Tambours likes those,' she told the orderly.

'Is that right?' the orderly asked. He smiled at Lily sadly, and took his palm from her forehead. 'Tell me more about this Tambours.'

As he folded his parka over her so that she would be

protected from the storm, the orderly listened carefully as Lily began to tell him about the grinning cat in her head.

As they left the shed, the sounds of Parker's rage echoed below them, his bellowings drowned out by the pounding rain. No one in the world above him could hear Otis Parker.

There was only one person who could possibly hear him now. And that was the devil himself.

THIRTY SEVEN

The monster raged. Parker's thwarted lust sought expression in a temper tantrum of epic proportions. The names he screamed as he railed against his unknown captors were so vile that even I, who had wallowed in the gutter while alive, had never heard them before. He uttered archaic, almost quaint, blasphemies that hinted at the centuries of evil stored inside him. But none of that evil could transcend Parker's body – and that body was trapped underground.

Outside the shed, away from his lunatic ravings, the rain gathered even more strength and hammered the earth in curtains of liquid fury.

I glimpsed flashing lights along the service road that wound through Holloway's acres. Men in yellow slickers were hopping from a truck at intervals, opening metal covers embedded in the earth and using crowbars to turn the gears concealed inside. They had been called out because of the storm and were adjusting the drainage water coursing through the network of pipes beneath Holloway's grounds, diverting the flow away from the overtaxed smaller pipes and toward the huge drainage pipe where Parker was trapped.

He had nowhere to go, nowhere at all, except one hope of escape.

Mullins was still crouched on the concrete overhang, frantically wrapping the chain of his wrench-like tool around the metal bars then pumping the handle, trying to bite through the iron even as the water from the pipe began to gather in strength, rising in volume until he had to wrap an arm through the bars to steady himself as the overflow tore at his legs. The water in the pipe was already a foot deep and the rain showed no signs of abating. Mullins looked up, alarmed, as sounds of Parker's fury reached him from inside the tunnel.

Parker had regained control by the time he reached the mouth of the pipe where Mullins worked frantically at his task. 'Move faster,' Parker ordered him. 'How much longer?'

Mullins looked up briefly and sensed a weakness in Parker's surface calm. A flicker of satisfaction crossed his face. 'You really think that was smart, making all that noise when we're trying to make a clean getaway?' he asked. The cutting tool had finally bitten through the bottom of one of the bars and Parker reached impatiently for it, bending it toward him as he tried to widen the opening.

'You're only making it harder,' Mullins said. 'You screw with the angle and it's going to take me longer to make the top cut.'

The water was rising steadily in the pipe, but Parker did not notice. He was angry at being deprived of Olivia and distracted by Mullins' satisfaction at his dilemma. He did not like anyone having power over him. He did not like that Mullins was free on one side while he was trapped inches away on the other. He did not like being told what to do by a man he saw as inferior, weaker and less worthy. In a flash, he had pulled the plastic wrist restraints from his back pocket and clamped one around Mullins' wrist and the other around one of the metal bars still blocking the pipe.

'Hey!' Mullins cried, nearly dropping his tool. 'Are you nuts? I need that hand.'

'You've got enough movement to finish. Just keep working at this bar,' Parker ordered him, pointing at the next bar in. 'Break through at the bottom and I can pull it toward me enough to get through. Hurry!'

Mullins stared at the pipe, then back at the restraint clamped around his hand. He had just enough leeway to reach the bottom of the bar, but the water was rising quickly and, if he didn't hurry, he'd soon be working underwater, making it that much harder to cut through.

He looked up at Parker. 'Take the handcuffs off or I'm done,' Mullins said.

Parker's temper flared. He was the master and he'd had enough of his sidekick. His hand lashed out as quickly as a cobra's strike. He grabbed Mullins by the throat and pulled him closer. 'You listen to me, you little piece of shit,' Parker said. His voice grew in timbre and deepened. 'You will obey me. Work faster. You will get me out of here now.'

It was too late. A rumble echoed in the darkness of the pipe, gathering in volume as the rushing waters drew nearer. A wave of run-off was approaching, gathering in momentum as the main flow reached each ancillary pipe and the overburdened system disgorged its flow.

Parker glanced over his shoulder and back at a terrified Mullins. The plumber flailed out, striking Parker with the heavy cutting tool. It bounced off Parker's skull, leaving a bloody dent. Parker swayed but recovered, tightening his grip around Mullins' throat.

'Get me out of here,' Parker commanded and, for the first time, I heard a hesitation in his voice, the smallest flicker of fear.

The waters behind him rushed closer and the roaring grew louder.

Mullins hit him again with the tool and Parker released his grip, rubbing at the wound on his head in astonishment. How dare Mullins defy him?

Mullins stepped back, eluding Parker's reach by balancing on the edge of the concrete platform below the pipe. But he was still trapped on the hillside by the plastic handcuff linking his left wrist to the pipe.

'You're a dead man,' Parker told him. He clawed at Mullins through the bars like an animal.

'You sure about that?' Mullins taunted.

The waters hit. A dark, roiling wave of run-off barreled out of the pipe behind Parker and hit him with the force of a train, slamming him against the bars. He fought the water and the water fought back, slamming his body again and again against the heavy metal bars crisscrossing the opening. It was brutal in its force. It was magnificent in its power. It was unstoppable as it pinned Parker against the bars and cut off all oxygen, trapping him in place.

Mullins could not escape, either. He was swept off his feet as the water found the edge of the platform and cascaded over the edge of it to pour down the side of the hill. Mullins sprawled on the ledge, held in place only by the hard plastic handcuff around one wrist. He gasped for breath and grabbed for an iron bar with his other hand. Dangling over the lip of the platform, he twisted and gasped for oxygen in the air pocket under the ledge.

Above him, Otis Parker was dying. The roaring waters bounced him about like a plastic toy. His upper body become jammed in the opening that Mullins had made in the bars, making it seem as if he was reaching for Mullins underwater. Perhaps he was. I had never seen such anger, such concentrated fury as I saw in Parker's last moments of life. It was as if his body had a will that transcended life itself and was seeking a connection with Mullins even as the rushing waters poured over both men.

Above this strange tableau, lightning flashed and a thunder-clap boomed, its echo rolling across the valley with a terrible power that no one, not even Parker, could challenge. It was a cry of triumph from the skies above. Lightning flashed again, illuminating the two men. Their faces reflected a pale light beneath the waters. Then all was darkness again.

THIRTY-EIGHT

I spent the hours until dawn stretched out beneath the pounding rain, feeling the drops bounce through me, enjoying the lingering trace of ions that filled me with a pleasant buzzing. I gave myself to the night and to the pounding rain. I gave myself to the wrath of a world I no longer lived in. She was awesome in her anger.

The rain finally stopped half an hour before dawn. When the sun rose, it spread tentative orange and red fingers across the eastern sky, as if seeking a way to part the lingering clouds so that the day might bloom in all its glory. I heard shouts on the road beneath the hill soon after as city workers, dispatched to check on the flood damage caused by the storm, spotted Mullins sprawled across the concrete lip beneath the pipe. Above him, the water had slowed to a steady trickle. Otis Parker's body had been pounded into a bloated, gray mass that was embedded between the iron bars and glistened with a thick coating of oily sludge.

Rescue workers and police arrived soon after. Maggie and Calvano were among the first to slide down the muddy slope to see what had happened for themselves. They both looked as if they had been up all night, searching for Eugene Mullins.

Well, they had found him and, astonishingly enough, he was still alive.

Eugene Mullins had found a pocket of air by twisting his head below the concrete lip and escaping the water's onslaught. He had somehow crawled back on to the concrete ledge when the waters abated and now lay, bloodied and unconscious, across its rough surface.

A crowd of hospital staff had gathered on the edge of the cliff above the pipe. The ground was so soggy and treacherous that they had to hook their fingers around the thick steel weave of the safety fence to keep from sliding down the steep slope.

The orderly with the braided beard was among the crowd, his gold tooth twinkling in the sun. He was at work early for someone who had clocked out so late, I thought. In fact, I realized, he always seemed to be at Holloway, no matter what time of day or night.

At least he always had been there until now. I took my eyes off him to verify that Connie's fiancé, Cal, was among the crowd and when I looked back at where he had been standing, the orderly was gone.

I would never see him at Holloway again.

It took a while to extract Parker's body from the bars and to locate a key that could free Mullins from the plastic restraints. Parker was covered with a plastic tarp and born away before anyone had stared at what was left of him too long. The emergency medical technicians lifted Mullins on to a stretcher and were about to attempt the tricky maneuver of

lifting him up the soaked hill when Maggie stopped the attendants so she could take a closer look. Satisfied that it was,
indeed, Eugene Mullins, she nodded and called in instructions
to have his hospital room guarded. She was taking no chances
that he would elude her again.

Calvano was a squeamish soul, but he was also taking no
chances, at least not when it came to Otis Parker. He followed
the two men who had lifted Parker's body up the slope, catching
up to them as they were rolling him into an ambulance for the
ride to the morgue. He crawled into the back of the ambulance
alongside the stretcher, then lifted the thick plastic covering
Parker's body and stared down at it for a long time. He barely
looked human, which I thought was fitting. Calvano asked the
attendants for help rolling Parker over and sliding down what
was left of his jeans. There, on possibly the only unmarred
part of Parker's body – his buttocks – was a colorful tattoo of
a cartoon roadrunner kicking up clouds of dust across Parker's
ass. Calvano nodded. He was satisfied. Otis Parker was dead.

The technicians stared at him, waiting for an explanation.
'Don't ask,' Calvano told them. 'Don't even ask.'

I returned to the top of the hill where Cal was talking to
Maggie away from the crowd. 'What happened?' he asked,
his voice making it plain that he feared her answer. It would
be up to him to put Holloway back together again.

Maggie shook her head. 'I don't really know,' she confessed.
'But Otis Parker is dead and I think we have the man who
was killing for him. It's over.'

Behind them, silhouetted by the morning sun, Gonzales was
striding toward Maggie with an expression of intense frustra-
tion laced with a non-specific anger. Cal saw him coming and
wisely hurried away, leaving Maggie to take the heat.

'Don't say a word,' Gonzales told Maggie. 'I want to see
for myself.'

'Sir, I was just going to say to be care—' Before Maggie
could get her warning out, Gonzales hit a patch of mud and
went down hard, sliding over the lip of the cliff and bumping
down the slope to an ignominious stop by the concrete ledge.
He clawed frantically for purchase and managed to right
himself inches from a startled crime scene specialist, who

froze in position above Eugene Mullins' toolbox, too shocked to do anything but stare at her suddenly arrived commander. She held a pink cell phone in one hand.

'Well?' Gonzales asked her.

'Sir,' she said, holding out the pink cell phone. 'I think this belonged to Darcy Swan.'

Before Gonzales could react, shouting broke out on the roadway below Holloway. Two frantic men in a yellow municipal pickup truck had flagged a squad car responding to the crime scene above. Both men were waving their arms and pointing down the road. Other squad cars were pulling over to see what the excitement was about.

Belinda Swan had turned up. Concealed only by a shallow grave too close to the river's edge, her body had been uncovered by the floodwaters, tumbled across meadows and fields, slid around boulders and shot through newly carved sluice channels until, finally, it lodged in the brush by the side of the road barely a hundred yards from where her daughter's body had been found. A crew dispatched to survey the flood damage had discovered her while clearing an access path of debris. Her miniskirt was pushed up over her thighs and her low-cut blouse was caked with mud. Her mouth gaped open at an odd angle and the responding officers soon discovered why: a thick wad of dollar bills had been shoved down her throat. Belinda Swan had choked to death on money.

I knew who had done it. I had seen the scratches on Eugene Mullins' face. He had probably used her, telling her that his son had killed her daughter and enlisting her help framing Adam for the attack on the school. But Belinda Swan was Belinda Swan, after all. She had been smart enough to figure out what really happened – and stupid enough to try and extort money from Mullins for her knowledge.

They would get Eugene Mullins for it. There was no doubt in my mind. Belinda Swan was a fighter and I knew she had gone down swinging. They would find his skin under her fingernails. They would make the connection and they would nail Eugene Mullins for murder. His career as a killer was over.

Otis Parker had been right after all – the man lacked a sense of style.

THIRTY-NINE

Eugene Mullins recovered. Indeed, he thrived. As the weeks to his trial passed, he grew larger and more imposing by the day. He was being strengthened by forces I did not understand – nor would I seek to understand them. My part in the battle had ended.

It was up to Maggie now. She made it her personal mission to ensure that Eugene Mullins did not get the free ride that Otis Parker had enjoyed. Whatever time Mullins had spent at Holloway, meeting with Parker in the recesses of the common bathroom, recognizing a kindred spirit, was over. Parker was dead and there was no way anyone was going to let Mullins end up at Holloway instead of prison.

Adam's grandmother turned out not to be as out of it as Eugene Mullins had assumed. She could confirm fights with Belinda Swan, that he had lied about his whereabouts the night Darcy Swan died and much more. She was a font of information on her son and she showed no hesitation in telling the police everything she knew. Unfortunately, the old lady also seemed to blame herself for what her son had done and she apparently could not live with that knowledge. She died a few months after Eugene Mullins had been convicted of both Swan murders, as well as the killing of Otis Parker's shrink.

I should have felt bad for Adam, but the truth was that I was relieved that he was freed from that dark, unhappy home that smelt of urine and beer and sorrow. Instead, I prayed that the old woman had gone to a happier world.

Maggie had never been big on loose ends. Even though Eugene Mullins ended up where Otis Parker had always belonged – in a tiny cell on a lonely hall in a dark corner of a prison where people spent each day waiting for their lives to be over – she reopened the investigation into the death of his wife. She was going to nail him for everything she could. She found that Adam had been right all along. His mother had not, in fact, left this world either willingly or by her own hands. She had been his father's first victim.

I suppose you could argue that finding out about his mother's death cost Adam Mullins his father, but Eugene Mullins had never been much of a prize in that department and, in a way, the truth was that it helped Adam regain his mother. He knew now that she had not left him by choice. I hoped it would be enough.

I thought the kid would be OK. Not once did Adam visit his father, not in the hospital nor in prison. I had no argument with that. His father's arrest and involvement with Parker hurt, I knew, but it could not have been much of a surprise to Adam. He had been trapped with his father in the little house they shared for years. He knew, better than anyone, what his father was capable of.

Besides, Adam had people who loved him and would see him through. He had Connie, who welcomed him into her house without hesitation, converting the guest bedroom into a sanctuary that Adam could make as tidy as the tiny space he had left behind. The room once designated as my place of banishment on drunken nights was transformed into a place of hope for a boy who had finally caught a break in life. And Adam's English teacher, Mr Phillips, was there for him, too, to be his advocate with Social Services and to make sure that Adam got the scholarship he had been hoping for.

In the end, Adam Mullins – who had been born on the wrong side of the tracks and, by all prescribed conventions of our town, doomed to die there, too – escaped Helltown.

My son Michael found himself while helping Adam through the difficult weeks of his father's trial. I think that all the months of being the boy whose father had been killed during a drug bust, under murky circumstances, had left Michael feeling like a character in a movie he did not want to see. Adam gave Michael himself back. He gave him a way to discover strength and compassion within himself and he gave Michael something bigger than himself to worry about. People call these byproducts of our suffering 'blessings in disguise.' But I think they represent so much more than that. I think they prove that there is, indeed, an evening outside of the

Universe, one that takes place in a hundred different ways in a thousand different places each and every hour of every day that passes in the plane of the living. It is a constant taking back of the world from the forces of darkness. Who or what oversees this balance, I cannot say. But it is an awe-inspiring power once you notice it.

The house where I had once lived was transformed into a noisy, teenage boy headquarters where Connie reigned supreme and sports equipment cluttered every room, and my youngest son, Sean, delighted in having another older brother – one who was actually nice to him.

They would all be OK, most especially Michael. He had left the darkness behind.

Connie continued to see Cal, but something had changed between them forever. Connie no longer needed Cal as much as she once had and Cal had seen Connie's astonishing inner strength, strength she had earned during her years with me. Whether they would stay together, I could not say. But I did know that, at least for now, I'd had enough of watching them and enough of contemplating what I did not have. I was constantly leaving Connie and returning to her, drawn by the need to spy on the life I had wasted. Enough. From here on out, I would fight that urge. It keeps me here, in this place, and I know that, no matter what, my mission now is to move on.

Holloway survived. It survived the murders and the chaos and the macabre sight of Otis Parker's body being toted across the lawn and disposed of like the garbage he was.

Holloway survived because it had to. My town, like all towns, needs a place like Holloway – a place where people who are lost can find their way back to a tentative truce with themselves; a place where people can make peace with the minutes that mark their days and find a way to go on living through the years. Those who remain at Holloway lead the simplest of lives. They walk, they see, they eat, they sleep. Maybe that is all the world can ask of them this time around. I have seen what thoughts they hold, what sorrows they harbor, what fears – often rightly – they run from. I understand. They need Holloway every bit as much as Holloway needs them.

It did not take long for order to return to Holloway, at least the level of order that was possible there. Soon, the short-term unit was filled again with people hoping to get back on the track of their lives. Harold Babbitt continued to spew his stew of words as he marched across the lawns and up and down the brick walkways. And he continued to astonish the weary aides who followed him around with occasional nuggets of wisdom that pierced through their exhaustion and gave them pause.

'Harold Babbitt sees an angel,' he said one day, staring at a fat aide whose skin was the color of walnuts and whose hair danced in braids when she shook her head. She was keeping him company as he marched across the lawn. 'Harold Babbitt sees an angel,' he repeated, pointing to her hair, 'and her braids shine like spun gold beneath a fiery sun.'

It was, in his own way, words of love – words that I knew the aide would never forget.

The staff returned his affection. They found a helmet for him made of a material that would protect his head while still allowing his wounds to breathe. He wore it rakishly, like a World War One pilot who has just gunned down another German ace. Someone with a sense of humor – my money was on a quiet nurse with light-brown hair who seldom spoke to anyone – gave him a long white scarf one day. Harold wore it wrapped around his throat so that it flowed behind him if he ran fast enough. All he needed now was a biplane.

Harold Babbitt was a man of the stars.

He and I seldom ended up in the quiet room with the padded corners anymore. He had found an identity, however improbable, and he clung to it with a contentment that trumped launching himself at walls.

I missed those moments alone in the padded room with Harold. It wasn't the same without him. Sure, I could go in and enjoy the quiet, but what I really missed was the feeling of Harold's frantic dissatisfaction transforming into contentment. It had seemed, somehow, to mirror something still unknown and restless within myself.

Lily did not remain at Holloway. Something had changed in her the night she ventured out into the storm. When a new

psychiatrist arrived to put Holloway back in order, he brought
with him a list of new drugs and found a combination of two
that held hope for Lily. As the days passed, and her mind
calmed, and it appeared that the grinning cat in the dark shad-
owed forest of her mind had been banished forever, her parents
made plans for her to move to a special school closer to their
home. It wasn't the same as living a normal life, but at least
Lily would be among others near her age. The day she left
Holloway, she held her father's hand and clutched her teddy
bear close to her heart. Someone – an aide, perhaps, who
wished her well – had embroidered bright-yellow daisies where
the mutilated eye holes had once been, transforming the
grotesque toy into a jaunty symbol of childhood. He'd be a
big hit at tea parties for sure.

Olivia, too, left Holloway, her journey back to herself
complete. One perfect spring morning a few weeks after
Eugene Mullins and Otis Parker had been discovered at the
lip of the pipe, Olivia rose, combed her hair, packed her suit-
case and sat on the couch in the waiting room, hands folded
in her lap and eyes fixed resolutely on the entranceway door.
I wondered who was coming for her. Her husband was dead.
Her child was dead. No one had ever visited her while she
had been at Holloway. But later that morning, as the birds
burst out in song, and the sun climbed in the sky, and the
tulips seemed to grow right before your very eyes, on a day
filled with new life and new promise, a plump older woman
with frazzled hair and a grateful look on her face spotted
Olivia and took her in her arms, sobbing without restraint at
the joy of seeing her daughter again.

It was Olivia who had imposed her own exile, who had felt
compelled to punish herself by locking herself up at Holloway.
There were people who loved her waiting for her, who knew
what she had been through, who would help her find her way
through the world.

I knew I would never see her again.

She opened the door and stepped outside, then turned back
to me as if to say goodbye. My heart leapt – until she looked
right past me to a corner of the room, where a beautiful old
woman with gray hair falling charmingly from her bun sat on

a chair, enjoying the sunshine that spilled through the French windows nearby. She was waiting for her knight to come bearing the yellow roses he always brought for her.

Olivia ran back to her and knelt in front of her, taking the woman's porcelain hands in her own. Olivia kissed each palm before placing them back in her lap. Then Olivia rose and turned to go, never seeing the miracle that I saw follow – a smile on the old woman's lips.

I followed Olivia and her mother out to their car and watched them drive away until they were nothing more than a speck of silver twinkling along the road that wound down to the valley below. It felt like she had taken my heart with her.

I stood for a moment on the street outside of Holloway, staring in through the front gate at the beautiful lawn and the aimless people wandering over its acres. They were lost, just like me. They wandered, just like me.

No wonder I'd felt like I belonged at Holloway.

But that was then and this was now. Yes, there were times when the lost souls of Holloway could see me, when their gazes lingered on my face and I could feel the heat of their recognition. It felt good, but it wasn't good for them. Too many of them wanted to join me here, in the afterlife. I could not become the wandering commander of a raggedy crew. They were not done with their lives and they were not why I was here. I had redeemed myself at Holloway, at least a little, but I would not find my answers on The Hill.

As I turned my back on the great house of secrets and began to make my way down toward town, I could hear Harold Babbitt behind me greeting a newcomer to Holloway. His voice drifted on the wind, reaching me like a gift: 'Harold Babbitt sees a crazy man,' he was announcing to all. 'Harold Babbitt sees a crazy man for sure.'

EPILOGUE

The storm raged, pounding the prison relentlessly. Thunder and lightning split the sky as if mocking the anger of the men trapped side. It had been an ugly evening, even for a place where ugliness was expected. A new prisoner, recently transferred in from a small town nearby, had been challenged at dinner by inmates far stronger and more experienced in the ways of institutional cruelty.

The new prisoner had surprised everyone. Although overweight and doughy, with a mournful face that seemed both sleepy and resigned, he had defended himself with a surety that took his attackers by surprise. Two of them were in the infirmary now, one with a fork wound in his eye.

Those who witnessed the fight pronounced the new inmate 'ferocious' and gave him the nickname 'Badger.' At the moment, though, he was simply Inmate #4372, confined to an isolation cell as punishment until the authorities could figure out what to do with him.

God, but he hated the rain. As soon as he was free from this hellhole, he was going to move to a desert town where he never had to see it or hear it again. He stood at the tiny window carved into the massive stone walls that confined him and stared out at the pelting rain, cursing his luck and, just for good measure, cursing the world itself.

He turned as a tinkling sound in the hallway approached. A series of clanks signaled the unlocking of his door. The heavily reinforced steel slab opened and a guard entered the cell. He was huge and his head was shaved so closely his skull gleamed beneath the cell's single light bulb. His uniform barely covered his bulging muscles and he had a red beard that had been twisted into small braids that dangled from his chin. Tiny brass bells threaded through the ends of the braids explained the tinkling sound.

The guard looked familiar, though the inmate could not quite place him. Had he known him on the outside? 'What the hell do you want?' he asked him. The guard made him uneasy.

'Not a thing,' the guard said cheerfully. He had a gold upper tooth that twinkled when he smiled. He was staring at the inmate as he smiled, his head cocked to one side and his massive arms folded over his chest.

The inmate stared back at him. 'What the hell do you want?' he asked again. His hands twitched. He was ready for anything.

'I just wanted to make sure you were in here all alone.'

'All alone?' the inmate growled back at the guard. 'No shit. I'm in solitary confinement.'

The guard nodded, satisfied. 'Better get used to it, my brother. I'm going to make sure you stay right here.'

'You can't do that,' the inmate said. He could feel the rage rising in him, like a beast that hungered to break free. What he wouldn't give for the chance to tear the guard's eyes out and rip his entrails from his body.

'Sure I can,' the guard said cheerfully. He dangled his keys just out of the inmate's reach and jingled them. 'I can do anything.'

He turned and left, locking the door behind him.

Behind the inmate, flickering against the gray stone wall, a terrible shadow coalesced and took shape. Dark wings swelled to life, magnificent in breadth, flexing and testing their strength. Just as quickly, they folded down into nothingness and the shadow disappeared.

The inmate never even seemed to notice. He moved to the window and stared into the night. Outside, the wind howled and the heavens thundered as the sky wept relentless, never-ending tears. There was nothing the inmate could do but watch the rain.

Eugene Mullins was alone.